# The Threshold

## Mike Owens

Blue Heron Press, LLC

# Prologue

They didn't bother to knock. They never did. They came and went whenever they wished, leaving Rosita locked in her room. Today there were two of them, a man so big his body filled the doorway, followed by a much smaller man with sad, downcast eyes. Rosita knew the smaller man as Gaudio, and he alone of all her visitors had treated her with kindness. But today he would not meet her gaze. He stared down at the floor.

The big man grabbed her wrist and dragged Rosita to her feet. He leered at her for a moment, slid his hand over the front of her gown, groping. "What a damned waste," he said. Then he pulled her toward the door.

"Wait, my shoes."

"You won't need them."

Rosita glanced back at her little cell. Small as it was, it seemed luxurious compared to all she'd ever known before. Here she had her own bed, clean sheets. The flush toilet puzzled her at first, but once she figured it out she thought it the most marvelous thing she'd ever seen.

Gaudio brought her meals on a tray every day. She was supposed to leave the tray by the door for him to pick up. Sometimes she kept the tray by her bed, forcing him to come inside to retrieve it, hoping he might talk to her, but still, she learned little more than his name during their brief snatches of conversation.

The only window in her room was covered over with a heavy black fabric taped to the wall. She managed to peel away one corner, enough to give her a glimpse outside. The area next to her building was filled with heavy construction equipment. Men wearing hard hats, carrying picks and shovels scurried about in a great hurry. Beyond the piles of upturned earth stretched a lush, green countryside, completely different from the parched landscape she'd known all her life. Far in the distance the sun reflected off a large lake.

They had kept her in the locked room for three days now. The first day a tall man wearing a white coat came in, pulled aside her clothing, and poked and prodded her in places where Rosita had not been poked and prodded before. He listened to her heart, then to her chest, then he checked her blood pressure. Why, she wondered? Was she sick? But he left without a word.

Soon after the man was gone, a young woman that Rosita guessed to be about her own age brought her the yellow gown she now wore. The young woman wore a white dress—a nurse? In addition to the yellow gown, she had a small tray of instruments that she placed on the bed beside Rosita. She pushed up Rosita's sleeve and swabbed an area high up on her right arm with alcohol. "This might sting a little," she said. The nurse took a thin silver tube from her tray. She stuck the tip into Rosita's arm and twisted it several times. "Be still," she said when Rosita tried to pull away. The nurse held the tip of the tube in a small vial of liquid, then tapped it a couple of times. Rosita watched a small piece of her own flesh, about the size of a match head, float to the bottom of the vial. The next day the nurse returned and repeated the procedure on Rosita's left arm.

Today was different. Instead of another puncture, the nurse wrapped both of the puncture sites tightly with clear plastic. "Have to keep them dry today," she said. Soon after the nurse left the two men came for Rosita.

She plodded down the hallway between them, Big Man in front and Gaudio following behind, her bare feet soundless on the carpet. They passed other closed doors. Were others like her locked inside, she wondered?

The corridor ended by a large door. Big Man had to use both hands to depress the lever that opened it. He quickly grabbed Rosita's arm and jerked her inside. The door closed behind her with a loud hissing sound.

The room where she now stood had bare white walls and a concrete floor, so cold that she hopped from one foot to the other to avoid contact with that frigid surface. She pulled her thin gown tightly around her, but it did little to stave off the cold. There were others in the room; the tall man in the white coat who had examined her on that first day stood next to the wall, beside him a shorter man wearing a gray suit. Just to their left stood three other attendants, none so large as Big Man, but large, just the same.

But it wasn't the other people that caught her attention. A large clear box only slightly taller than Rosita herself filled the center of the room. She could see right through it. She could see the reclining chair inside, bolted to the floor. She could see the restraining straps that looped around the arms and legs of the chair, and the thicker band that ran across the seat.

"No," she screamed.

She fought as hard as she could, and it took all of the attendants to force her into the box, then strap her into the chair. They closed the door of the box and left her inside, freezing, terrified and clueless. She spotted Gaudio in the corner. He covered his face with his hands and turned away.

There was a roar, then a gush of icy water that covered her feet and crept rapidly up her legs. She screamed again, but her futile cries were drowned out by the noise of the onrushing torrent. Within moments the water had reached her neck. She gasped for what she knew would be her last breaths. They were killing her. Why? What had she ever done to them?

The cold, at least, was merciful. In the moment that it took for the water to rise above her head her struggles ceased as her shocked body shut down, her brain went into a state like hibernation. Far off in the distance she saw a point of light that seemed to be coming closer.

# Chapter 1

Sometimes whether you make it through the day or not depends on whether your good luck outweighs your bad luck. It can be a simple matter of balance. Take John's decision to go ice fishing, for instance. Just bad luck? Maybe. Plain stupid, others would say. John's oldest and closest friend, Herman Poulos, said John had some sort of death wish, that the lake had him hooked like a fish, always dragging him back, and Herman knew John's personal history better than anybody.

John had plenty of reasons to change his mind about the trip. There was a storm coming; he could feel it in his bones. But he'd already gotten up in pre-dawn darkness to plow a path in the fresh snow from his back door down to the barn, tended his horses, then loaded his gear into his truck. It would take more than a change in the weather to scare him off. He called Herman one last time, but got the same answer.

"I'm telling you, John, that warm spell thinned the ice out. It's over, man. You better pack it in and wait 'til next year." Herman's voice was plaintive, like he was trying to coax a jumper off a ledge.

"Okay, limp dick. Stay home, see if I care." John stirred his coffee with the end of his spoon. From where he sat at his kitchen table he could see a low-lying bank of clouds in the west. Yeah, storm probably, but he'd seen storms before. Besides, there was a storm brewing inside him, had been for years, blown by forces more fearful than anything visible through his window.

"Hey, if you fall in and drown, can I have your snowmobile?" Herman's idea of a joke, as usual, a bad one.

"Fuck you." John laughed and hung up, but the laughter was forced. "How about you, Rebel, you gonna back out on me too?" His large mixed-breed dog hung close by, brushing against the side of John's

5

leg. Two years before when he'd turned up at John's doorstep in a thunderstorm, wet, skinny and—John discovered later that same day— flea-ridden, he didn't look like he'd live through the night. Now, at just over one hundred pounds, he ruled the ranch. Once again Rebel pressed against him, making a whimpering noise. "What's got into you, boy? We're going ice fishing. You love that, remember?"

Outside John flipped up his collar against the frigid morning air as he checked his fishing gear, now covered by a thin layer of snow. Satisfied that he had everything he needed, he pulled onto the gravel roadway and headed for the lake. The snow alongside the rutted track had turned to gray slush, almost the same color as the cloudbank building in the west. His truck stalled twice before he'd driven a mile. Damn, first Herman, then the dog, now the truck. What next? At some level he probably knew the answer, but he wouldn't stop, he couldn't. The lake drew him like a magnet.

Shortly after nine A.M. he parked by a snow-covered ramp on the northern tip of Canandaigua Lake, one of the eleven so-called Finger Lakes that had been gouged deeply into the earth some two million years before by southbound glaciers. The lakes were long, narrow and deep; the floor of Seneca Lake, so John recalled from high school geography class, lay over six hundred feet beneath its surface. As late as the eighteenth century—also from his high school memory—the road over which John drove would have been part of the domain of the powerful Iroquois Nation, but they had long since been vanquished, their reign marked primarily by the picturesque names they bestowed on the lakes.

During the brief upstate New York summer this lot on Canandaigua Lake would be filled with vehicles and empty trailers while the powerboats they had launched raced up and down the lake But winter was the season coveted by ice fishermen. John scanned the lake— no one else around. Two weeks before, when he was last here, the frozen surface of the lake looked like a parking lot, with all the ice fishing vehicles scattered around. One guy had even towed his gear out with a riding lawn mower.

But things had changed since that last visit. A brief southerly airflow had swept through, and the more prudent fishermen had packed it in for the season. John had the place all to himself, and the icy expanse stretched out in front of him, cold and silent as a tomb.

John towed his apparatus, along with a concrete block he used to anchor his shelter, out onto the frozen lake, then set up his gear about one hundred yards from shore. He'd barely started drilling a hole in the ice when his augur broke through. Damn, the ice was really thin. An impartial observer would look at his situation, out on the ice alone, thin ice at that, storm approaching, and say something like "idiot." Yeah, he knew that, and he couldn't disagree. But such an observer wouldn't have John's own personal history, wouldn't share his ghosts, and wouldn't understand why he couldn't leave even if he wanted to.

The storm shouldn't have caught him by surprise. Anyone who had lived through as many upstate winters as he had knew well enough when to duck and take cover, but he plunged ahead, almost daring the weather fates to strike him down. Now, if he didn't get off the lake pretty damned quick, that was exactly what would happen. He grabbed as much of his gear as he could carry, then untied the rope that connected his shelter to the concrete block anchor. He wrapped the rope around his free wrist, but the force of the wind made it impossible to pull the thing behind him. In fact it overturned and acted like a parachute, dragging him across the ice with Rebel following closely behind barking like a banshee.

John dropped his gear and held on to the rope with both hands. He didn't want to lose the shelter—no telling where it might end up with this wind. But he couldn't stop it. His boots provided no traction on the frozen surface, and he was headed straight for the thinner black ice at the edge of the lake. The coils of rope around his wrists held like a noose.

About twenty yards from shore, just when he thought he might make it, the ice cracked beneath him, and he broke through. The sudden cold took his breath away. His down-filled jacket soaked through instantly, pulling him into the depths of the lake. He had to get out of the jacket, but the zipper wouldn't budge. He stripped off his gloves. Instantly his fingers were frozen, useless. The zipper stayed stuck.

He clawed at the jacket but, as advertised, the rip-stop nylon refused to rip. A sheath knife at his belt was useless in his frozen hands. He kicked and thrashed, none of which slowed his descent. At near-freezing temperatures it didn't take long. Soon he couldn't move at all. Right at the end he saw a brief glimmer of light. At first the light looked far, far away. Then it seemed to envelop him like a warm cocoon. There were faces, but he couldn't make them out. Then everything went black, just like before.

So it all comes down to a matter of balance, good luck versus bad. Falling into an icy lake is bad luck by any measure; body heat is lost through such exposure at a rate twenty to thirty times faster than it would be lost from exposure to cold air, so John's chances of surviving the event should have been nil. But nature, perhaps through evolution, interceded on his behalf, even where his better judgment had failed him. From the moment he entered the icy water his body went through what has been termed the *mammalian diving reflex*, a protective mechanism that kicks in when the victim hits cold water. Almost immediately he experienced tight laryngospasm, preventing him from aspirating water into his lungs, a terminal event. His heart rate slowed immediately, and within moments he was in full cardiac arrest. Another critical part of the protective mechanism involves the brain. Without oxygen, brain death at normal temperatures begins within three to five minutes, but at cold temperatures the brain may survive intact for up to forty-five minutes, even longer in some cases. But even with these protective mechanisms in place, he was still submerged in very cold water, and no natural processes could keep him alive indefinitely.

Fortunately John had a few other good luck chips falling his way. His friend, Herman drove out to the lake, partly out of guilt, moreso out of concern. He got there shortly after the storm had blown through and saw no sign of John. What he did see was Rebel close to shore, running around a hole in the ice, barking his fool head off. Thank God for 911. Both the Canandaigua Fire Department and the regional EMT service were on hand in minutes. The grappling hook snagged John's jacket on the third throw. Whatever hope his rescuers might have had must have been dashed by the sorry appearance of the form they dragged from the depths—cold, blue, pulseless, not breathing, pupils dilated; dead for sure.

If they had taken a vote on what to do at that point, they would have simply wrapped John's body in a blanket and taken him to the morgue, but there would be one dissenter, the EMT who had taken the time to read the memo that came from Dr. Paul Pierce's office on procedures to follow with victims of cold water drowning. He would have been in a great hurry get John into the ambulance and to the hospital ASAP, sirens blazing, emergency lights flashing. There would be an argument, of course. "What's the rush? This poor guy has had it. Anybody can see that."

But the memo reader prevailed, and he saved John's life.

#

When the ambulance carrying John Merritt backed up to the emergency entrance to Upstate Medical Center, Dr. Paul Pierce stood by the door waiting on them. Snow, which had been falling heavily through much of the morning had slacked off a bit only to be blown sideways into drifts by a swirling west wind. Pierce waited alone on the platform outside the ER, the gusts whipping his lab coat around his knees, while the rest of the staff huddled just inside the door, seeking shelter until the last possible moment before they had to dash out into the frigid air.

The ambulance, belching blue exhaust as it backed up to the ramp, was pasted halfway up its sides with a gray slush accumulated on its forty-five minute race from Canandaigua, a small upstate New York town at the northern tip of the lake by the same name.

If Pierce made note of any of this, or even cared, he gave no sign. He clenched his hands in his pockets, eager with anticipation. He was about to do something remarkable; he was going to bring someone back from the dead. Cases like this maintained his status in the medical center and beyond. Tomorrow, if all went well, there would be an article in the Rochester Chronicle, a photo of Pierce standing at the bedside of an alert, smiling John Merritt. Another miraculous save by Dr. Paul Pierce. Of course, he would give full credit to his team, but they would not be seen in the photo, just Pierce himself, as always.

"Not much hope, Doc. Must have been under for half an hour, maybe more." One of the EMTs nodded toward the cold, blue, lifeless figure strapped to the gurney. "Danged fool, out on the ice like that, this late in the season."

Danged fool was probably accurate, but such fools provided Pierce with a steady supply of cold water drowning victims--victims, he always called them that, almost never patients. As he saw it, they had passed beyond the status of patients; they were clinically dead, after all. That distinction raised his achievement above the classification of mere medical intervention. His success was god-like in comparison.

"But we kept him cold, just like you said." The stocky EMT driver shuddered in the icy wind.

Do not warm. The victim must be kept cold. Pierce had disseminated this critical information to all the EMT units in the area. Simply wrapping the unfortunate individual in warm blankets, as had been done in the past, led to a further rapid, and often fatal, decrease in core body temperature, known as the *afterdrop*. Pierce had first-hand experience with this phenomenon, and his past mishaps had gone straight to the morgue, which was why he insisted that the EMT teams transport the victims of cold water drowning in the same frigid state as when they fished them out.

"Thanks, guys." Pierce pointed with his thumb to a cubicle just off the main entrance, a space reserved exclusively for his own use. Most of the regular emergency room staff stopped at the door. The area into which they wheeled John Merritt's gurney was Pierce's private domain, and those present were there by his orders only. No interested observers allowed.

The small windowless room was already full almost to capacity with equipment. The most important piece of apparatus, the portable cardio-pulmonary bypass machine, sat beside the bed obstructing the path of anyone trying to wedge past, but no one dared suggest that it be moved. The bypass instrument, a squat, metallic box sporting an array of digital signals already in full operational mode, was a scaled down version of the essential technology found in every operating room where cardiac surgeons plied their skills. Inside the device a thermal unit had already warmed the coils of tubing powered by roller pumps that would perform the task that John Merritt's own cardiovascular system now failed to do.

That such a mechanical marvel could be rendered both compact and portable for use in an emergency room was, in large part, a tribute to the dogged brilliance of the young Chinese national known only as Chang who now manned the dials on the front of the bypass machine. But Chang, with his limited English skills had reaped few accolades for his accomplishments. Those laurels were reserved for Pierce himself. If the inventor's name appeared at all on the reports that Pierce published it was added only as a footnote, in small print.

Of all the staff packed into the small cubicle, only Chang himself seemed immune to the excitement that emanated from Pierce and spread through the others like an electric charge. They stood on tiptoes, hyperventilating like sprinters before a race. But Chang's reaction was altogether different. That he and his magical apparatus were about to accomplish what could best be described as a resurrection didn't appear to arouse him at all. He focused on the instrument's various dials with no more apparent emotion than if he were trying to dial in his favorite radio station.

Jammed into the corner at the head of the bed opposite the bypass machine, a technician sorted through the maze of wires that ran from an electroencephalogram. She would shortly attach these leads to various sites on John's skull, providing a continuous monitor of his brain activity.

The remaining members of Pierce's official team were three: an EKG technician who would report on John's cardiac status, a nurse who would insert cannulas from the bypass machine into his blood vessels, and, off in the far corner, a petite woman with a clipboard in hand who would record the events as they transpired in the room. In her left hand she clutched a single syringe containing ten milliliters of opaque liquid. If you looked closely at the barrel of the syringe, the label read Dormistan.

The EMTs stopped at the door and waited while Pierce's staff freed the restraints holding John to the gurney, then rolled him onto the waiting bed. The team went into action without hesitation. Time was the enemy now. The more quickly they accomplished their assigned tasks, the better the chance of a good outcome. Within moments John's sodden clothing was stripped away, and, aside from the towel someone had thought to drape across his genitals, he lay as bare as the day he came into the world. One glance at his blue, unresponsive figure should have been enough to cancel out any further attempts at resuscitation, but the team plunged on, just as Pierce had instructed them.

The ER nurse inserted a temperature probe into John's rectum. "Body temperature fifty-seven," she said.

Within moments one tech had EKG leads attached to John's chest. "Flat line," she called out soon after.

From the head of the table, the EEG technician echoed the call, "Flat line."

In other words, John Merritt was as dead as dead could be.

"Got it," the bypass technician said, as she successfully threaded a catheter into John's femoral vein high on his left thigh. Ordinarily this did not require an announcement, but since John had no pulse, the femoral artery which lay beside the vein, and which she most definitely did not want to puncture by mistake, could not be used as a landmark. She had only her technical skill and experience to guide her. She quickly switched over to John's right side, swabbed his upper thigh with Betadine, and pierced what she hoped was his femoral artery with a large-bore needle. Ordinarily she could tell from the color of the blood return whether she'd hit her target. The bright red of the arterial blood would contrast sharply with the darker hue of the venous circulation. But that difference in color was due to the higher oxygen content of the arterial blood, and oxygenation depended on cardiac and pulmonary function. Both of these vital systems had shut down shortly after John plunged into the icy lake water, so all of his blood looked the same…cold and blue, like death.

The staff members, with the exception of Chang who was already hard at work, looked back to Pierce for confirmation. They were ready to start. The bypass machine hummed as John's blood began to circulate through its coils. In addition to supplying circulatory assistance, the apparatus allowed controlled re-warming of John's body temperature, a process that had to proceed from the inside out—first the core, then the extremities.

Pierce took up his position by the door. like a conductor waiting for the precise moment to bring his orchestra to life. He stood above the fray, watching his team carry out their tasks. Indeed, he had not even touched the patient lying on the gurney, and would not until the process of resuscitation was complete. Establishing the standard doctor-patient relationship would have to wait until John Merritt, whoever he was, had crossed back into the land of the living. Pierce nodded to the woman holding the Dormistan syringe.

"Let's go," he said.

#

Dr. Paul Pierce was quite familiar with the marvelous physiologic protective mechanism that somehow preserved the spark of life even in the presence of clinical death. He had staked his modest professional reputation on successful resuscitation of such victims with the use of the portable cardiopulmonary bypass machine.

"Sixty-seven degrees." The technician monitoring John's vital signs made a note of the temperature. Indeed it was the only value she transcribed. The rest of the data that would ordinarily be logged—blood pressure, pulse, respirations, and such—were absent.

Pierce stood off to one side, watching his team at work. At this point he was more like a conductor, someone directing the activities of a group of skilled professionals. He took a long look at John Merritt; was it still appropriate to call the subject of their labors by his name? Would it be better to refer to it as John Merritt's body, or John Merritt's remains? Because most certainly, the life force, whatever it was, was gone now. But he, Paul Pierce, M.D., was going to retrieve it, to reinstall it in the moribund body that lay before him.

He checked his watch; twenty-six minutes. Twenty-six minutes since the gurney bearing John Merritt had passed through the door; that was the number that counted. He could just as well have designated a starting time as the point at which they switched on the bypass machine, but that was not the way he worked. From the moment a patient entered his medical domain, that's when the clock started. He accepted full responsibility from that point on.

"Seventy-four degrees."

Waiting was the hardest part. He was confident that his medical regimen would successfully revive his patient; a return of cardiac and respiratory activity would tell him when that had occurred. But there was no way of knowing about the patient's neurological status. At normal body temperatures, the brain deprived of oxygen would degenerate quickly. The situation was altogether different when the victim was submerged in cold water. Just as other body systems shut down and survived lack of oxygen for extended periods, the brain did likewise. People submerged for thirty minutes and longer recovered with normal neurological function.

This return of normal neurological activity was the most miraculous aspect of what was taking place now. That incredible database stored in the human brain, where did it go when someone pulled the switch? If you lost power to your computer, chances are you lost whatever data was floating around at the time. How could the brain be so much more efficient? Was there some sort of evolutionary advantage to having such a capacity? Pierce pondered these questions as he watched his team carry out their assigned tasks. He had no answers, of course, no one did. All that mattered was his ability to restore that mental function, an ability shared by a precious few. You're a lucky man, Mr. Merritt, Pierce said to himself.

"Eighty-two degrees."

"We have something." The technician following John's EKG pointed to the monitor where the flat line tracing began to show a series of slow but regular beats. An irregular heartbeat, sometimes even fatal arrhythmias, occurred often enough during this phase of the recovery, but Pierce wasn't concerned. The Dormistan injection would take care of that problem, and others as well.

Moments later the EEG tracing showed some activity. The technician who monitored the recording turned and gave Pierce a thumbs up.

"Eighty-nine degrees." By now John had a regular pulse and a blood pressure to go with it. His EEG showed a mixed pattern of slow waves, as if he were waking from a deep sleep. Pierce checked his watch. Thirty-seven minutes had elapsed since John had arrived.

"Okay, let's get him up to the unit."

# Chapter 2

For a man who, a short while ago could have been pronounced dead on arrival, John Merritt was feeling surprisingly chipper. He sat up in bed, his face covered in lather, while the young nurse shaved him. Sure, he could have done it himself, but this was every man's fantasy, right? Lying in bed while some sweet young thing dressed in white fussed over him? He had pushed himself over to the far side of the bed, not to get away from her, but so she had to practically crawl in with him to reach his face. Yeah, every man's fantasy. He lifted his knee to hide the erection he felt creeping upward. Damn, that thing had a mind of its own. Every time something in a white skirt swished by it had to stand up for a better look.

If he weren't enjoying himself so much at the moment, he might have wondered about all this new sexual energy. After all, he hadn't always been this way. His present state of almost continuous arousal was completely at odds with the shyness that had characterized him for so many years. Oh, there had been plenty of opportunities. He attracted lots of attention from the opposite sex, but, when it came down to the act itself, John usually fumbled the ball. Premature ejaculation, they called it. After a number of embarrassing and very sticky encounters he decided the humiliation just wasn't worth it. The worst part, his brother, Christopher—never Chris--never seemed to have any problem at all. "How do you keep from, you know…too soon?" John had asked.

"Too soon?" Christopher said. "No problem. Just get it in, that's all that counts. The rest doesn't matter."

It was a lot easier then to stand back and let his brother be the ladies' man, something he was really good at. Of course, Christopher was good at almost everything he tried, or so it seemed. That's what people expected, anyway. John, a year younger than his illustrious sibling, was doomed to a life of second place.

"Why can't you be more like your brother?" If he'd heard that once he'd heard it a thousand times. Or worse still, "Hard to believe you two guys are brothers." That one stung because sometimes he wondered himself, how could they be so different just one year apart?

But all that seemed far in the past now. He lay back and closed his eyes as the nurse applied soft strokes of the razor beneath his chin. The scent of her wrapped around him like a pleasant fog. He wanted to grab her, pull her beneath him and….

"Mr. Merritt, are you okay?" the young nurse asked. She sat close beside him on the bed, her hip pressed against his own.

"Huh? What?"

"You were moaning."

"A little dizzy, that's all."

"Maybe I shouldn't have raised the head of your bed so high." She pushed a button at the bedside, and John was lowered down flat, except for his knee that he kept raised to conceal his obvious arousal.

"Here, let's straighten your leg out." She pushed down on his knee.

"No, it's okay, a little cramp."

"Then it should be out straight." She pressed down with both hands. The leg went out straight and all was lost. His erection caused a tent in the middle of his bed sheet that left no doubt about his current feelings.

"Oh, my goodness, Mr. Merritt. Oh, my goodness."

#

*Stacey Patterson, M. D., Upstate Medical Center.* She clipped the nametag to her white jacket and frowned at her reflection in the mirror, trying to look stern and professional. But the frown didn't last. It never did. It was as if the facial musculature that might tug downward at the corners of her mouth was missing. The grin popped back into place. She couldn't help it.

Buxom, blond and bubbly—she got it all from her mother. Of course, Mom by now had gone a bit past buxom, quite a bit past, and her blond hair was being overcome by a siege of gray, thanks mostly to Stacey's three older brothers. But her perpetually upbeat personality hadn't changed in the least, neither had Stacey's during her undergraduate years at Syracuse University, or during four long arduous years of training at Upstate Medical Center.

Stacey's appearance had marked her from the day she entered her current post-graduate training program. "There," said the surgical chief resident who was inspecting the new crop of trainees, "is your basic corn-fed midwestern beauty." He added a prediction that he would nail her before the Thanksgiving holiday. He was wrong on all counts. To begin with, Stacey was not from the Midwest. She had grown up on a dairy farm just northeast of Canandaigua, New York, and she didn't like corn at all. The corn she knew was destined to become cattle feed. She didn't like the surgeon either. So far as she cared, they could use him for cattle feed too.

Now in her second year of postgraduate training she managed to maintain her "glass-half-full" outlook. True, she had taken her share of lumps and bruises along the way; almost daily contact with death and dying made such things unavoidable. But along the way she had grown. What might have begun as wide-eyed optimism had deepened into a personal constitution that could embrace joy and despair on equal terms, most of the time.

It was changeover day for the residency staff. Stacey was finishing her tour on the renal service, which she hated, and was headed back to the internal medicine wards. She scanned the list of patients that would become her own and dropped her clipboard when she saw his name— John Merritt. It couldn't be. Not the John Merritt from Canandaigua High School. Not the John Merritt who had left her blubbering like some fool kid who had just had her ice cream cone snatched away.

Stacey retrieved the clipboard, then pulled John's hospital chart from the rack. Next she looked for a chair; her knees were wobbly. John had been transferred up from the ICU earlier that morning. She flipped through the pages of medical information only half aware of what she was reading. Twenty-nine years old, the age was right. He had been a year ahead of her at Canandaigua High.

"Are you okay?" One of the nurses patted Stacey's shoulder. "You look a little shaky."

"Too much coffee," Stacey said.

"Hope that's it." The nurse laughed. "You're way too young for hot flashes."

Stacey was shaky all right, and it had nothing to do with coffee. It had everything to do with the emotional rush going on inside her, and she had never been good at concealing her emotions. She and John Merritt had a history, and after all these years she'd never been able to get past it. Even now she felt like a silly schoolgirl mooning over an upperclassman. Get a grip, girl, for God's sake, he's a patient, you're a doctor—his doctor, not his old girlfriend.

She put the chart back in the rack and went on to the next patient on her list, but it was no use. For all the concentration she could muster she might as well have been reading the comics in the Sunday paper; he was in her head and she could think of nothing else.

Memories rushed in like a snowstorm, coming from everywhere at once--John Merritt, so shy at first that if she even looked at him he would duck his head and scurry away like a frightened rabbit. Somehow his shyness made him all the more attractive to her. Then the attraction grew with all the fragile power of a rose in bloom, and he filled her world.

Those winter months they shared were magical. One night in early February he parked by the edge of the path, now buried in snow, that led to the barn.

"A barn?" she said. "You're taking me to a barn? You sure know how to show a girl a good time."

"Come on, it's a surprise."

They struggled down the path through knee-deep snow, arms wrapped tightly around each other. They fell, whether accidental or on purpose, no matter. They rolled around like a pair of otters until she finally managed to get astride him.

"Got you now," she said. Then she leaned down and kissed him.

"Get off me, woman." He laughed. "You haven't seen your surprise yet."

"Is it better than this?"

He pulled her closer. "Nothing could be better than this, but I'm freezing."

The barn was warm and musty. "Oh, my gosh," she said. "I can't believe it." She walked around the sleigh, a two-seater that sat between the horses' stalls. "Where on earth did you find this?"

"It was in the shed out back. I put in a new seat, cleaned it up a bit."

"And bells. You put on bells." She ran her fingertips along the row of shining ornaments that lined the sides of the sleigh. "But I thought the bells were supposed to go on the horse."

"Tried that. Scared the hell out of him, so I had to put them on the sleigh. When did you get so picky anyway?"

"Just giving you a hard time. It's beautiful. But how are you going to keep me warm?"

"How do you think?"

They rode west through the pines where snow from overhanging limbs sifted down on them until they were both cloaked in white. When they turned into the pasture the sleigh flipped, dumping them both. They lay side by side, laughing until they could laugh no more.

"I believe your horse thinks we're crazy," she said.

"I believe he's right."

But the happy days ended that stormy afternoon on the lake; Christopher drowned, John survived. She knew John blamed himself for his brother's death, and knew just as well that he was blameless. It was a horrible, tragic accident, but no one could convince John of that. He built a wall around himself and stayed there. His blue eyes, once a source of so much joy and merriment became lifeless pools.

John went into a shell that nobody could crack. Heaven knows, Stacey tried, and the trying almost killed her.

Finally, her own mother ended it. "I forbid it, do you hear me? You will not see him again." She'd grabbed Stacey by the shoulders, shaken her hard. "Look at yourself. You look awful. Your teachers call me every day. They're all worried sick about you."

She wrapped Stacey in her arms. "I know you love him, honey, but this has to stop. You've done all you can do."

So, she stopped, but she didn't forget.

#

But that was all years ago. She had changed a lot since then, gone off to school, became a doctor. I'm a different person now, she said to herself.

Bullshit. The word popped into her mind as if from nowhere, and everywhere. And it rang true. In spite of the nine years during which she hadn't laid eyes on John Merritt, even seeing his name now sent her into a tailspin. Bullshit was right. You better be very careful, girl, she told herself, knowing well enough she was right on the edge.

She patted her nametag again. Dr. Stacey Patterson. That's who I am, and I can take care of business. I know I can. Then from somewhere, that distant echo…bullshit. No, not really, she hadn't changed at all, not when it came to John Merritt. She stood up, steadying herself for a moment. She had to see him.

She touched the nametag one last time, reminding herself of who she was and what she was. Reminding herself that if she wasn't very careful she might make a complete fool of herself. She would be seeing him every morning on rounds, and probably several times after that. Could she keep things professional? Did she really want to?

How did that old refrain go, hurt me once, shame on you. Hurt me twice, shame on me. If it were only that simple.

#

The day before John's transfer to the medical ward Herman Poulos snuck in to see him. Only family members had visitation privileges in the ICU, but Herman had bluffed his way through by saying he was John's uncle and his last living relative. This statement was only a mild stretch of the truth; although he had no blood tie to the man, Herman was the only human John allowed inside his protective shield. John wrapped the little man in a bear hug and squeezed the breath out of him. "Damn, I'm glad to see you."

"Then why are you trying to kill me?" Herman wheezed in John's grip.

John let him go, and Herman backed a safe distance away from the bedside. "You look pretty good for a dead man," Herman said. "That's what you were when they fished you out, you know."

"They said if it hadn't been for you I'd still be at the bottom of the lake. I owe you big time, man."

"Hell, I never should have let you go out there in the first place. I knew better. You did too." Herman shoved his hands in his pockets, like he always did when he was frustrated.

Neither spoke for a moment. The issue was one they had gone over many times before, why a perfectly reasonable man would go fooling around on thin ice all by himself was one thing, but there had been other equally foolish acts on John's part, most of them involving that damned lake, or, the scene of the crime—his crime—as he thought of it.

"Won't change nothing," Herman said finally.

John had no answer for that. How could he atone for a death, how indeed?

"I'm only going to say this once more; it wasn't your damned fault. Not that you ever listen to me."

John reached out and Herman took his hand. "Maybe you're right, but sometimes it seems like I just can't help myself. Maybe I was born stupid."

"All the more reason you should take my advice." Herman chuckled, a dry, rattling sound that sounded like footsteps in dry leaves. "Okay, that's enough chit chat. When are they gonna let you out of this nuthouse?"

"I think they're moving me out to a regular bed next day or so. Honest, I haven't thought much about leaving. Have you seen the nurses here?"

"Ah." Herman rolled his eyes upward. "That's why you're looking so frisky. Never figured you for that type. You never were before. They put something in your food?"

"Damned if I know, but every time one walks by I want to latch onto her. And would you look at this." John pulled up the sleeve of his hospital gown revealing three small puncture marks all in line. "Skin biopsies, they called them."

"Why'd they do that?"

"Don't know, but the little girl who did them, cute as a button. Wouldn't mind a bit if she came back and did it again."

"Hate to spoil your fun, but you got a ranch and a business to run, remember?"

The Merritt legacy—a small ranch of about fifty acres, mostly in pasture, and a construction supply business just off Main Street downtown, next to the post office. Aside from a reduction in acreage, a visitor to the ranch would swear it hadn't changed a bit in the past fifty years. The only buildings, a three-bedroom house forged from hand-hewn logs and a barn with a roof that sagged in the middle, had been painted and repaired over the years, but basically unchanged. About one

Mike Owens

hundred yards south of the barn the remains of a vineyard spread over a hillside that sloped eastward. In years past John's dad had planted rows of cabernet grapes there, supported by posts he'd cut from the surrounding woodland. It was all part of a master plan, a family vineyard that he would expand and pass on to his sons. But Christopher's death and its tragic aftermath had dashed those plans, and the small stand of grape vines lay untended and unnoticed. Any fruit the vines bore was consumed by birds and raccoons.

Time had also taken its toll on the office and storage space that housed the Merritt Construction Supply business. Flanked on either side by newer brick buildings, it looked like a quaint relic, maintained only for historical purposes. The cash flow for the business was mostly historical too. In good years John broke even. Most years weren't good.

A mammoth chain store, twice the size of his shop, had opened just outside town two years before, and Merritt Construction Supply had been bleeding red ink ever since. His old customers, passed down from his father, and his grandfather before him, were retiring, and all the new business was gobbled up by that new store with all its bright lights and free parking.

"How are my animals?" John asked. His livestock holdings now consisted of four horses—two of his own and two that he boarded for his neighbor—and his dog, Rebel.

"Horses are fine. Damned dog won't eat when you're not around."

"Well, guess I better get out of here then. There's got to be women outside the hospital somewhere."

"Women? What's got into you, John?"

#

John's last couple of nights in the ICU were more eventful than he would have liked.

One evening, after the nurse had taken away his dinner tray, he saw them for the first time. Shadowy figures, first one, then three of them, hovered around his bed. Only the upper parts of them were distinct. The lower parts—what should have been legs and feet—were all haze, as if they were standing in fog. When one drew close he tried to touch it but his hand passed directly through, like touching smoke. Damn, the place was getting to him for sure. Either that or he was going

22

crazy. Almost an hour passed before he worked up enough courage to report this to the nurse.

"What you think you're seeing are just hallucinations," she said. "That's quite common in the ICU."

"How are you so sure they're not real?" John asked.

"We have a video monitor in your room that shows everyone who goes in or out. If there were any extra people around, they'd show up on the monitor. Don't worry about it. They'll all go away when you're moved to the regular floor."

"When will that be?"

"As soon as Dr. Pierce says you can safely be transferred."

But the next night, the three figures reappeared. They were more distinct now. Dressed in hospital gowns, they looked like patients. One was a very old woman, standing alongside a black man about fifty, and the third, a young child. The child was completely bald, and John couldn't tell whether it was a boy or a girl. The apparitions stood at the foot of his bed and stared at him. "Who are you?" he asked. "What do you want?"

They moved toward him, passing right through the solid sides of his bed. He could hear no sound, but there was definitely something going on. It was as if someone were speaking from behind thick glass; he could see it but couldn't hear it, not yet. He rang for the nurse.

"What's wrong now, Mr. Merritt?" a tired voice asked over the intercom.

"They're back."

"Who's back?"

"Those people I told the nurse about this morning. They're all here in my room."

"Mr. Merritt, you're having hallucinations again. Your monitor doesn't show anyone in the room but you. Shall I come and give you something to help you sleep?"

#

They moved John out of the ICU about nine the next morning. And—joy of joys—his new room was right across from the nurses' station. All morning he watched them parade back and forth in their pristine white uniforms. There were other ways he could have entertained himself, watching TV, reading a book, counting the ceiling tiles, but he couldn't tear himself away from the angels of mercy.

He was now in a semi-private room and had a roommate—the town drunk. John recognized the man who for years had meandered up and down the streets of Canandaigua in various states of inebriation. One morning he and Herman had arrived at the shop to find the man passed out in their doorway. Herman grabbed him by the collar and chunked him into the street. Herman did not care for drunks. The man was quiet for most of the morning. Apparently the nurses kept him sedated.

A little past ten the technician from Dr. Pierce's lab arrived with John's special medication. She was the same one who had delivered a single pill for him each morning while he had been in the ICU. Unlike the nurses and other staff, she dressed in jeans and a blue work shirt. Only her nametag identified her as a hospital employee. When John questioned her about the pill, she said "Dr. Pierce wants you to continue it." When he asked her what it was for she told him to ask Dr. Pierce.

Suddenly the drunk woke up and started singing. His screech startled the technician who dropped the medicine cup. While she searched the floor for the errant pill John enjoyed the best laugh he'd had in weeks. He rolled over to the edge of his bed to get a better view of the technician's backside as she bent down to retrieve the pill, and, when he looked up he saw someone he never expected to see again.

Couldn't be, could it? Then the rather stern face, obviously a ruse, dissolved into a familiar grin, complete with a giggle. It couldn't be anybody but her.

"Hi, John, Stacey Patterson. Remember me?"

Oh, yes, he remembered. And the memory hit him like a punch in the gut.

The technician stood up. "Got it. I'll be right back with your pill."

"A clean one, right?" John said.

"Wait, what pill?" Stacey asked.

"Some pill Dr. Pierce wants me to take," John said. "I still don't know what it is or what it's for."

"I'm Dr. Patterson." Again, the stern face, aimed squarely at the technician. "I'll be taking care of Mr. Merritt, so I need to know about his medications, all of them."

The technician paused, obviously not enjoying the questions. "It's

24

called Dormistan."

"Never heard of it," Stacey said. "What's it for?"

"Best you ask Dr. Pierce." The technician left in a huff.

"Stacey Patterson, I can't believe it," said John. "After all these years. And you're a doctor now."

She shifted back and forth from one foot to the other as if unsure what to say next.

The drunk broke the tension. "Hey, sweetheart, when you're through with him, how about you examine me?" He raised himself as far as he could in his restraints. "I got a lot of pains."

"You *are* a pain." John threw a magazine at him.

Stacey drew the curtain that separated their two beds. "I took a quick look at your hospital chart. You've been through a lot."

"My own fault," he said. "Just plain stupid going out on thin ice. Should have known better."

The silence that ensued was even more awkward than before, as though neither of them knew the ground rules for this new relationship. What was it to be? Doctor-patient? Old friends? Sweethearts?

It bothered him that she knew intimate details about him, that stuff that finds its way into medical charts. Of course, she would know his old history too, all about Christopher's death. It didn't seem quite fair, but there was nothing he could do about it.

A beeping noise. Stacey took her pager from her pocket. "It's my team. I'm late for rounds. Look, I'll check up on that Dormistan for you, see what I can find out." It seemed she couldn't get out of the room fast enough.

The drunk struck up another tune, something about a long lonesome road. Yeah, John knew that song.

That last night, what, nine years ago, she'd screamed in his face. Then she'd slapped him, hard. Then tears, a veritable flood. She took his face in her hands. "Are you in there, John? Can you hear me?"

"You don't understand." It sounded completely lame, but it was the best he could do.

"No, I understand perfectly." She blubbered as tears ran into her mouth, and she spat them into his face. "You can't get it through your thick skull. It wasn't your fault. You have to let it go. You have to let Christopher go."

25

He tried so hard to think of something to say, something sensible that wasn't gibberish. But anything that came out of a brain as muddled as his stood no chance. So he said nothing.

"John?"

More nothing.

And nothing was what he felt when he watched her stumble away, out of his life, because inside he was dead now. Wherever feeling should have been lay as barren as any desert, and a dry, powerful wind howled across its surface.

#

"Go ahead, measure it."

"I'll do no such thing."

The two night nurses, one a grizzled veteran just a year from retirement, the other a middle-aged matron who worked nights so she wouldn't be around when her husband got home from work, stood at John's bedside gazing at the very impressive erection that had become a nightly occurrence with him. They had been warned by the ICU nurses about his nocturnal tumescence and had gathered round to watch, sort of like watching the moon rise. Soon they were joined by a third nurse, a much younger woman who had only started work at the hospital two weeks before.

"Oh, my God," she said. "Is it real?"

"Grab hold, see for yourself. Better still, measure it." The older nurse thrust a measuring tape into the new arrival's hand. "He's not going to wake up. He had enough Seconal to put a horse to sleep."

The younger nurse unrolled the tape and stretched it alongside John's erect member.

"I think I'm in love," said the nurse who had given her the tape.

The desk clerk, who was their lookout, rushed into the room. "She's coming," she said.

"Yeah, so am I," said the veteran nurse, and the entire group convulsed in laughter.

Stacey rushed through the door. "What's the big emergency?"

The nurses, who were laughing too hard to speak, stepped away from the bedside revealing the small tent arising in the middle of John's bed. "We thought you should check this out. It looks dangerous." More laughter.

Stacey stomped her foot. Her anger was real enough, but her physical appearance gave her away; it always did. Her complexion was so fair that, when she blushed, it was as if someone had poured red dye into a clear liquid. Even in the semi-darkness of John's room everyone could see her distress.

"This is not acceptable," she said. "What do you expect me to do about that?"

"We thought you'd know. You're a doctor, right?"

# Chapter 3

John's stay on the medical ward was brief. On the afternoon of his second day Dr. Pierce arrived with his small entourage and announced he was setting John free. He pulled a chair up to John's bedside and laid out the ground rules. "I only require two things of you when you leave."

"Anything, Doc. Without you I wouldn't be here at all."

But John's gratitude was tempered by a growing dislike for the physician. He wasn't even sure of what exactly about Paul Pierce rubbed him the wrong way. It was more like some visceral aversion, the kind of reaction he'd seen from his dog; some people he liked, some people he didn't, simple as that.

Like many other patients, he was willing to overlook some of the behavioral quirks exhibited by medical professionals—and Pierce had many of those—in view of their seemingly miraculous abilities to save and preserve life. He'd heard from any number of the hospital staff that the only thing that had stood between him and a slab in the morgue was Dr. Paul Pierce. He had entered the hospital stone cold dead, and now he was leaving, alive and feeling great. How could he not be grateful for that?

Well, gratitude was one thing, trust was another. Trust was that bond he shared with his friend, Herman Poulos. But Paul Pierce? Not even close.

Pierce handed him a bottle of pills, the same ones John had taken every morning. The label only gave instructions—one tablet each morning before breakfast—but nothing else. "There are sixty tablets here," Pierce said. "When you run out you'll have to come back to see me for a refill."

"Can't you just give me a prescription?"

"You can't get this by prescription," Pierce said. "But it's absolutely essential that you take it every day. Do you understand?"

"Sure, whatever you say."

"The other thing is, no alcohol. And no drugs."

"I'm not a drinking man," John said. "Maybe a beer once in a while, but that's about it."

"And every couple of months we'll repeat your skin biopsy." Pierce stood and shook John's hand, then turned to leave. "Carol will give you a list of your return appointments." The same technician who had brought John's pill each day handed him a printout. He would be coming back the first Wednesday of each month. It seemed like a hell of a lot of return visits, but considering that Pierce had saved his life, maybe not too much after all.

He wasn't overjoyed, either, at the prospect of more skin biopsies. He'd already had three during his hospital stay. When he asked Pierce about them all the doctor would say was that the tissue samples helped them monitor the effects of the medication. The only upside was Alicia, the Asian girl who did the biopsies. If she were any cuter John might have jumped her right there at the bedside.

Stacey had not been in Pierce's group the afternoon when John was discharged. She had come in earlier to say good-bye. Things hadn't gone as he had hoped between the two of them. Her visits had been brief and infrequent and completely professional. When she did show up she seemed distant, almost embarrassed as she performed her daily physical examination, checking John's heart, lungs, poking around on his abdomen. He had tried to get her to loosen up a bit, talk about old times at Canandaigua High School, but she would have none of it.

"So, Dr. Pierce is letting you go today," she said. She kept her gaze riveted on his hospital chart, as if she dared not look him in the eye.

"Yeah, finally. Be good to get back home."

"Is someone coming to pick you up?"

"Yeah, Herman. You remember him?"

"Of course. How is he?"

"Great. Herm's just great."

"Well, uh, good luck then." She stuck out her hand for a shake.

So, that was it? A handshake?

She turned to leave, her face a glossy crimson.

30

At least the nurses didn't seem to find him so repulsive. They had waited on him hand and foot, even when he no longer needed any assistance. They couldn't do enough for him. On the day he left several of them, some considerably older than he, had come by to leave phone numbers, addresses with him, just in case he ever needed anything, anything at all. Even a couple from the ICU came up to say goodbye, to wish him well. More phone numbers on small strips of paper slipped into his open hand. Damn, what a nice group of ladies. It was the kind of attention his brother Christopher would have expected, but it was all new to John, and he liked it.

One thing, though, he would be all too glad to leave behind— those damned visions, or hallucinations, whatever they were. He thought he'd be rid of them when he got out of the ICU, but they had followed him to the medical ward; three of the original ones from the ICU along with a couple of new ones. What bothered him was, they were becoming much more distinct. He could see their faces clearly now. As they hovered around his bed he got the clear impression they wanted something from him. He even asked his roommate, the town drunk, whether he ever saw things that weren't really there.

"Oh, sure, all the time."

"Do you recognize them?" John asked.

"No, nothing like that. Mine are mostly animals."

Surely these things, whatever they were, would have the decency to stay in the hospital. No way they could follow him home.

Later that morning Herman picked him up at the hospital entrance. 'How are you feeling?" The brisk air was a shock, and John was grateful for the jacket Herman had remembered to bring.

"Great. Ready to get back to work." As they drove away John glanced back, half expecting to see specters waving at him from the front lawn. But none of those appeared; he saw Stacey instead, standing there with a very perplexed expression on her face, like there was something she wanted to say and had just missed the opportunity. She didn't wave or anything.

#

"Stupid, stupid, stupid." Stacey slammed her heavy medicine textbook down on the library table.

"Hey, who are you calling stupid?" The medical student whose

31

coffee she had sloshed looked up at her.

She grabbed some tissues to mop up the spill. "Not you…me. I just did something really incredibly stupid."

"Dang, you look like you just lost your best friend."

"Yeah, that about says it."

"You want to talk about it?"

"No, thanks, but no." She looked down at the offending hand, the one she had extended to John Merritt a short while before. A handshake? That was the best she could offer? For God's sakes, she'd wanted to climb into the hospital bed with him. Instead, she'd shaken his hand.

Now what? Her gut twisted itself into little knots. All those opportunities she'd let slip away. All those times she'd walked into his room with a little prepared speech in her mind, only to have it evaporate as her brain turned to jelly when she saw him. All those years in school, what was the point of it all when she stood face to face with the man she loved and couldn't even tell him? Stupid, stupid, stupid.

#

Canandaigua was a small town after all, a place where things didn't change so much as they evolved slowly. The summer months got crazy with all the tourists, but the rest of the year one day was much like the next. People liked it that way, and when something shifted about quicker than expected they sat up and took notice, and they soon noticed John Merritt cruising down Main Street on a brand new jet black Harley Davidson.

"Just like his brother," they said, and it wasn't said kindly. They shared rumors about John tearing around the countryside on his new bike.

"That boy must have something against living," they said. "Right out of the hospital, and now he's found a new way to get himself killed."

Several of the locals had asked Herman about this newer, wilder John Merritt. Perhaps that long spell underwater had addled his brains? Herman's answer was always the same: "All he needs is some time. He's been through a hell of a lot." Herman offered to fight the man who'd made the comment about John's brains being addled, but the man wisely rescinded his speculation.

But they couldn't fault John for lack of effort. The first couple of weeks after his discharge from hospital he worked like a man possessed. By sun up every day he had fed and watered his horses, cleaned out their stalls and turned them out to pasture. By the time Herman got to the shop John had already been at work for an hour or so. He had gone through all the bills, paid about half of them and tossed the others aside until next month.

Merritt Construction Supply was getting some business from a new complex called the Upstate Longevity Center under construction a couple of miles south of town, but the contractor had been slow with his payments, making John even slower with his own.

"Guess when he sees you riding around on that new bike he figures you got plenty of cash," Herman said late one morning as he handed John a cup of coffee.

"Don't make any difference what he thinks," John said. "He better pay up soon or I'm going to start making life hard for him."

Around one o'clock in the afternoon, John and Herman usually broke for lunch. John stuck a sign on the door saying they would be back in one hour, although it seldom took that long. Coburn's, their destination, was down one block and across the street. The eatery had been in operation almost as long as John's own business, and it showed. The hand-painted sign out front, now so faded that only the first two letters remained legible, gave no hint of what lay behind the front doors. But the locals knew, and, like John and Herman, they came, every day.

The early April air was still brisk, and John turned up his collar. Herman trudged along beside him, hands jammed in his pockets. For as long as John had known him, Herman wore the same uniform every day—a brown khaki shirt with a red emblem that said Merritt Supply on the breast pocket, and khaki pants of the same brown color. The only time John saw him dressed differently had been at family funerals, and there had been far too many of those.

The rattle of dishes along with the earthy aroma of Coburn's luncheon meatloaf special greeted them at the door. The lineup of regulars were perched on stools at the counter, working men with grime under their fingernails, shirts worn thin at the elbows. Membership at the Coburn's lunch counter was not automatic. It might take years before a newbie was allowed to join in the friendly banter these men shared each day. It might never happen at all. John had more or less inherited his spot from his father, who had inherited it from his grandfather before him. And Herman, he had been around forever, and belonged anywhere he chose to sit. He was almost a part of the décor, like the worn tables and chairs that never seemed to change.

Ronnie Coburn, the third, or maybe fourth owner of the eatery, had tried a small upgrade once, nothing drastic, just some new plates and cutlery, but the regular customers complained so much he finally retrieved the old stuff, chipped and bent as it was, from the storage bin out back. This group liked things the way they were, the way they'd always been. Why change?

John polished off his meatloaf in nothing flat, then eyed the untouched roll beside Herman's plate. "You gonna eat that?"

"Go ahead." Herman pushed the bread plate over toward John.

John slathered the dry roll in butter then popped the whole thing into his mouth. But he still wasn't satisfied. He gazed up at the rather unappealing assortment of pies behind the counter. That wasn't it either. Then it hit him. He realized what was missing at Coburn's. The only woman in the whole room was Ronnie's twin sister who looked exactly like her brother except with longer hair. John found her no more appealing than the contents of the pie rack.

In less than thirty minutes John and Herman were back on the street, headed back to the shop. Diners tended not to linger at Coburn's; these were men with places to go, paychecks to earn, and there was always someone waiting for a seat.

"You know, I been thinking," John said. "Maybe we ought to try some place new for lunch. What do you think?" Some place a bit livelier with at least a few younger women was what he had in mind, but of course, he would never mention that to Herman.

No sooner was the question out of John's mouth than Herman stopped dead in his tracks. "What the hell are you talking about? We always eat at Coburn's. Your daddy ate there, his daddy too. I don't know what's got into you lately."

"Okay, forget it. I was just thinking, that's all."

"Well, don't think. You make me nervous when you think."

It turned out that, the next afternoon, what John was looking for came looking for him.

"Hi, boys." Janie Sells' voice rang through the shop like a siren's song, and most likely she wasn't there to talk about construction supplies.

John left his office, partly to rescue Herman, partly to watch the show, even though he'd seen it all before. As Janie sashayed up the aisle, all work activity came to a halt. Herman missed the second step on the ladder he was climbing and almost fell on top of her. He was the most capable man John had ever been around, with everything except pretty girls, that is.

Times past, John had been much the same himself, but that was all changed now.

"Be careful, Hermie." Janie patted his thigh as she walked past.

John covered his smile with the back of his hand. He'd get no more work out of poor Herman today. But the carnage wasn't to end there.

"Hi, Johnny." Janie headed straight for him, her short spandex skirt riding up a little higher with each step.

Much like every small community had a town drunk, such as John had seen in the hospital, most also had a town tease. That would be Janie. She had played her role for several years now, causing fights and occasional traffic accidents, but no one knew for sure whether she ever did more than entice. She had certainly made John's life miserable on a number of occasions with her insufferable teasing, but today was going to be different. Janie was about to get what she'd been asking for all along.

"Saw you cruising around on that big bad bike of yours. How come you haven't given me a ride yet?" She perched on tiptoes and gave John a kiss, ran her fingertips along his neck. Ordinarily this was enough to make him turn crimson and forget his own name, but not today.

He sent Herman home, took Janie's arm and led her into his office. In a moment he had her stretched across his desk with her spandex skirt bunched up around her waist.

A person walking past the partially open window in John's office would have heard a medley of barnyard sounds. There were grunts, groans, squeals, and, once, something that sounded like a dog barking. It ended with a dazed Janie staring up at the ceiling praising God and several saints John had never heard of. She was never quite the same after. Just before she left she asked John for her underpants, which he held in his hand. He shook his head. "Souvenir," he said.

35

He watched Janie weave her way toward the front door, wobbling like someone who knew they were drunk, but didn't want it to show. She probably wouldn't be back his way again, but then again, maybe she would.

When he tossed her underpants into the bottom drawer of his desk he discovered several other pair, four to be exact. His recollection of the women who wore them and how they had gotten there was fuzzy at best. He plopped into his chair and stared up at the same ceiling Janie had stared at a short time before.

So much change, so fast. The John Merritt who went into the hospital near death and the one that came out a couple of weeks later seemed to be two different men. It was as if he had a devil whispering into his left ear, and an angel doing the same on his right. More and more often the devil got the upper hand.

He hadn't taken a lot of time yet to consider this drastic change. At the moment he was enjoying himself too much. In a short while he had gone from being a quiet guy whose idea of a great day was one spent in the company of his horses and dog, into someone else entirely, and it didn't take a rocket scientist to figure out who.

Now he knew what it felt like to be Christopher, or so he thought, and it was different from what he expected. His brother always seemed like the happiest guy in town. John never saw him alone. There were always guys and girls—girls, mostly—hanging on Christopher wherever he went. Was that what he really wanted? John never got a chance to ask; then one day on the lake it was too late. It would always be too late. He cracked open the desk drawer and peered again at the pile of underpants—his trophy case. Wonder if his brother had had one too?

# Chapter 4

On one of the rare Sundays when she was completely free from clinical duties, Stacey decided to celebrate with a morning run. As a bonus, an early cloud cover had burned away, and by the time she reached the trail the temperature was already in the low seventies, and climbing. That brief, glorious phenomenon known as spring in the Upstate region had arrived with a flourish, and she meant to enjoy it while she could.

She started with a leisurely jog for a hundred yards or so, then picked up her pace and sprinted past a small stand of young maple trees just beginning to show buds that lined her path. The main purpose of her morning run, aside from burning off a few calories, was to clear her head, and usually it did just that. The four mile track along Irondequoit Bay had enough hills to leave her gasping before she was halfway around, and there was nothing like being severely short of breath to clear all that extraneous detail from one's mind. All her focus narrowed to a single point—oxygen.

Stacey slowed to a walk for about a hundred yards or so where the track leveled off. A few of the lilac bushes on a low ridge to her right were in bloom early and their subtle fragrance wafted down to her courtesy of a soft breeze. Ordinarily this would be enough to attain that clear-headed state she sought, but not this time. As soon as she caught her breath thoughts of John Merritt intruded once again, and along with those thoughts, more confusion. If she hadn't known him years before as a shy, soft-spoken, completely charming boy she would have written off immediately the John Merritt she encountered in the hospital. This new guy, her own patient, no less, was boisterous, a little aggressive, and far too sure of himself to suit her. Hard to believe they were the same person.

Even so, she felt it was worth a phone call, but not to John, that would be too risky. She couldn't trust herself, what she might say. She had a second cousin, Bev Giordano, who still lived in Canandaigua. They usually touched base around the holidays, and Bev always filled her in on doings of former classmates and acquaintances. She knew too that Bev once had a thing for John back in school days, but that should be ancient history now; Bev was married and had two beautiful daughters.

Stacey waited until early afternoon to make the call. She had made up a list of leading questions in case she had to pry information from Bev, but didn't need them. All Stacey had to do was mention John's name, and Bev was off and running.

"You're shitting me. John Merritt? You saw him? What did you do? What did you say? Oh, God, I wish I had been there for that. You two, after all these years."

When Ben paused to catch her breath, Stacey broke in. "Nothing like what you're thinking, Bev. It was strictly professional. He was admitted to my medical service. I was his doctor, that's all."

"Yeah, right, in a pig's eye." Bev howled. "This is too much. Tell me everything, and don't even try to lie to me. I remember how many nights you cried on my shoulder after you two broke up."

"Bev, I haven't even seen him for almost nine years now. We didn't really get a chance to talk much. I just wanted you to catch me up, you know, fill in the blanks." Stacey propped her feet on a sofa cushion and settled in for what she was sure would be a long session.

"Where to start? Let me see. You know, he was still like a zombie after you left. I mean, it was really creepy. He went off to community college in Binghamton for a couple of years, but came back to help his dad."

"He just dropped out?"

"Sort of. You know about his mom leaving, right? Well, from what I hear she raided the family bank account before she took off, and John's dad just couldn't keep up with things, I mean, the ranch and the business too. So John came back to help. From what my dad says he was always the one that kept things going over there, even when he was in school. Like, his dad was always full of big ideas, but John was the one that did most of the work."

"I wonder why they just didn't sell out. Would have been a lot easier," Stacey said.

"My dad says it was a family thing. That ranch has been in the family for years and years, and I think John couldn't let it go. That meant a lot to people around here, how he pitched right in, never complained. Now, if it had been Christopher, he would have sold out in a heartbeat."

The conversation ran on—Bev talking while Stacey listened--and Stacey became more and more concerned over the differences in the old John Merritt she had known before and this newer, flashier version.

Bev shared her confusion.

"What on earth did you all do to him?" Bev wanted to know. She went on and on about how John used to be the nicest guy on the planet until he went for that swim in the frozen lake. "Did he have brain damage?" Bev asked. "Must have been. I never saw anybody change so much so fast. The whole town's talking about him."

Bev never paused long enough for Stacey to answer her questions, but that was nothing new. When she was on a roll the only thing you could do was put your feet up and wait until she ran out of gas, or air.

Even so, Stacey was taken aback by Bev's description of John's escapades. Several husbands around town had taken to coming home for lunch, apparently to make sure their young wives were keeping house, not playing house.

"And he used to be so shy," Bev went on, and on. "Remember how, in school, if you said boo to him he'd almost wet himself? From what I hear, any girl who does that now will find her pants down around her ankles in no time flat. That's what I hear, at least. Spitting image of his brother, if you ask me."

For the briefest moment Stacey wondered whether Bev might be speaking from experience, but no, not with a nice husband and two great kids, no way.

"Brain damage." Bev gave her diagnosis one last time. "Got to be it."

"So, now, the big question," Bev said. "When are you going to see him again?"

"We didn't make plans or anything. Like I said, it was just a doctor-patient thing."

"You are the world's worst liar, you know that?"

Maybe, Stacey thought. Worse still, she might be lying to herself.

After she and Bev exchanged promises to get together over the summer, Stacey rang off and poured herself a cup of lukewarm coffee. She spilled a few drops of liquid on the notepad where she had written John's name a half dozen times during their conversation with Bev.

She considered Bev's summation once again—brain damage, no that wasn't it. There had to be another explanation. Medication, she wondered? She still had no information at all about the mysterious pills Dr. Pierce gave John.

Dormistan, they called it. She had checked the hospital formulary, but it wasn't even listed. For sure she was going to find out.

\#

"Hi, fellas. Remember me?" John called over his shoulder as he backed into the EMT on-call office, a small room with an entrance adjacent to the hospital's emergency room, lugging a case of beer. It had taken him the better part of the day to find out the names of the two who had kept him alive after he was dragged from the lake, but he figured he owed these guys big time. The office reminded John of his old college dorm room, dirty clothes strewn about, a couple of old pizza slices left lying in an open box. Apparently the staff was all male, as no woman would likely tolerate such squalor.

Neither of the men sitting at the table playing cards showed any immediate sign of recognizing him.

"I'm John Merritt. You fellas pulled me out of the lake about awhile back. At least, I think it was you guys. I guess I was out cold when you were working on me." John sat the case of beer on the table in front of them. "I don't suppose either of you drinks beer, but maybe you know somebody who does."

"You're that guy," one of the EMTs said, rising to shake John's hand. Instead John grabbed him in a bear hug.

"I'm Jeff, that's Larry there," he said, although the breath was effectively squeezed out of him by the exuberance of John's hug. "Jesus, watch him, Larry, he's strong as a bull. I think he cracked one of my ribs."

"Not bad for a dead man." Larry extended his hand but kept the table between John and himself. His uniform shirt hung unbuttoned revealing a generous abdomen protruding beneath a hairy chest.

"We tried to see you at the hospital, but they wouldn't let us in. Some doctor claimed you couldn't have visitors. They've never done that before." Jeff, almost as tall as John and at least twenty pounds heavier, rubbed the side of his chest.

"Dr. Pierce?" John said. He was relieved to know that some people cared enough to try to visit him, but why had Pierce kept him in virtual isolation?

"Yeah, I think that was his name."

"Pierce is a weird duck, but I guess he saved my ass, so I can't complain too much. You guys really did it for me, though. If you hadn't pulled me out and kept me alive there wouldn't be any story to tell. God knows, I can't thank either of you enough for what you did."

"No problem, man. It's great to see you up and about, and able to break Jeff's ribs." Larry fumbled beneath the table and retrieved a pair of slippers.

"Sorry about the squeeze. I got carried away. I'm just so grateful to you both." And he was. The two men facing him could just as easily have pronounced him dead on the spot, and no one would have questioned their call.

"Look, we've only got a few more minutes on shift. Is that beer cold?" Jeff asked.

"It is, and I'm gonna be real put out if you don't start drinking," John said.

"I'm not gonna argue with a man as strong as you are." Jeff tore open the top of the case. "Three tall ones coming up."

"Say, guys, you've pulled other people out of the drink like that, haven't you?" John asked. He dragged a chair to the table and sat, took a few deep breaths to calm himself. Sure, his gift of beer was welcome enough, but he had an agenda too. He wanted information, and these two seemed a likely source.

"Not in a while," Jeff said. "Larry is the big expert, though."

"I don't know about expert." Larry took a long swig then set his bottle on the table. "Years ago, I did some work with the Navy in Scotland on the effects of cold water submersion. Several of their divers developed some weird effects after being under for a long time."

"What kind of weird effects?" Maybe this was it. Maybe he was about to get an explanation for some of the weirdness he'd seen in the hospital. John twisted in his seat, and the chair creaked beneath him. These guys seemed to know what they were talking about.

"Well, I don't guess this is classified information or anything. Some of them developed cardiac problems, and a few of them had really bizarre central nervous system effects."

"What do you mean, central nervous system? You're talking to a small town boy here." John took a swig of his beer.

"Brain stuff, hallucinations, and things like that."

"That's it," John yelled. "I've been seeing some weird shit. I thought it was the medication that Pierce has me taking, but maybe it was just being in the cold water. How long did those effects last?"

"Not long. They cleared within a few days."

"Oh, God," said John. "I fell through the ice a month, maybe six weeks ago, and I'm still seeing things. What kind of stuff did they see?"

"Flashing lights, colors, stuff like that. Why? What have you been seeing?" Larry set his beer aside and stared at John.

"People. They're not real clear sometimes, and…," his voice drifted off.

"And what, man?" Jeff said.

"They look like they're dead."

#

The beer was a mistake, a bad one. Pierce had warned him about alcohol or any kind of dope, as he called it, but dammit, it didn't make sense that a guy couldn't have a few beers with people who had saved his life. And John, true to his word, not usually a drinking man, consumed several on this occasion. Now as he walked down the hall toward the parking lot the bright fluorescent lighting shimmered before him, like heat rising off the road in midsummer. The straight lines of doorways wavered, bent, then went back straight again. Fuzzy things scurried across the hallway in front of him, things that seemed to pass right through solid walls. When he got outside, things got worse. He'd parked up the street from the hospital. All the spaces near the ER entrance were marked Reserved for Physician, Reserved for Chaplain, Reserved for Laboratory Technician…none were Reserved for John.

The lights that glared down on the parking lot were all wrong. He didn't remember them being green when he came in. And the people around him, they weren't distinct like before. They looked fuzzy, like the things he'd seen inside, and they didn't seem to be going anywhere, just drifting around. When one of them walked through a car and emerged on the other side, without opening any doors, John broke into a run.

Where had he left his truck? A cold sweat soaked through his clothing. He ran down another street. No truck. He retraced his steps. From the corner of his eye he saw movement, but when he turned, nothing. A shadow loomed off on his left; he whirled toward it, but again…nothing. He leaned against a vehicle--his own truck, he'd walked right past it. He fumbled for his keys, and then he vomited.

"You okay, buddy?" A security guard stared at him.

"Yeah, just something I ate." John needed both hands on the roof of his truck to steady himself.

"You don't look so good. You been drinking?"

Had the guard smelled beer on his breath? "Just one beer. One lousy beer." Okay, maybe a few more, but why tell the cop?

"You don't look fit to drive, boy. Want me to call a cab?"

John crawled into his truck. "I'll be okay, soon as I get away from here."

"Why are you looking at me like that?" The guard stepped back, away from John.

"You're real, aren't you?" John asked. He reached out to touch the guard, to see if he was solid.

The guard stepped farther back. His hand dropped down to the sidearm at his waist. "Fuckin' loony," he said. "Get the hell outa here."

#

Naomi Welles was riding her snowmobile through the woods not far from her cabin when it happened to her. Being stuck behind a desk processing insurance forms three days a week paid the bills but such confinement was torture for this energetic twenty-three-year old. She'd grown up on a farm in upstate New York and loved the outdoors, especially the winter excursions on her snowmobile. Speeding through the forests, snugly encased in a snowsuit that looked fit for space travel was her release, her reward for the week's travails. She had a beautiful day at her disposal, probably the last one of the season.

A cold front, one last sneak attack by old man winter, had pushed through the night before, and now the sky was a crystalline blue, not a cloud in sight. But it wasn't the pristine sky that lifted Naomi's spirits; it was the fresh unmarked blanket of snow that had fallen during the night. It would melt quickly this time of year, and she planned to make the most of it while it lasted. "Thanks, Canada," she said looking up. She'd gotten that habit from her father who'd always reminded her that winter cold came down from Canada. Whenever she said it to herself now, it brought back memories of him and their upstate winters together.

She veered off the path and headed for the deeper woods. Over eight inches of new snow spread unblemished before her. As she sped along she left a cloud of white powder behind her. She wasn't exactly sure of where the shoreline left off and the edge of the lake began, because the snow was so deeply drifted over the usual landmarks. When her machine plunged through the soft ice into the lake her first thought was that she had simply plowed into a drift. Then the icy waters dragged her under. In her heavy snowsuit, she never had a chance.

The other thing her father had taught her was to never go out alone. She didn't particularly like going out with Freddie, but he was the only person available who liked riding snowmobiles as much as she did. The main reason that Naomi didn't like Freddie was that he was so cautious. He'd always lag behind, letting Naomi race ahead and break a trail. He'd even brought a cell phone along on their trip. That combination of caution and preparation saved her life…barely.

#

The fire department got there just before the EMTs did. After having fished John Merritt out of a similar mishap just a short time before, there were a few crude jokes about an epidemic, but that didn't stop the crew from doing their jobs.

"She's a goner for sure, Harvey," the chief said to his partner. They were throwing grappling hooks into the water, having nothing else at hand. "You'd think people would have more sense."

"How long has she been under, Freddie?"

"I called you at one o'clock, so it's been almost half an hour." He pulled up his sleeve to get a look at his watch. "There was nothing I could do."

"We know that, Freddie. If you'd gone in after her we'd be fishing out two bodies instead of one. Nobody could survive in water that cold."

"I think I got something." Both men pulled on the chain that held the grappling hook, and the lifeless body of Naomi Wells emerged from the lake, the nylon shell of her down parka snagged by a single prong of the hook.

"Quick, get her in the ambulance." The EMTs were in a big hurry.

"What's your rush boys, she's gone. Look at her."

"We're supposed to take her directly to Upstate."

"What the hell for? We've got a funeral home right here."

"They're doing something new there. They've saved several people like her. But we gotta keep her cold until we get there."

"That shouldn't be so hard. She's frozen stiff already."

\#

When Naomi woke up in the ICU at Upstate Medical Center, everybody looked fuzzy. By her third or fourth day in hospital, some definitely looked fuzzier than others. By the end of the week, she was spooked. The fuzzy people outnumbered the normal ones.

"You look real enough," she said to the nurse, "but he doesn't."

"Who doesn't?"

# Chapter 5

John slept in as long as he dared. He had things to do, and they wouldn't get done with him lying in bed. Being Sunday, Merritt Supply was closed for the day. Of course, the big box store at the edge of town was probably wide open, probably busy too. But he had other things to worry about just now. When he finally got out of bed his hangover was still bad enough that he had to stop frequently and hold onto something solid, anything to make the world stop spinning so violently. He got even shakier when he recalled the events that followed his drinking binge with the EMTs. It was just too weird, too crazy. Of course Pierce had warned him about booze, but the idea that he got what he deserved didn't help much just now. He wondered if that sort of thing was what the town drunk went through whenever he tied one on.

After he finished up his barn chores he decided to tackle the house. He didn't particularly like house cleaning, hated it, in fact, but things around the Merritt place had gotten pretty shabby over the past few weeks, and he couldn't put it off any longer. He started in the kitchen because, when he was indoors, that's where he spent most of his time. With the windows open to let in fresh air the only sound was episodic bursts from a screech owl that had taken up residence in the oak beside the house.

The various components in John's kitchen—to call them appliances would give them more credit than they were due—were a mix of things old and things older still. The sink was a long porcelain affair chipped in so many places that it appeared to have been dropped from a considerable height. Both John and his brother had, according to their mother, been bathed as babies in that very sink.

The small stove and refrigerator were the only items that required electric power, except for the microwave oven John had bought two years before. The stove had replaced a three-burner wood-burning relic that now sat rusting in the barn.

Much of the kitchen space was taken up by a hand-hewn table made by John's grandfather from boards six inches wide and over an inch thick. Even after generations of wear the saw marks from where the boards had been cut remained visible. John's dad had carved his own initials in the surface years before, and John and Christopher had added their own in later years. When John was a high school freshman his mother had demanded removal of "that ugly piece of junk" from her kitchen. She replaced it with even uglier pieces of junk—a smaller table covered with lime green formica and chairs with padded back rests.

The ancient wooden table went to the barn where it sat alongside the wood-burning stove until just after John's mother skipped town leaving him the sole occupant of the Merritt Homestead. Then John, with Herman's help and hearty approval, lugged it back to its proper place in the kitchen, along with the same chairs his grandfather had made. They carted the formica table off to its proper place as well—the city dump.

By early evening he paused and checked things out. Not bad, he thought, looks a hell of a lot better. He rummaged through the refrigerator and came up with a frozen dinner. No telling how long it had been there, but he was very hungry so he popped it into the microwave. He paused by the window and inhaled deeply. This was familiar, comfortable. This was normal. He felt safe here.

That is, until his dog started raising hell. John interrupted his sweeping chores long enough to swat his dog on the butt with the broom. "Rebel, you keep barking like that and you're gonna sleep in the barn."

The dog snarled at the back door. Then he backed across the room and cowered behind John's legs.

"What's got into you, boy?" John put his hand on the dog's broad back, now arched, hackles raised. "You're trembling, hell, you're shaking all over. Something out there you're scared of?" But even as he asked the question, he knew he didn't want an answer. Rebel feared nothing. If the dog was scared, something truly dreadful must be up and about. If the dog was scared, he should be too.

Then John saw it too, the source of Rebel's fear. Oh no, not in his own home. Rebel retreated to a corner as the apparition floated through the closed back door. How could it have followed him here? The nurses had told him they were just hallucinations, stuff that would go away when he got out of the hospital. He rubbed his eyes hard thinking maybe it would vanish, but it didn't.

The hazy figure standing by his kitchen table looked to be a girl of ten, maybe eleven years old. Slowly, she became more distinct, looked solid, almost. Colors became apparent, but that only made things worse. Her blonde hair hung in clumps, matted with red dirt, the same dirt that was smeared across her face.

Her neck showed a gaping wound where it had had been slashed, probably several times. A reddish halo surrounded an open wound in her chest. The arm with which she beckoned to John had no hand. In fact, both her hands had been cut off, leaving only coagulated stumps.

None of the specters John had seen before had appeared in such sharp detail, or so horribly wounded. He lurched backward and knocked his TV dinner off the table. "Who are you?" His voice came out as a hoarse croak.

"Help me."

Had he really heard a voice, or had the message simply appeared in his head? He wedged a chair between himself and the figure as she moved around the table. "Stay away from me."

Again, "Help me."

This time he was sure there was no sound. She definitely was in his head. "Leave me alone, damn you." He picked up a large kitchen knife, brandished it, then put it back down. Hell, she'd already been stabbed to death.

She drifted closer.

"No." He was screaming now because he could see her much more clearly, see the tears that coursed down her muddy face. "You can't cry. You're dead. Leave me alone."

Rebel whimpered in the corner.

#

Just before daybreak, John awoke in his bed, fully clothed, boots included. He lay there for a moment, rubbed his eyes. How had he gotten there? Had he really seen a ghost or just imagined it? He staggered back

49

into his kitchen, leaning against the walls for support like a drunken man. The lights were still on, just as he'd left them.

His fears were confirmed when he found the turkey tetrazzini dinner he'd knocked over as he tried to get away from the little girl with the slashed neck. Rebel, who usually kept the floor clean of even the smallest crumbs, wouldn't touch it. He circled around the mess, growling as if it were responsible for the ghastly visit from the night before.

"Enough." John scooped the gelatinous lump off the floor, tossed it, then collapsed into a chair at his kitchen table. Whatever was going on, it was getting worse instead of better. He'd never dreamed the ghosts would follow him home, and the one in his own kitchen was the worst yet. How on earth would he fight off these unwelcome visits? Padlocks, solid walls offered no protection. His hands shook—hands? Hell, he shook all over when he thought about it. But the weirdest part of it all, the girl, the spirit, he never got the feeling it meant to do him harm, not even once. Her plea, "help me," still echoed in his brain. What did that mean? How could he possibly help her?

He lay forward on the table, head cradled in his arms. The question he didn't want to acknowledge kept pressing into his consciousness: was he going crazy? He'd been under water for forty minutes, almost dead from what Dr. Pierce told him. What might that have done to his brain? And he hadn't even told Pierce about the earlier incident, the other time he'd nearly drowned. Was remaining normal after two submersions too much to hope for?

He pushed himself upright, walked over to the sink and ran a glass of water. Time for his medication. He retrieved Pierce's pill bottle from the cabinet above the sink. For the first time, he took a close look at it. The label was blank. He had no idea of what he was taking, or why. All he had was Pierce's firm admonition that it must be taken every day.

In the small room off his bedroom that he used for a home office, John turned on his computer. He looked up drowning, then intensive care, then hallucinations, and finally, ghosts. All he found was stuff he already knew. Yes, hallucinations occurred in patients kept in intensive care, but they resolved after the patient was transferred, and most definitely did not follow them home. Ghosts didn't fit into the equation at all. The apparitions that now dogged him seemed to have no connection to anything that had gone before.

He turned the pill bottle over in his hand, stared at the blank label. All medications had side effects, he knew that much, at least. But he didn't even know what he was taking. He smacked his hand down on the desk, jostling the small cup where he kept loose change. Pierce had made a point of telling him almost nothing about the pills, and John had let him get away with it.

Now he had to find out. The pills, whatever they were for, were all that stood between him and a diagnosis of being crazy as hell. If the ghosts weren't some weird medication effect, he'd lost it for sure. He thought about going back to Pierce's office; maybe a few smacks upside his head would make the good doctor more informative. More likely it would just get John thrown in jail. He rolled up his sleeve and ran his fingertips over the small indentations that marked the sites of the skin biopsies Pierce's technician had performed. Why, he wondered? Another question he couldn't answer.

He had to have help, and he knew only one person he could ask—Stacey. But she had seemed so distant in the hospital, like she couldn't bear to be around him.

#

It was still too early to call her, and if he wasn't crazy to start with, sitting around waiting would drive him nuts soon enough. He went to the barn and wheeled out his Harley. He pushed it halfway up the drive before he turned on the ignition. Rebel hated the bike. The dog ran alongside nipping at the tires, but when John started up the engine Rebel retreated to the front porch. Traffic was light at that early hour so John opened it up on the flat stretches of farmland that neighbored his own spread. God, but it felt great flying along, just beyond the limits of real control, something he would never have done before, and shouldn't have done this time either.

Until recently his preferred mode of travel about the countryside had been on horseback. Such rides alongside his father were among his most pleasant memories. They seldom spoke on these short treks; there was no need for words. Their bonding, to each other and to the land over which they rode was of a more basic sort. The power of the land itself extended upward unbroken through horse to rider. It extended back in time, through generations of Merritt men, and in it John could see his future as well.

But in one day, one stormy afternoon when Christopher had struck out to swim for shore while John screamed at him to stay with their upturned boat, all was shattered—past, present, future, everything. Now he needed speed. He needed escape. He didn't even glance at the speedometer on the Harley. He didn't care. If he could go fast enough, nothing could catch him.

Ahead in the road, a baby rabbit no bigger than his fist hopped into his path, and John veered off into a freshly plowed field. The fall dazed him, and he sat for a minute, staring around him. The bike had some rear fender damage but otherwise appeared serviceable. The soft dirt had saved him from losing a lot of skin. If he'd landed on asphalt instead of a plowed field he'd likely resemble a partially peeled tomato about now.

Luckily no one saw him fall, so he didn't have to explain what he was doing tearing around the countryside like a crazy fool so early in the morning. The only person who needed an explanation was John himself. What indeed was he doing? Had he just found another way to try to kill himself, like people were saying?

#

Stacey answered his call quickly. Just hearing her voice lifted the pall that hung over him. Even Rebel looked a little relieved. But then there was that awkward silence, just like before. She had little to no new information about his medication, or why Dr. Pierce insisted he continue taking it for so long. She promised to keep trying, even though, as she said, Dormistan hadn't turned up in any of the places she had looked.

But there was something else he had to ask her about, and he hated the thought of doing it. He had to ask her about ghosts. Either they were real or he was crazy, and neither alternative was very pleasant.

"What, John? What else?" she asked when he hesitated.

"In the hospital I was having hallucinations."

"Yeah, that's pretty common in the ICU. They go away when you get moved out."

He took a deep breath. "Mine didn't."

"What?"

"I still see them." He didn't dare tell her about the horror, the mutilated little girl, about how she got into his head, had talked to him. Only a complete lunatic would admit to seeing what he'd seen and heard.

52

But Stacey had no answers for him either. "Just give it a little more time," she said. "You've been through a lot, remember?"

That seemed to be the answer for everything. "You've been through a lot." As if time would solve all his problems. Well, dammit, he'd been waiting for nine years now, and things were getting worse instead of better.

#

Stacey balanced her massive medicine textbook on her knees as she polished off the cup of blueberry yogurt she'd bought for lunch. But the section she was reading on cardiomyopathies failed to hold her attention; her thoughts kept finding their way back to John Merritt. There was no point in pretending any longer that hers was just professional curiosity; it was personal, very personal.

Relationships were seldom a simple matter, she knew that well enough. But this one had gone from complicated to just plain weird. John's behavioral changes were bad enough, but now he was seeing things that weren't even there, couldn't possibly be here. Yeah, there was something else going on. Hallucinations? She couldn't buy that one herself. There had to be more.

Stacey didn't tell John that she'd checked into the hospital medical records department after he was discharged. She first tried the hospital computer but the message came up, "Access Denied," so she tried again, with the same results. She negotiated with a senior resident for his password. That didn't work either. When the computer approach failed she went directly to the records department and signed in using the name of an attending physician. Maybe having the actual record in hand would provide her with the information that she wanted.

"I'm sorry," the records clerk said, "but we have no record under that name."

"Are you sure? Did you check the social security number?"

"Yeah, checked it both ways. Even if he was in under another name—people sometimes do that--the social security number should work, unless you copied it down wrong."

"That's possible, I guess. Thanks." But Stacey didn't make mistakes like that. She'd double-checked and knew very well that she had the right number.

The only remaining source of information was the hospital billing department. If anything, the billing clerks were even more compulsive about files than the medical records department, so if there was information to be had, they should have it. Unfortunately they were no more willing to part with it than were the other departments in the hospital, so Stacey conjured up believable story about needing some demographic information about the patient. She even went so far as using Dr. Pierce's name, saying she was gathering data for him.

The clerk entered the identification data that Stacey gave her. "Nope," she said. "Nothing here. You sure you have your information right?"

"I guess I must not have the right name, after all." Stacey threw up her hands and trudged out of the billing office. It appeared that, to the Upstate Medical Center, John Merritt did not exist. But he existed to her, very definitely.

#

Oh, crap, Stacey said to herself as her pager buzzed in her pocket. She was well into her initial interview with her new patient, a forty-seven-year-old man admitted with his second myocardial infarction. Cardiology, she had decided, was her thing. She was, in fact, among the final group of applicants for a plum fellowship position in Boston.

But her patient was being particularly difficult. After a long period when he'd just stared at the ceiling, either answering her questions with grunts or ignoring them altogether, he had finally begun to open up to her, to talk about his wife and two young daughters. What would happen to them if he wasn't around? All that stuff, the fear and anger that she knew he had bottled up inside had begun to seep out. This was the time, that crucial point at which trust was established, or lost forever.

Her pager buzzed again. STAT. DR. PIERCE'S OFFICE. NOW.

She bit her lower lip to stifle the profanity that almost slipped out.

She ran up the two flights to his office, then paused for a moment to catch her breath, also to let some of her own fear and anger subside, because the emotions she felt were not too far different from those her patient was experiencing.

Pierce's outer office was almost as large as the entire office space allotted to most full time faculty members, and the arrangement was not exactly warm and fuzzy. The room was finished off in dark panels with no ornamentation whatever. And, in spite of the space, there were only two chairs sitting against the far wall.

In the center of the room sat the receptionist's desk, like a command post under the strict control of a woman who, so far as Stacey knew, never smiled.

"You took your time getting here." The woman spoke without looking up.

"I was with a patient."

"Whatever. He's waiting for you."

Dr. Pierce sat behind his spacious desk thumbing through one of the folders the medical department kept to monitor the progress of members of the residency staff, Stacey included. Although Pierce didn't say as much, Stacey felt sure the folder he held in his hands was her own. In effect, he held her career in his hands, and the thought brought beads of perspiration coursing down the middle of her back.

"Tell me, Dr. Patterson, why have you been snooping around in my private affairs?"

"Sir? I haven't done anything of the sort." At the moment she would have given anything to be somewhere else, anywhere, just away from those terrible half-hooded green eyes.

"I don't appreciate dishonesty any more than you might. Odd, such aberrant behavior has never been noted in your file before."

Stacey stared at her shoes. Her feet were numb. She had no idea what was going on, only that it was bad.

"I happen to know, for instance, that at three-thirty PM, on the eleventh, you logged into medical records and requested information on my patient, John Merritt. Would you like to deny that?"

"Oh, no, I wasn't snooping. I followed John, I mean, Mr. Merritt when he was on the medical ward. He was a very interesting case, and I was just trying to learn more about him."

"So, you went behind my back when you should have come to me with your questions. I'm assuming your interest is professional, not just personal. Is that correct?"

"Oh, yes, sir. Absolutely."

As his stare bored into her, Stacey felt herself flush. For certain, there was not a square inch of her skin that wasn't glowing crimson.

"I don't tolerate snooping, Dr. Patterson, whatever the reason. If, in the next few moments, you haven't told me exactly why you chose to sneak around I shall consider terminating your contract here. Moreover, this nice cardiology fellowship that you fancy will be gone. In fact, I will make sure this incident follows you wherever you go. So speak up now, or start thinking about a general practice, say, with the Indian Medical Service, say, someplace like South Dakota."

She fumbled for words. The best she could come up with was, "I'm sorry."

"Not good enough."

"Mr. Merritt was having hallucinations. He thought he was seeing ghosts. I couldn't explain it, so I wanted to look at his chart, check on his medications."

"Medications indeed. It's very simple. If you had taken the time to perform a more conventional inquiry into the medical literature—as opposed to prying into my private files—you would have come to what must be an obvious conclusion. Mr. Merritt has undergone what is called a Near Death Experience. It happens with some frequency in the patients I treat. Hallucinations are a common complaint, as are often bizarre personality changes. You didn't need me to tell you all this. You should have found out for yourself."

"I didn't mean to snoop. I just wanted to find out if these changes, these hallucinations go away."

"Information that is also readily available in the medical literature, had you taken the trouble to look. Often they become permanent aspects of the victim's personality. Now, you've taken up quite enough of my time. But don't think that this ends here. From now until the time you finish your residency here, you will be on probation. I will personally monitor your behavior, and if other such incidents arise, you're out. Furthermore you will not mention this conversation to anyone. If I find that you have violated my confidence in any way, you're though. Do you understand?"

Stacey nodded, then turned for the door. She stopped there for a moment to steady herself against the wall. Pierce's attack had taken her by surprise, and it was so unfair. Most attending physicians welcomed interest in their patients. Upstate was a teaching hospital, after all. But Pierce had treated her as if she were acting with some kind of criminal intent. Why? What was he trying to hide?

Not until she was out in the hallway did she realize that neither of them had mentioned Dormistan.

# Chapter 6

Paul Pierce watched from his chair as Stacey Patterson turned and left his office. Her skin color had changed rapidly from a crimson blush to a ghastly white, and he wondered for a moment whether she might faint dead away. But she seemed to regain some degree of composure, enough to allow her to leave his immediate area. Then she became someone else's problem, not his.

Even so, this one would bear watching. She was smart and too inquisitive by half. She would figure out soon enough that a Near Death Experience could produce some but not all of the manifestations seen in their mutual patient, John Merritt. She would realize as well that his own verbal assault was mostly bluff. Unless he could produce some real evidence of malfeasance on her part, Pierce could not possibly force her dismissal from the residency program.

In short, they were both vulnerable; Stacey Patterson because of his assumed power over her employment, and Pierce himself because in her investigation, which most likely would continue, she might actually stumble upon the real reason for John Merritt's aberrant behavior.

Oh yes, Pierce knew all about such transformations and the fact that they most certainly did not arise from Merritt's having been clinically dead, a condition from which Pierce had saved him. He knew, for instance, that whatever Merritt's personality might have been like before, now he would be highly active, confident, even aggressive.

Pierce chuckled to himself as he considered other aspects of the new John Merritt. If young Dr. Patterson had not discovered already, Merritt would now possess an almost uncontrollable libido. Surely she could not complain about that.

And yes, Merritt would receive visits from the dead—ghosts, spirits. Pierce had heard reports of such visitations from other patients he had treated. True, this manifestation could be distressing, but it paled in comparison to what they would receive in return; the gold ring, the grand prize…an indefinite life span.

How long might Merritt and the others live? Pierce had no idea, only that so long as Merritt continued taking his medication, the natural aging of his body had been brought to a virtual standstill. He would, barring some unfortunate and unexpected event, remain just as he was now, indefinitely.

Why must we grow old and die? That was the most important question of all, wasn't it? The search for a way to prolong the human life span indefinitely has consumed untold amounts of labor and resources. Early on there was the idea that eradication of known causes of death— infection, cancer, heart disease and the like—would add years of longevity, and, to an extent, that proved true.

Almost every generation has been able to look forward to more years of life than has its predecessors. But mankind is a greedy animal, and the addition of a few years here, a few years there, has not satisfied the longing for something more substantial. Seekers of immortality have arranged to have themselves frozen at death and stashed away for future use, but none of these bizarre methods have had any real impact on the aging process. Immortality was well and good, but perpetual youth was something altogether different. And now the answer to that riddle seemed close at hand.

And that answer was Dormistan, that mysterious pill that John Merritt and all the others took once a day, without any idea of the supreme benefit that had been bestowed upon them. Dormistan worked its magic through inhibition of an obscure but vital bodily process called Apoptosis.

*Apoptosis*—programmed cell death, was wired into the human genome, into the genomes of all living things, for that matter. In time, all living things would grow old and die. Apoptosis. The word hung there as if it were enclosed in a giant balloon. Apoptosis and how to manipulate it had become the holy grail for many scientists, had been for years.

Body cells could die in several ways. Traumatic cell death, such as that which had occurred in a tragic head-on collision on the New York

Thruway two days before, was most dramatic, but this was an unpredictable event. A more predictable occurrence, a certainty, in fact, was that body cells age and die. In time this aging process would also consume the body that hosted these cells. On the death certificate some specific cause would be listed—heart failure, kidney failure, respiratory failure—but the common element underlying most of these various terminal events was aging. Youthful hearts rarely fail; youthful kidneys typically continue their delicate adjustments of the body's fluid and electrolyte balance; youthful lungs go right along taking in oxygen and expelling carbon dioxide.

Apoptosis, or "cellular suicide," as some called it, would, after a certain period of time begin to wreck the cells' internal machinery. These effects would be microscopic at first, but after such assaults on a few million or so cells, the result would become apparent to any observer— old age. The entire sequence was hard-wired into the genome. Aging and subsequent death, unless brought on prematurely, were inevitable, and apoptosis appeared to be the primary culprit. To inhibit apoptosis might, just might, be the way to hold the process of aging in check.

Dormistan effectively halted aging due to apoptosis, but that effectiveness required that the body's homeostatic mechanisms be shut off temporarily, rather like having the power to an electrical circuit shut down, then restarted. Cold water immersion of at least thirty minutes brought about this biological marvel, but there was a catch. Always, there was a catch. Immersion in near-freezing water for thirty minutes was a fatal event, unless appropriate resuscitative measures were applied by expert hands. That's where Dr. Paul Pierce and his portable cardiopulmonary bypass machine came in.

His career had been a long series of near misses. He had been hard at work on a portable cardiopulmonary bypass machine for use in the emergency room, when a report was published by a group in Texas who had not only engineered such a machine but had used it successfully in six cases. Pierce's own findings, published later, and a direct result of Chang's efforts, merely confirmed the success of those who got there first; there was no prize for second place. The Texas success, and subsequent patent, meant that Pierce could use his own machine and collect clinical data, but could not sell it to any of the manufacturers of medical instrumentation. In other words, his own machine was a bright, shiny toy, one that would never net him fame or fortune, not in the conventional sense, at least. But then he met a man to whom the machine might become immensely profitable.

#

A few weeks before his fifty-eighth birthday—a bit too late in his career to hope for the lightning bolt of success to strike bringing him fame and fortune—Paul Pierce had a visitor. No appointment, no advance notice, the man simply showed up at his office one afternoon in late March.

"I am Professor Hans Riegler."

The man was about five feet eight inches, Pierce guessed. His clipped accent came with strong Germanic overtones. He stood ramrod straight and carried a polished brass walking stick, although he didn't appear to need it. His suit looked expensive, very expensive, the kind of garment Pierce craved for himself but could never afford.

"I have been reading your reports about your work, Dr. Pierce, and I wonder if you might spare a few moments to discuss it."

"My work?"

"Yes, I find your success in treating victims of cold water drowning intriguing, in particular your development of the portable cardiopulmonary bypass instrument."

Pierce had made a modest name for himself by successful treatment of cold water drowning victims, modest because the event occurred infrequently, and so was not considered a major public health hazard. So far as he knew his own clinical reports had attracted minimal attention. A couple of his successes had received coverage in the local newspapers, but this was hardly enough to bring him any scientific acclaim.

"Your bypass instrument, is it available? Might I see it?" Riegler asked.

"Of course." Pierce led his guest down the hallway to the elevators, eventually ending up in a cluttered area that stored equipment used in the emergency room. Pierce had to move aside several large items and a half dozen folding chairs to clear a path to the bypass machine, which sat in a corner beneath a stack of hospital scrub uniforms still in their brown paper wrapping.

"Sorry about all the mess," Pierce said. He shoved aside the stack of scrubs, then wheeled the bypass machine out into the hallway. "Less dusty out here," he said.

Riegler dropped to his knees, then unwound the vascular lines that ran from ports on top of the machine. "You use a femoral-to-femoral attachment, I presume?"

"Yes, right."

"As much as I would like to see it in operation, I understand that is quite impossible."

Was the man making a statement or asking a question, Pierce wondered? Was he asking for a demonstration?

Before Pierce could answer, Riegler bounced up and gazed at the clutter around him. "Such a fine instrument with such great potential deserves a space of its own, don't you think?"

"Oh, yes, I agree completely, but space is so limited here."

Riegler turned to him, and for the first time Pierce felt the burning power of those gray eyes. This was a man who was accustomed to getting exactly what he wanted, exactly when he wanted it.

"Such problems can be remedied, Dr. Pierce, with much less difficulty than you might think. Now, shall we return to your office?"

"Have you heard of Dormistan, Dr. Pierce?"

"No."

"Few people have. I have worked with it for a number of years now. Some of my results will interest you, no doubt."

As he listened to Riegler, Pierce found himself trying to stand straighter, sit straighter. Riegler never slouched, never leaned against anything—walls, desks, the backs of chairs. You could drop a plumb line from the back of his head to his tail bone, and his spine would follow it perfectly.

"I am asking for a week of your time, Dr. Pierce. You will be compensated, of course, quite handsomely.'

"Okay, I guess. What do you have in mind?"

"A bit of travel. I want to show you my lab in Zurich. But first I need to stop off at my apartment in Paris. You wouldn't object to a few days in Paris, would you?"

What could he say? Pierce wouldn't realize it until much later, but at that moment what he would come to call "that unholy alliance" had been formed. He had just been bought.

#

Of course, Paul Pierce had heard of the Concorde. Who hadn't? He just never believed he would be flying on such a luxurious aircraft. Champagne at ten o'clock in the morning. A flight attendant who called them by name, treated them as if they were royalty, which, for all he knew, Hans Riegler might well be.

This was the life for which he'd been intended. This was the life he deserved. If only those twerps at Upstate could see him now, those mental midgets to whom he'd had to go hat-in-hand pleading for space, pleading for technical assistance. No more. Finally he'd found someone who appreciated his genius.

Pierce gazed around him at the other occupants of the first class compartment. These were people to whom luxury was not some special treat, but a daily occurrence. This was where he belonged.

After a ridiculously smooth landing at Charles de Gaulle, Pierce tagged along behind Riegler who followed their driver out to a limo parked squarely in a No Parking zone.

"But, our bags," Pierce said as the driver held the door open for him.

"All taken care of, sir."

Yes, this was where he belonged.

#

But even the luxury of his trip over did not prepare him for Riegler's plush apartment on the Rue Fabert. From the west balcony he had a perfect view of the Arc de Triomphe. Finally, Pierce felt he had arrived.

Riegler had business appointments during the afternoon, so he had his driver take Pierce to a very exclusive shopping area. "I have most of my clothes made there. If you see anything you like, feel free. Just give them this. They'll send your purchases to your home address."

He handed Pierce a small card with a barcode and Riegler's own name in large print. Pierce hesitated at first, having no idea of the exchange rates of francs and dollars, only that he probably couldn't afford anything he saw. How quickly his inhibitions melted away. Surely Riegler would not have given him the card if he didn't mean for him to use it, so use it he did.

But after all the glitter of Paris, the trip to Zurich was a big letdown for Pierce. No Concorde on this journey; he and Riegler travelled by train. Oh, it was a very nice train, even luxurious, but still a train, and Pierce was not partial to trains. From the moment they left the Paris Gare Lyon, he felt his spirits drop. What should have been a seven-hour trip took two days because of the sightseeing stops Riegler insisted on making. The overnight compartment in which the gentle course over the rails was supposed to rock him to sleep had the opposite effect. He awoke feeling downright crotchety; he had caught a cold.

Pierce was becoming restless. All he'd seen during the train ride was cattle grazing on hillsides, all quite picturesque at first, but in time, boring. The small village where they disembarked had no name that Pierce could recall. He was tired, hungry, and had no idea about the source of Riegler's barely contained enthusiasm. Riegler had a car waiting at the station, a short drive, more cows, more hillsides, and they arrived at last, in the middle of nowhere. Pierce looked around for shops, restaurants, hotels, but saw nothing of the sort.

"There, what do you think of them?" Hans Riegler pointed to a group of six boys chasing a soccer ball around a small playground. A chain link fence topped off by coils of razor wire enclosed the area like a steel moat.

"You brought me all the way to this godforsaken place to look at a freaking bunch of kids?" The wind gusted and Dr. Paul Pierce turned up his collar. He sneezed a couple of times. "I can watch kids back home in the 'States, without freezing my ass off. And what's with this fence? This place looks like a prison camp." Pierce turned on his heels, scowling.

"The fence is necessary," Riegler said.

"Necessary for what? There's not even a gate."

"Very observant, Dr. Pierce."

"You mean they can't get out? Ever?"

Riegler shoved his hands into his pockets. "I'm cold," he said. He walked toward the car.

"Wait a minute." Pierce trotted after him. "Those kids are prisoners? What on earth have they done? What's wrong with them?"

Riegler stopped and turned back toward the playground. Someone close to the main building blew a whistle. The boys formed a line and marched inside the main building. "They look quite normal, don't they?"    "Sure, I guess, but why do they have to be fenced in? Are they dangerous?"

"No, not dangerous."

"Why, then?"

"It…it is necessary."

"You said that before. Jesus, whatever you're doing, you'd never get away with this in the 'States."

"We're not in the 'States, Dr. Pierce." He pulled the collar of his topcoat closed and held it shut with his hand. "How old do you think they are?"

"I'd say six, seven years old, just kids."

"What if I told you the youngest is thirty-nine and the oldest is forty-three?"

"I'd say you were crazy," Pierce said.

Riegler closed the gap between them with two quick steps and stood very close to Pierce. "What I say is true."

"That doesn't make sense. They're kids. There's no way they can be that old."

"And how old do you think I am?" Riegler asked.

"I don't like this game."

"How old?"

"Okay, maybe mid-forties, fifty, at the most."

"I'm eighty-three. I'll be eighty-four next month."

"That can't be." Pierce shook his head "No way."

Hard to believe, of course, but Dr. Pierce would learn, in time. Riegler clapped him on the shoulder. "We're going to do great things, Dr. Pierce, great things."

"What about those kids?"

He got into the car, leaving Pierce standing in the cold.

They talked little on the drive back to the train station. A hot meal and a couple of glasses of white wine helped Pierce see the possibilities of Riegler's little demonstration. Fame and fortune seemed to have jumped into his lap all at once. When Riegler asked if he wanted in, Pierce didn't hesitate.

"I'm concerned about what will happen if somebody finds out about what we're doing," Pierce said. Perhaps he'd jumped on board too quickly. Those boys Riegler had brought him to see should now be middle-aged men, but Riegler, if he was being truthful, had somehow managed to halt the aging process.

"What will happen, Dr. Pierce, is, you'll have more money than you ever dreamed about. You'll be a god in the medical world you think so highly of. If you want something to worry about, worry about that."

#

Hans Riegler gazed out the window at the rolling countryside. Off in the distance sharp mountain peaks rose, piercing the clouds. He wondered about Pierce. Did the man fully grasp the enormity of what he'd just seen? Godforsaken, that was the term Pierce had used. Not true. There was a god at work here—Riegler himself. For his small group of boys Riegler had stopped the biological clock. Who else but God could do that?

He'd made regular trips back to the encampment for over forty years now. Beyond the enclosed playground a former military barracks that served as a dormitory for the boys squatted like a giant gray toad. It was hard to imagine a less inviting edifice, but the setup inside that bland building was far more lavish than ever seen by the Swiss infantry troops who had occupied it many years before. The dormitory kitchen turned out quality meals enjoyed by few in the neighboring city. Inside he'd installed a complete gymnasium plus a swimming pool. Nothing was too good for his boys, nothing except freedom. How many years had it been now? Did it really make any difference? Nothing changed, ever. Over his many visits, only the staff had grown older. For his boys, and for Riegler himself, time had stood still.

No matter, really, whether Pierce appreciated the miracle Riegler had wrought. Pierce, at his core, was a shallow man, easily manipulated by promises of wealth and fame. The surgeon possessed some talent, of course, but it was his flaws that made him ideal for Riegler's plans.

#

As soon as they returned, Riegler set to work, building an empire for his puppet, Paul Pierce. In addition to his private area in the emergency room, Dr. Pierce soon acquired exclusive use of two beds at the west end of the intensive care unit. This unusual situation raised a few eyebrows among the staff—a lot of eyebrows, actually—but no one dared question him about his apparent eminent domain, because Pierce had friends in high places. This special arrangement was forged earlier during a visit to the medical school dean, Donald Westbrook, by Pierce and Riegler, himself.

In return for his sole use of these two rooms, a promise was made and kept to completely refurbish the entire intensive care area. Nothing was written down; there was no paper trail, at least, none that was apparent to the dean. In times past they might have referred to it as a "gentlemen's agreement," but such arrangements no longer held any validity, and designating this small gathering as gentlemen was also questionable. Rather, they closed the deal in a more conventional means, with a smooth calfskin valise that Dr. Riegler passed over to Dean Westbrook.

The bag itself was handsome enough, but inside was more cash than Westbrook had ever seen at one time in his life. He clutched the bag in his arms; he asked no questions. Money was tight. He'd just completed a fund-raising drive for the medical center with results so meager as to be an outright embarrassment. His personal financial picture, already stretched to the breaking point, was not much better. And the answer, temporary thought it might be, had just fallen into his lap. Oh, yes, Dr. Pierce could have his private spaces, and anything else he wanted.

The cash in the satchel that Riegler passed across the desk to Westbrook was no more than an opening gambit. Westbrook might have looked upon it as a single transaction, payment for services rendered, but he was quite wrong.

Riegler would return, frequently, with new demands. Westbrook would never know which to expect, the carrot or the stick. Sometimes Riegler would bring cash, other times he would bring copies of sales receipts, even deposit slips from Westbrook's personal and, heretofore private, bank account. Riegler, it seemed, knew more about Westbrook's finances than did Westbrook himself. He knew, for instance, that Westbrook regularly dipped into that portion of faculty research grants set aside as overhead costs, never amounts large enough to draw attention, just enough to make ends meet. But making ends meet was becoming harder and harder, so Westbrook's petty thefts were becoming ever less petty. If anyone ever found out…

So Riegler, when he came, never came with any overt threats. He simply spread the incriminating documents across Westbrook's desk. Westbrook's gut turned to jelly as he realized that in future meetings

Riegler's demands would no longer be subject to negotiation. Westbrook would comply without hesitation, because he had no other choice.

# Chapter 7

Stacey felt a slight tug at her sleeve. Charlie Tucker, the intern with whom she had worked so frantically through the evening, now well into the night trying to save the life of a young leukemic patient stood at her side, his eyes almost tearful. By now he looked as if he could barely stand. Stacey guessed she didn't look much better, maybe worse. Running on fumes, they both were now.

"Can't we sedate her? She shouldn't have to go through this awake," Charlie said.

"You mean, put her down? That part's in God's hands, and you aren't God, not yet. So get back to work." Her words, the harshness of her own voice, surprised them both.

Charlie looked as if he'd been slapped in the face.

"Sorry," Stacey said. "I shouldn't have said that." To add to the numbing mixture of fear and fatigue that weighed on her, she now had to add remorse.

The ability to work under stress, to function when one's reserves—physical, mental, emotional—had been drained, was an unwritten component of the medical training program. Their work was overseen by more experienced clinicians, but that made the process, almost military in nature, no less arduous. There was also a corollary to the code, as Stacey was learning quickly: Just when you think things can't get any worse, they usually do. Stacey might have hoped for a brief respite after her grilling by Paul Pierce, but she worked in a hospital among patients whose problems made her own seem small and of little consequence by comparison. Knowing that didn't make things easier either.

Wilma Whitaker, the young woman with acute leukemia, was the same age as Stacey, and very likely they shared many of the same hopes and dreams about the future. But Wilma would not live to see any of hers come true.

Stacey knew Wilma from an earlier hospitalization some three months before. Wilma, mother of a precocious and precious two-year-old daughter, Betsy, had been moving her belongings into their new home, just down the street from her parents in Elmira, New York. Both young and strong, she and her husband had decided to handle the move themselves to save money. Wilma had just lugged a couple of boxes into the kitchen when she simply gave out. She had to bend over to catch her breath. That's when she noticed the large bruises spreading over her legs.

"Maybe you're coming down with something," her husband said. So Wilma bedded down at her parents' house while her dad pitched in to help with the move.

The next day the bruising was even more prominent. When she blew her nose she began bleeding profusely. The family doctor's office was only a few blocks away. He did a quick exam, then drew some blood work. The venipuncture site in Wilma's forearm continued oozing, and he had to wrap it in a pressure bandage to staunch the flow.

"Probably just a virus," the doctor said, but his facial expression said otherwise. Wilma and her husband waited in his office for the results from the lab.

The print-out that the doctor showed them had a series of light green boxes where the normal blood counts would fall. None of Wilma's were even close. Her platelet count and red cell count were perilously low, and her white blood count was off the chart. The technician had written a short note: "over ninety percent blasts." In other words, acute leukemia.

The doctor brushed aside most of her questions. "I need to send you to Upstate," he said. "I can't handle this here."

"But can't we wait until after we've moved in?" Wilma asked. "All our stuff is still in boxes. I haven't even unpacked Betsy's toys, her clothes."

The doctor shook his head. "You have to go…today." Shortly after noon the following day, after a very painful bone marrow biopsy, Wilma had acquired a new label: acute myeloblastic leukemia. In the matter of a few hours her life had flipped completely. She'd grabbed her daughter, clasped her to her breast with such force that the child cried out.

"Mommy, not so hard. You hurt me."

For safety's sake her husband seized Wilma's hands and pried the child from her grasp. They'd sat in the hematologist's office, huddled together like victims of a storm while the dread diagnosis—acute myeloblastic leukemia—enveloped them. Hopes, dreams, indeed, their future, all up in smoke.

By that final night Wilma had already undergone several rounds of chemotherapy which, although it left her completely bald and aged her ten years in just a few months, failed to halt the progression of her disease. Instead of producing those life-sustaining cells that carried oxygen, fought infections and prevented bleeding, her leukemic bone marrow continued spewing out malignant cells. All through the night Stacey and her assisting intern had pumped blood products—red blood cells, platelets and fresh frozen plasma—into the young woman, trying to keep her alive. But as fast as those fluids ran in, it all surged out again from her nose, her mouth, her rectum.

She was dying and everybody knew it. Worst of all, Wilma knew it. The fear in her eyes burned into Stacey like a hot light.

Charlie's suggestion no doubt arose from his own feelings of compassion. Where, Stacey wondered, were her own? Besides, Charlie was one of the good guys. Stacey had chatted with his wife, a petite blonde who hated the long upstate winters and couldn't wait to get back to South Carolina. Stacey envied Charlie, having a shoulder to cry on when this was over. She had no one. John Merritt was a hour's drive away, and emotionally even more distant than that.

Sometime during that long fatal night Stacey's emotions, even her basic feelings of humanity, were quashed by fatigue. She was going through the motions of care without actually feeling it. The dying girl became a case, no longer a wife, a mother, a friend, but a diagnosis. Grief, guilt—that would come later. For now, fatigue blocked out everything else. Stacey was a machine, doing what she'd been trained to do. Briefly, as she made yet another frantic run to the blood bank, she recalled a lecture on stress management from her first year: "Put yourself in a happy place—the beach, a forest, a family holiday." But that little trick was only a band-aid. Besides, Wilma Whitaker deserved a happy place too, and look what she got—a blood-soaked sheet pulled up to her neck.

The situation reached its inevitable end just past five A.M. Wilma coughed one last time, soaking Stacey's scrub suit in bloody froth. "Write up your note," she said to Charlie. "I'm going to talk to the family."

Charlie tugged at the bloody lapel of her jacket. "You should change your coat first."

They were all waiting for her in the small room that served as a chapel, Wilma's family and friends. A vase of lilies, probably set by the altar the previous day, hung limply over the sides of the container. Their aroma, still pungent, reminded Stacey of a funeral parlor.

All those upturned faces clinging to hope, except for Wilma's husband who sat with his face buried in his hands. Indeed, what good news could come at this ungodly hour?

So Stacey, as gently and as kindly as she could, dashed their hopes, brought them the other side of hope—grief. She did it with two words: "I'm sorry." Of all the tens of thousands of words at her command, only two came forth. Maybe this was not a time for words.

As she looked around her, she felt as if she were there and not there, both at the same time. She had already begun the process of building a wall around the tragedy.

Memories of Wilma's husband, her daughter and Wilma herself would be locked away. She did it in spite of knowing better. Like many in her profession Stacey kept a growing number of such losses sealed away in compartments deep inside herself. The senior clinicians had warned her and her classmates against doing this, citing statistics on alcoholism, drug addiction, even suicide, among physicians who suppressed such feelings, but Stacey felt she had no other choice.

When she thought about it, John's own mechanism, going into a shell and staying there, was not so very different. And look what his efforts had brought him to, a plunge into a freezing lake. Had she had time to reflect more, she might have better understood John's own reaction to tragedy, his brother's death, how building a wall around the experience might be the only way to deal with it. She would have thought about how one revisits that locked room, hears scratching on the walls. Something wants out.

But that moment when she might have experienced an epiphany, even a small one, got caught up and swept away. There was no time for grief; she had work to do.

As it was, she barely had time to get home for a quick shower and change of clothes before she was due to meet with her rounding team. The regular workday was beginning, and she was already running on empty. She gulped down a cup of coffee as she hurried to catch up with her group, but had to make a quick detour to the bathroom where she vomited it back up. Yeah, this was going to be quite a day.

She might have pulled it off—this wasn't the first time she had worked straight through the night and wouldn't be the last—but she was covering for another resident who was home with the flu. Stacey knew the medical details of her own patients very well, but had not had time to review the charts on the other patients she would be responsible for on rounds. She caught up with her rounding team as they turned the corner toward the last patient for the morning. Dr. Paul Pierce, the attending physician who was making rounds with the group, glared at her.

"Dr. Patterson, since you've seen fit to finally rejoin us, perhaps you'll enlighten us regarding this next patient."

"Sir? Yes. Mrs. Ellison is sixty-three years old…no, twenty-nine." It was all so unfair. The very first patient, not really hers, but still her responsibility, and Stacey had never laid eyes on her. All she had was a few notes the other resident had given her. Protesting that she had been up all night and hadn't had time to review the new charts would get her nowhere. This was part of the training process; complaints and excuses were not acceptable. All she could do was suck it up and hope that the next patient discussed was someone she knew something about.

"What is it, Dr. Patterson? We'll find out soon enough," Pierce said.

Little chuckles erupted from the rounding group; Stacey Patterson, the sharpest resident in her class, got caught on a routine detail.

"It's twenty-nine, sir. I'm sure."

"That's a good start." His smirk became more evil. He was enjoying her discomfort. Earlier in the year Pierce had seemed friendly enough, but since the incident where she'd made inquiries about John Merritt, resulting in Pierce's threat to have her thrown out of the program, had become decidedly hostile. Now he had her in his sights and, at least for morning rounds, seemed determined to make her life miserable.

"Besides her questionable age," he said, "do you have any other information you might wish to share with us? Surely, she's come to the hospital for some reason."

The chuckles grew to outright laughter.

Her face burned. She fumbled with her notes. "I believe she has pneumonia, sir."

"You *believe* she has? Is that an affirmation of faith on your part, or do you have some data that might lead the rest of the flock here to *believe* as you do?"

The words on her note cards blurred and she watched, trance-like, as they all fluttered to the floor like so many falling leaves. Someone said, "Catch her." Then blackness.

#

"I'm okay, Judy. Just help me get up." Stacey pushed up to her elbows, struggling against the restraining hands of the nurse.

"You'd better stay put for a while. You were white as a sheet when they brought you back here."

"God, why did they have to bring me all the way down to the ER?" Stacey looked around her, the familiar sights, sounds, and smells of the emergency room suddenly different from her current viewpoint as a patient lying on a stretcher.

"They brought you here because you scared the crap out of them upstairs, that's why. From what they said, one minute you were talking, the next minute you were in the middle of a swan dive. At least they caught you before you hit the floor."

"What's this?" Stacey tugged at the garment that had slipped off her shoulder. "A hospital gown? You put me in a hospital gown?"

"Yes. You know the procedure. All I'm doing is following the rules. The doctor can't examine you with your clothes on."

"Doctor? Someone examined me?"

"Yes. That's what we do here, remember? Dr. Wilson saw you. In fact, here he comes now."

"Glad you're awake. How are you feeling?" Instead of the scowl she expected, a smiling Mark Wilson, head of services in the emergency

76

room, pulled up a chair beside the gurney where she lay. He took her hand, held it for a moment longer than seemed necessary.

"I'm fine, really. I just want to get out of here."

"I'm sure you do. And I want you to stay that way." Wilson pulled a small penlight out of his pocket, directing the beam into Stacey's eyes. "Pupillary reaction is normal now. It was a little sluggish before." He turned to the nurse. "Is her blood pressure back to normal?"

"Back to normal?" Stacey's eyes opened wider. "What do you mean, back to normal? What was wrong with it before?"

"Below normal, and not just a little. That's why I started the IV.'

Stacey looked down at her arm at the intravenous needle. "I didn't even notice." The IV bag hanging at her bedside was almost empty. "God, how long was I out?"

"About fifteen minutes," Judy said. "Out is the right word, too. You weren't responsive at all when they brought you in."

Stacey rolled onto her side, tears beginning to build in her eyes. "I'm okay," she said in a soft whisper. "I know I am." She'd been so caught up in the stress of Wilma's care that she'd eaten nothing for at least thirty-six hours. That had to be it, she thought. All she needed was a nap and a meal.

Mark Wilson scratched his chin and looked at the nurse. "Cancel the CT scan."

"CT scan?" Stacey said.

"Yeah. You were out so long that I thought we ought to be sure, and I ordered a CT scan of your head. You probably don't even remember Dr. Pierce coming to see you."

Stacey sat upright, catching the hospital gown just before it fell off her shoulders. "Dr. Pierce came here and saw me?"

"Yes. He seemed very concerned."

"Where are my clothes? I've got to get out of here."

"Here's all your stuff." The nurse handed Stacey her clothes and a little carton containing her personal belongings. "I'll stand by the door, make sure nobody bothers you."

"Judy," Stacey spoke slowly, haltingly, "how long was Dr. Pierce here?" Her skin crawled as she thought of herself helpless, unconscious with him leering over her.

"Just a little while, ten, fifteen minutes, maybe."

"Were you with me when he came by?"

"Yeah, but he chased me out, said he wanted to check you out in private. That seemed a little strange. Most of the docs insist on an escort when they examine a female patient. I'm sorry. I know I should have stayed in spite of that SOB. He's creepy."

"God." Stacey felt her knees go weak, and she grabbed the edge of the gurney for support.

"Hey, you okay there?"

"Yeah. I just slipped."

"Okay. Since you're almost finished, I'll duck outside. I hear a lot of commotion in the hall, so something must be going on."

Alone in the cubicle, Stacey sank down onto one of the chairs. Why had Pierce come? What did he want? What did he do? On impulse she looked through her wallet. Everything seemed to be there, but the order wasn't right. She always kept her credit cards on the left side, separate from her license and other professional cards. Now they were all mixed together. Pierce? She ran to the door and into the hallway, almost colliding with two attendants who were trying to restrain a bloodied, apparently inebriated man who seemed intent on wrecking the ER.

An hour later she was still wandering around in a fog, numb with fatigue, confused by what had just happened to her. Mark Wilson found her in the hallway. He took her by the shoulders. "What are you doing here?" he asked. "Go home. Get some rest."

"But I can't, not yet. There's so much to do."

"Believe it or not this hospital can still function without you, for a few hours at least," he said, still holding her. "Now get out of here. That's an order." But it was an order delivered with a smile.

She never even made it to the bedroom of her apartment, just collapsed on the sofa. Late afternoon she woke with a start. The brief nap had done little to relieve her fatigue and even less for her confusion. The thought of Pierce touching her made her skin crawl.

She doubted Pierce could make good on his threat to have her tossed out of the residency program, but he obviously could and would make her life miserable at every opportunity. There was only one explanation for his hostile behavior as she saw it. He was worried. No, he was scared.

The spiteful bastard was up to something that he didn't want found out, and John Merritt with his crazy behavior was right in the center of it. If she played her cards right, and very carefully, she might just be able to give Dr. Pierce the kick in the ass he so richly deserved, and get her guy back to normal at the same time.

# Chapter 8

In the second week of April a warm air mass laden with moisture from the Gulf of Mexico swept northward and collided with a low pressure system that howled down from the northeast. The two systems met just off the upper east coast and sat there like two gigantic tops spinning in opposite directions. For the first two days the coastal regions took the brunt of the tempest with flooding and erosion that sucked the foundations from beneath hundreds of structures built along the shoreline. Then the competing air masses, as if jockeying for position, moved inland and pounded the northeastern states without mercy for four additional days. Rainfall totals of over eight inches pushed rivers well past flood stage. Small streams usually of no consequence became torrents, sweeping away bridges, vehicles and sometimes, people. Ancient oaks, their roots no longer bound by firm soil, were blown over, blocking roadways, bringing down power lines, crushing houses.

The town of Canandaigua was not spared. John called Herman to tell him to leave the shop closed until the storm had run its course. The need for construction supplies would come later on, not now in the midst of the weather's fury.

For the time being, John was marooned. The bridge over the only reliable roadway connecting him to the village was washed away on Friday, and the secondary roads he might have used were all flooded. Overall he weathered the storm well enough. His cupboards were well stocked with canned goods, and his faithful microwave functioned throughout. He spent most of his days in the barn where there were always repairs to be done. A few shingles blew off the roof, but he simply collected the incoming rainwater in a tub so the inside stayed relatively dry. Once he'd run out of chores to keep him busy, he found an old set of barbells that had belonged to Christopher and pumped iron until his arms were rubbery.

Ordinarily he would have remained quite happy with this sort of activity in the company of his dog and the two horses he kept. How many rainy days had he spent in this same barn working alongside his father, perfectly content? But things were different for him now. He had urges, carnal urges that had kicked into overdrive. Fatigue brought no relief from the burning in his loins. What he wanted so desperately just now was not to be found in his barn or his house.

What would Christopher have done in a situation like this, stranded with no company except horses and a dog? John chuckled at the thought. His brother would never have tolerated this kind of isolation. He would be foaming at the mouth about now. In all their years together, he had never known Christopher to spend time alone. Always there was a crowd, mostly girls. And the members of Christopher's entourage were always changing, never the same girls twice. He moved from one to the other like a bee sampling pollen from different flowers.

Now, alone with little to do but think, John could not escape the fact that, since his discharge from the hospital, since he'd been taking those pills from Dr. Pierce, he had become more and more like his brother. Now he had all the girls he wanted, and like the members of Christopher's harems, they were almost always one-night-stands. He couldn't recall a single girl that he'd been with more than once. He seemed to be following his brother's motto: "Just get it in. Get it over with and move on. Keep it simple." Yeah, that pretty well summed things up. As soon as he got his pants back on he was looking around for somebody new.

That approach had seemed to work out well enough for Christopher. He always appeared to be the happiest guy around. But it wasn't working for John. He wanted more. He needed more. A sexual conquest provided only a momentary satisfaction, then he was looking for something else. But what else?

When the realization finally hit him, a thought that had crept in from the corners of his consciousness, it was like all the air had been sucked right out of his lungs. What if he had been wrong about his brother? What if Christopher's happy smile was just a mask? Was it possible that underneath, his brother might have felt the same emptiness that John felt now, that all his escapades, all his conquests were just attempts to latch onto something that always eluded his grasp? In no more time than it took for him to let out a gasp, John's world turned inside out.

Could it be that this brother he'd kept on a pedestal—hell, everyone kept him on a pedestal—had been desperately unhappy all along? Maybe, just maybe, in spite of his constant crowds of admirers, he had been one lonely guy.

"No, no," John cried out. "Christopher was happy. Everybody said so."

But what if he wasn't? What if was all an act? And what if John himself, his own brother, had marched right along with the rest of them, proclaiming Christopher as the greatest guy in town?

All the guilt he'd carried since Christopher's death suddenly multiplied ten times over. How could he not have seen it?

He dropped to the floor. Tears were a new sensation for him. He couldn't even remember the last time he'd cried. Now they flooded his face as if he were standing outside in the downpour. At Christopher's funeral service, the Baptist preacher had said something about Christopher's "brief but happy life." What if that brief life had been an unhappy one? The thought unhinged John. The comforting recollection that had held him together in the aftermath of his brother's death, and his own role in the tragedy, was that belief in his brother's happiness, that "brief but happy life". Now he had to face the possibility that this brother whom he loved, idolized, now emulated, might have been fighting a desperate battle against loneliness, and he himself, who might have helped had let his brother down, again.

John lay on the floor and bawled like an unhappy child. Rebel whimpered at his side, licked his face, but to no avail. The truth had reared its ugly head and beat upon John without mercy. The old wound of his brother's untimely death was opened wider than ever before, and he knew of no way to close it.

And, like a child, he cried himself out. But afterwards, while a child might shrug off the whole episode and perhaps top things off with a nap, John lay curled in a ball on the floor. When he finally stood, he did so with difficulty. His world had been shaken badly. His anxiety about his own near death was nothing compared to the churning grief over his brother's passing. If he had to choose a word to describe his present state it would be emptiness. In the past hour or so he'd lost something, a thing he could not name precisely. The idea that he could recreate his brother in himself was gone, just as Christopher was gone.

He became aware that the rattle of the rain on the roof had stopped. When he looked up at the hole where several shingles had blown off he glimpsed a clear blue sky. "Come on, Rebel, I got to get out of here."

He had no conscious thought of heading to the lake, but that's where he wound up. The road had a thick gravel base so he was able to coax his truck down to the clear space that functioned as a parking lot. The water's edge had crept halfway across the lot, so John ventured out only a couple of steps. Even then he sank in mud above his ankles.

Farther out, some thirty yards from where the shoreline used to be, he looked at the spot where he must have gone through the ice months before. The accident, that's what they called it. Was that the right word, he wondered? "Maybe it would have been better if they hadn't fished me out after all," he said.

By the time he got back to the house the sun was touching the pine tops. A deep hunger gnawed at him. Part of that hunger would never be satisfied by food, but, on the other hand, a can of beans, maybe a couple of hotdogs mixed in, would sure go good about now.

#

She was waiting for him in the kitchen, floating there as if she had no real connection to the floor. He'd had no ghostly visitors during the storm, even hoped he had seen the last of them, but not so. He had no idea how this one or any of the others knew how to find him, but she had. God, didn't time or distance have any meaning for these weird things?

The door was still closed, just as he'd left it, but the thin lady in the hospital gown with bare feet probably didn't bother with the front door of his house. She must have passed right through it; they usually did, these ghosts. She sort of flowed right up to John and hovered there in front of him. He set his coffee pot back on the kitchen counter and retreated as far as he could. Rebel, hackles raised, teeth bared, trembling tail tucked beneath his legs, cowered in the corner.

Then, as if he were addressing a neighbor who'd just dropped by for a chat, John asked "What?"

She, like the others, made no sound, but her communication appeared in John's mind as surely as if she'd shouted it in his face. "Tell Stacey I'm grateful for all her kindness, and I left something for her in the table beside the bed."

"Who are you?" John recoiled. As soon as questions formed in his mind, answers appeared right alongside them. This ghost was one of Stacey's patients. She'd come to John because she couldn't communicate directly with Stacey. Now she was asking him to pass her words along. "How did you find me"? Indeed, how did any of them find him?

"I'm Mrs. Arthur. Stacey will remember. Please, just tell her there's something for her in my nightstand, top drawer, in the back."

"Look, you're a ghost, right? Let's get that much straight at least."

No response.

"How come I can hear you, but I'm not sure you can hear me?"

Again, no response.

He stepped to the side, and the ghost appeared to be staring at the same spot he'd just left. "Hey, I'm over here now."

No movement, no response.

"You're not very scary. Aren't you supposed to be, a little, at least?"

"Please, you mustn't forget. This is very important."

"I don't know about this," he said. "She thinks I'm crazy as it is. If I do what you say she'll know for sure I've gone off the deep end."

Even without words or gestures the urgency of her message came across loud and clear, and there was no way he could deny her request.

"Okay. I'll call her. I promise." What else could he say?

He couldn't be certain, but, for a moment he thought the ghost smiled at him. She reached out and grazed his bare forearm with thin, skeletal fingers. It felt like someone was blowing softly on his skin.

"Don't worry so much," the ghost said.

Don't worry? Who was she, or it, to tell him not to worry? How did she know anything about him? This whole bit was beginning to piss him off, like his private thoughts were suddenly public property.

"Wait a minute, you weren't out there in the barn before, were you?"

"Don't worry so much," she said again. Then she melted silently through the closed front door. No sooner had the ghost disappeared than she emerged once again from the wall. "And you take care of that sweet girl," she said.

"Who? What girl?"

"You know who I mean." Then she disappeared once again.

That girl, it could only be Stacey. But how would a ghost know about them? Maybe Stacey had mentioned him some time before Ms. Arthur died. Whatever, a recommendation from a ghost hardly formed a basis for a relationship.

After she was gone he ran his fingers along the solid walls of the old ranch house, walls built by his great grandparents from timbers hewn right from the forests that encircled the pastures, walls that over the years had withstood all manner of storm and hardship, now breached so effortlessly by the floating figures that visited him.

Locking the doors and checking the windows would not deter the sort of visitors he had. They came whenever they wanted, melting right through solid structures as if they weren't there.

And come they did. Rebel knew, too. When he set about growling, his hackles up, John knew they'd arrived, whether he saw them or not. In fact, if it weren't for Rebel's outbursts, John would have been sure he was slipping into insanity. As it was, he still wondered. But the dog saw them too, so somebody or something was out there, had to be.

"Rebel, old boy," John said as he tried to calm the dog after another midnight arrival had come and gone, "if they were out to hurt us, something would have happened by now."

The odd thing was, he became less and less afraid. Even though each visitation seemed more frightful than the last—like the week before, the man standing on his front porch who had no head—there was no feeling of impending harm, just a deep hollow sadness that seemed to have no bottom. For sure, he wished they'd go away, wished he'd never seen them in the first place, but having heard their cries, he simply couldn't turn his back and walk away.

So, when the visitors talked—not talked, really, communicated-- John listened. Instead of breaking his body, their laments more often threatened to break his heart. More and more he asked, "What can I do? How can I help you?" It bothered him less and less that he was posing this question to a corpse, a ghost, some form of dead thing. For certain, they wanted something from him, but what?

But the question he voiced more and more frequently was, "Why me?" Why were they drawn to him? How did they know where to find him? Did they talk to one another? Share information? It was as if he carried some internal beacon that guided them to him.

Up until now he'd been able to keep the new visitors in his life pretty much to himself. Everybody seemed fairly comfortable with the idea of hallucinations, especially since, as everybody agreed, "He'd been through a lot." But if he started delivering messages from those hallucinations that would blow the lid off for sure. People who'd been willing to cut him some slack before would consider him downright crazy. He certainly didn't want Stacey to think he was nuts, but he'd made a promise, and, unlike some, he made a point of keeping his.

#

Thank God, the storm was finally over. For four days Stacey had slogged through the downpour, reaching the hospital soaked to the skin. Her umbrella blew inside out the first day, and after that she covered herself with whatever she had handy, one day, a plastic garbage bag through which she cut holes for her eyes and mouth. At least her apartment was on the second floor. The unfortunate tenants below her had abandoned their own place when water began to seep under the door.

At the hospital she managed to find a quiet alcove, and, armed with a fresh cup of coffee, began to review her patients' charts. That's when the call from John came. His tone was non-committal. He had called to deliver a message, nothing more. He expressed gratitude from one of Stacey's patients, a Mrs. Arthur, for her kindness, and told Stacey she had left something for her in the top drawer of the cabinet beside her hospital bed. No problem so far, except that Mrs. Arthur, after a long struggle with breast cancer, had died two days earlier. When Stacey told John about her death, he said, "I know."

Stacey's knees began to buckle, and she sat down heavily. Her fear and surprise came out as anger. "What is this, a joke? You know very well that if she died two days ago she couldn't have given you a message yesterday. What are you trying to pull?"

"I guess I knew all along you wouldn't believe me." He hung up.

She took a few deep breaths and latched on firmly to the table beside her. This was crazy. Hallucinations were one thing, but dead people with messages? Nuts, absolutely nuts. John Merritt was a menace. He should be locked up. But then, how did he know anything at all about Mrs. Arthur?

When she felt it was safe to stand, Stacey made her way back to Mrs. Arthur's former room. As soon as she walked through the door images flashed of that valiant woman trying to smile through what Stacey knew was agonizing pain. On nights when she wasn't on call Stacey often went by her room and read to her, since the poor woman was far too weak to even hold a book steady in front of her face. But she hadn't been there for her that last night, and the guilt of it gnawed at Stacey like a persistent headache.

Stacey's hands trembled as she reached for the drawer of the nightstand. She opened it slowly, half expecting something to leap out in her face, some cruel joke, but nothing of the sort happened. She slid one tentative hand toward the back of the drawer, and her fingers contacted a small parcel. Wrapped in several layers of tissue paper was a small locket that Mrs. Arthur had worn every day. Stacey had commented on it several times, and now it lay in her hand, a gift from a dead woman. And the common denominator, the connection between the living and the dead, was John Merritt.

She cradled the locket in her palm. What she held was hard proof of something she didn't really want to know about, and she didn't want John to know about it either.

#

Stacey needed a treat. After getting kicked all over the landscape for the past week she really needed one. That meant a nice long soak in a hot tub, a glass of wine or two, some soft music with a few candles for atmosphere. She'd just settled in, let the hot soapy water work its magic, when the phone rang.

She ignored it for as long as she could. "Crap, might be the hospital." She wasn't on call, but that didn't mean she wasn't still responsible for her patients. And besides, she had to be extra careful with Pierce on her case, looking for some way to trip her up. She did remember to bring the wine glass along.

"Hi, it's me, Bev. Just calling to see how you made it through the big storm."

"Storm?"

'Yeah, where have you been? We practically got washed away."

"Oh, right, the storm. I got wet, everybody did, but that's about it. You really called to talk about the weather?"

Bev laughed so loud Stacey had to move the phone several inches from her ear.

"Okay, you got me. I really called for an update on your love life."

"Love life? What love life?

"Oh, this must be good. Start talking, and don't leave anything out."

"Honest, Bev, I haven't seen John for over two weeks. He called once, but it didn't amount to much. Seems like every time we start getting somewhere things get all crazy again."

"Keep talking."

Stacey hesitated. What was she supposed to say, that John Merritt just gave her a message from a dead lady? That he was not only seeing ghosts, he was talking to them? Worst still, they talked back?

"There's this guy, one of the attending docs, he's really been on my case lately."

"You mean he's trying to get into your pants too?"

"No, nothing like that. He's just been making my life miserable."

"That still doesn't mean he's not trying to get into your pants. Sounds like that hospital soap opera I watch on Wednesdays, everybody doing everybody else. Wow, when do you have time for work?"

"No, no, no, Bev. You've got it all wrong. It's nothing like that."

"Then how is it? Tell me, and don't leave out the juicy parts."

"No juicy parts, just work. You'd laugh if you knew just how dull my life really is."

"And whose fault is that? You've got a handsome young stud mooning over you. All you have to do is snap your fingers, and he'll come running. I should be so lucky."

"It's that easy, you think?"

"Sure, but you better hurry up before some other girl gets her hooks into him. There's a lot that want to. Hey, who is this other guy, the one that's out to get you?"

"He's a real bastard. I think he's up to something, but I don't know what. Worse yet, he's John's doctor, the one that revived him after he drowned."

"Why is he trying to get into your pants, as if I couldn't guess."

"I wish you'd stop saying that. Believe me, if he ever tried anything like that I'd cut it right off."

"Wow, you sound pissed, cousin. What's this charmer's name, in case I ever run into him?"

"Paul Pierce, but you probably never will."

"Paul Pierce from the Longevity Center? That Paul Pierce?"

"Hold on, what are you talking about? What's the Longevity Center?"

"Lord, girl. You've got to get out more. Don't you even read the papers? Dr. Paul Pierce is medical director of that new Longevity Center they're building right outside of town. There's a sign out front with his name on it. It's going to be huge. The dean from your own medical school, some guy named Westbrook, he came down, and there was a big ceremony. Your Dr. Pierce must be a big deal. Next time he tries to get into your pants, maybe you should let him?"

"Screw you, Bev. When can you come up for lunch?"

# Chapter 9

Dammit, why did this one keep turning up, following him around, John wanted to know? All the others had appeared once or twice, then no more. But this one, the pathetic ghost of a pathetic little girl, with its slashed neck and missing hands, this one wouldn't leave him alone. When he got ready to leave for work, it was standing by his truck. When he got to the shop, there it was, hovering a few feet off the floor back by the bins of loose bolts and screws. On Tuesday night he'd awakened to find it floating by his bed, close enough to reach out and touch. Scared the hell out of him. "Stay away from me," he'd yelled.

Yelling seemed to work, for a few days at least. Then Saturday morning, just as he laid his breakfast bacon strips into the cast iron fry pan, it appeared again, at the end of the table, right behind his chair. When he stepped toward it, the ghost floated farther across the room. That was the other weird thing about this one, it was persistent, but also shy, like a child. Well, for crying out loud, it was a child, or had been before some bastard carved it up. How many times he had thought that, if he could ever lay hands on the monster that did this, he would send him straight to hell where he belonged. But now he'd gone and yelled at a child, and, ghost or not, that wouldn't do.

"Look, I'm sorry about before, yelling like that. I didn't mean anything by it. You just scared me, is all."

The ghost floated closer, right through the oak table as if it wasn't there.

His bacon was beginning to sizzle, and John flipped the strips over. "I don't guess you eat breakfast, do you? I could always cook up some more." He smacked his forehead with his palm. God, he was going totally stupid. Ghost didn't eat. Everybody knew that. But then, his ghosts did all sorts of things they weren't supposed to do. They talked to him, or maybe communicated was a better word. And this one the little girl, cried. Every time he saw her tears formed little rivulets in the dried blood on her face.

And always, the message was the same, just as now: "Help me."

He moved the pan off the hot burner. Breakfast would have to wait a bit. "I don't know how to help you. What do you want me to do?"

"Tell my mother."

"What? Tell her what?"

"That I'm all right."

"All right? You're not all right. Look at you."

She moved closer, closer than ever before, until there was no boundary between them, and John was enveloped in a warm aura. Inside was peace. She didn't say so, but he knew: That was the message for her mother.

"Who are you?" he asked, only the question was in his head, never reaching his lips. And just as quickly, the answer was there.

"Elizabeth."

He had other questions, but they didn't seem important. Besides, he'd know the answers soon enough. He was sure of it. He didn't have to ask.

The aura dissipated slowly, and the little girl specter with it. But this time John didn't want it to go. Unlike his upside down life for the past few months, for a brief moment he'd found a place of perfect peace, and he liked it. The feeling of warmth and caring was much like the sensation he'd found in the depths of Canandaigua Lake. In that moment all that he'd struggled for and against was set aside, replaced by a state of perfect bliss. But it wasn't his place, not yet. He knew that, too.

Now the child specter had a name and a request. What would he do about it? He had already given Stacey every reason in the world to think he was crazy, delivering that message from her dead patient, but running up to a total stranger and saying, "I just saw your daughter and her throat was cut and her hands were gone, but she said she was okay," would get him jailed or committed or both.

But how could he deny a request like the one he'd just received? Somehow, when the time came—and it would come, he was sure—he'd have to find a way.

Then, three days later, when he saw the picture in the paper, he knew without question that he was looking at Elizabeth's mother. Margaret Simmons, a local attorney, had just been elected president of the Upstate Medical Center board of directors, and John Merritt had a message for her.

He had to do it. He just didn't know how. He made several laps around his kitchen table hoping for some resolution that failed to appear. Finally, with no particular plan in mind, he dialed her office and made an appointment. In response to the obvious question about the reason for his visit, all he could come up with was "personal."

#

Late morning, under a sky that threatened rain, John dusted off his jeans and climbed back into the saddle, still a little woozy after the toss Nacho had given him. He'd chosen the gelding over the Harley, hoping to regain some of the equilibrium that seemed to be slipping away from him so fast. A ride around his farm seemed like good preparation for his meeting with Margaret Simmons later that afternoon. God knows, he needed it. The phone conversation had been awkward, but even if he'd planned it more carefully, how could it have been otherwise? When she'd insisted on meeting with him, John knew his involvement was going to get complicated.

He reached forward and patted the horse on the neck. "Should have figured you'd be a little rambunctious after being cooped up for three days, but I didn't think you'd buck me off like that."

John let the big gelding pick his way along the path through the woods on the northeast corner of his farm. The scent of pine needles carried on brisk northern air cleared his head in no time.

They reached a clearing and Nacho stopped for a drink from the little stream that meandered through the open meadow. John stood in the stirrups and looked at rolling hills in all directions, the same view that generations of Merritts had enjoyed before him. A few times, when they were kids, he and Christopher had gone out together on horseback rides, but coming-of-age, better known as puberty, ended all that. After the hormonal surge took command of his brother, John rode alone, occasionally with his father, but most often by himself.

His dog ranged up ahead following the course John usually took when he saddled up Nacho. Riding around the farm, feeling the gentle undulation of the horse beneath him grounded John, connected him to his past in a way that nothing else could. Yeah, he needed this, especially now.

Back at his house, the ancient pick-up truck, the one that had neither air conditioning nor a reliable heater and so was uncomfortable in all seasons, sat in his driveway, MERRITT SUPPLY barely legible on the door.

Herman Poulos leaned on the fender waving at him. "Hey, John. Figured I'd come out and see how you're doing."

John guided Nacho over next to the truck and dismounted. "How's it going, Herman?" He turned and flipped one stirrup over Nacho's saddle.

"That's your granddaddy's old saddle, ain't it?"

"Yeah," John said, running his hand over the worn leather.

"How'd you get so dirty?" Herman said, pointing to John's backside. "Nacho didn't buck you off, did he?"

"As a matter of fact, he did just that," John said. He patted the gelding on the neck.

"Didn't think I'd ever see a horse that could throw John Merritt. What got into him?"

"I didn't take him out for several days, just didn't feel up to it. So when I finally got around to it, he was probably pissed, and he let me know."

"If you say so. When you reckon you'll be comin' back by the shop? There's some stuff there needs your signature. Otherwise, we're okay."

"I have to drive up to Rochester this afternoon to meet a lady. I'll stop by then."

"A lady? And who might that be?" Herman pushed his hat farther back on his head.

"Nothing like you're thinking. It's an older lady."

"Older? Hell, John, that's even better. The older ones, they got some experience, and, best of all, they're grateful for the attention."

"Herman, you got a one-track mind. You're the horniest man I know." Which wasn't true, of course. Until recently John's own exploits were the talk of the town. But he could feel himself losing interest. They were just conquests after all. He longed for something with actual feeling, someone he could build something with. He wanted a relationship. Maybe the same thing his brother had looked for but never found.

John loosened Nacho's saddle girth. The horse responded with a prolonged emission of flatulence.

"That's why he threw you off." Herman cackled. "You bound him up with that girth when all he wanted was a good, long fart."

"You might be right. Now if we could just solve your problem with something that simple...."

"Problem? I don't have a problem." Herman climbed into the truck. The hinges squeaked loudly as he closed the door. "We might have to think about a new truck someday, John."

"Maybe. See you later." At least Herman hadn't mentioned the Harley. They'd already had a heated discussion about John's purchase of a "damn fool bike" when their only truck was practically falling apart. It was an empty argument, of course. Herman was just expressing his frustration with John's behavior. Neither of them wanted to replace the truck in the first place. The ancient vehicle was another link to the past, and some days that was about all John felt he had left.

#

He hadn't been in the Wishart Building since his father's death, that long afternoon with the family lawyer when, as sole surviving Merritt, John became heir to the farm, the family business and a big stack of overdue bills. When Margaret Simmons asked him to meet her there, he could think of a dozen reasons for not going anywhere near the place, but he could not deny her request any more than he'd been able to deny her daughter's ghost.

Margaret Simmons, Attorney-at-Law, he learned soon enough, had her own suite of offices, and, not one, but three secretaries.

The one closest to the door, a pert blonde with blue eyes and a red ribbon in her hair, looked up and gave John a bright smile when he walked in. "May I help you?" She looked him up and down, apparently pleased with what she saw.

"I'm John Merritt. I'm supposed to see Ms. Simmons."

She clicked on the intercom. "Ms. Simmons, Mr. Merritt is here," still flashing that bright, inviting smile.

The tall woman who opened the door held onto the handle like she needed the support. Her suit looked expensive, but maybe a size too big for her. She beckoned to John. He took a deep breath and followed.

She motioned to a chair, then walked over to the window, her back to John, her arms clasped tightly over her chest. After what seemed like an eternity, she said, "What do you want, Mr. Merritt?"

"I'm supposed to give you a message, from Elizabeth." He could hear her gasp all the way across the room.

"My daughter? She's been missing for four months." She turned toward him, her eyes narrowed to slits. "I said, what do you want?"

John gripped the arms of the chair and checked to make sure he had an unimpeded path to the door. "Elizabeth said to tell you she's okay."

The woman walked over next to him, blocking his exit. "You know where she is."

"No. I don't know that."

"You've seen her, though?"

"Not exactly."

She stepped closer, her fists clenched. "Mr. Merritt, you'd better start making some sense very quickly. If this is your idea of a joke, I'll make you sorry you were ever born."

"She said to tell you she's okay. That's all." He hung his head, speaking softly. "This was all a mistake. I never should have come."

"Why did you?"

"I had to. She kept coming back, asking me to help her. " He hung his head even lower until his chin rested on his chest. "I'm sorry. I can't explain it. It won't make sense to you, and it doesn't make sense to me either."

The woman leaned against the desk. Her breathing became labored, a pained groan. "She's dead, isn't she?"

"Yes, m'am."

"How did she die?"

John shook his head. There was no way he would ever describe the ghastly circumstances of the little girl's death to anyone, let alone her mother.

"Did you kill her?"

"No."

"Where is she, her body?"

"God, I don't know. All she said was her name was Elizabeth. I don't even know for sure she meant you."

He could hear her breathing, coming now in short gasps, but he could not meet her gaze. What had he done? What if he was wrong?

At the very moment he was about to bolt and flee from the room, she pulled a chair alongside him and fell into it. She grabbed his arm and he felt hot droplets hitting the back of his hand, tears she made no attempt to divert. "I knew it would be bad news, sooner or later. She came to you, after she died? Is that what you're telling me?"

"Yes. Look, I know this all sounds crazy. You probably think I'm a complete nut case, and you might be right."

Her fingertips dug into his arm, and she looked straight into his eyes, as if she could see right through him, read his mind. He thought for a moment she might attack him. Then the lines in her face softened. She took several deep breaths. There was a connection now. The words didn't matter so much.

"No. I don't think you're crazy, Mr. Merritt. At first I thought you were a crook, but I don't think that any more. If anything, you seem to be hurting as much as I am. If I didn't believe that, you would be a bloody mess by now."

"I'm sorry, I...."

She leaned forward and put her arm around John's shoulders. "She's all right, you say?"

"Yes, ma'am."

"Then I guess that's all I need to know, for now." She kissed John on the forehead. "Thank you."

There were other questions, of course, had to be. The poor woman had just received the worst possible news from a complete stranger who claimed he'd heard it from her daughter's ghost. John had no idea how she could accept such a message, but she had, and knowing, hearing from her daughter seemed to have lifted a terrible burden.

"I knew someone would come. In a way, I've been expecting you."

After a moment she shuffled back to the window, stood there looking out. It was time for him to go, but he knew he would see her again.

After he left Margaret's office John walked from one block to the other, not knowing where he was going or why. Just before five o'clock, he went into a small shop on the corner and ordered coffee. Some of the fog in his brain was beginning to clear. He understood a few things now, while others remained unknown and probably unknowable. Just like the message he had passed on to Stacey, what he had just said to Margaret Simmons seemed crazy, impossible, but he had done it because he chose to, not because he had to.

He sat for a while swirling his coffee in his cup. As he gazed into the depths of the brackish liquid he came to understand that he wasn't the only one with pain, not the only one who had experienced tragic loss and now had to live with regrets about things he could never change. In Margaret's case he felt he'd been able to ease the pain of her loss. Maybe he had done the same for her dead daughter, passing along something she would never be able to say herself. If this was lunacy, so be it.

The pieces of his personal puzzle were ragged and oddly shaped, but somehow they began to fit together. He had a job to do, even if he was nothing more than a glorified messenger. He had no idea who or what had selected him—maybe he had selected himself—but for now he had a special ability, one that allowed him to alleviate at least some of the world's pain and suffering, both for the living and the dead, and he wasn't about to ignore it. He'd carried the guilt of Christopher's death around for years, and now perhaps he saw a way to atonement, if not for his own grief, at least for that of others who had suffered as he had.

"Coffee okay?" The waitress pointed to the cup John hadn't touched.

"Yeah, it's great," he said. "Best ever." He watched as she walked back toward the counter, the little bounce in her step, the white skirt of her uniform stretched snugly across her buttocks. Couldn't be a day over seventeen. Probably making a few bucks working after school. The thought crossed his mind, but he dismissed it; the war inside him, conquest vs. compassion, today came out on the plus side. He left her a generous tip.

# Chapter 10

Even at one hundred and thirty-five pounds, fully dressed, including work boots, Herman Poulos got into fights. Often as not he started them, particularly when he was in a bad mood, and lately his mood was stinking. He'd promised John's dad that he would look after his son, but now John was slipping away from him, and he didn't know how to stop it. He hoped at first that the crazy behavior—tearing around the countryside on that new bike, jumping on any girl who didn't have the sense to get out of the way—would run its course and he'd get back to his old self again. It didn't take a trained psychologist to see what he was doing, acting like his brother. John had worshipped Christopher, hell, everybody had, but in Herman's mind John was twice the man his brother was. Christopher needed the limelight, needed the attention. John never did. Character counted with Herman, and if he needed someone to help him out of a tight spot he'd pick John every time.

But now John had gone off the deep end with no sign he would be coming back soon. It put Herman in a real funk, and Herman in a funk was Herman looking for a fight. He spotted two out-of-town construction workers, big beefy hard hat guys, taking up the whole sidewalk, forcing the local pedestrians to either hop into the street or get run over. Just what he needed. Herman crossed the street and set himself directly in their path. He put his head down and walked straight into the man closest to the curb. The big guy shoved Herman aside and must have been very surprised when Herman, standing on his tiptoes, punched him squarely in the mouth.

John walked out of Merritt Supply just in time to see Herman get tossed into the street. Both of the big guys headed for Herman, apparently planning to do some serious damage. John charged straight in and dropped the lead guy with a right cross. Herman would say later it was the prettiest punch he had ever seen, but things went badly from that point. When Herman rolled over to get to his feet he tripped John. The second guy kicked John in the head, and he landed on top of Herman, out cold.

Herman launched himself at the man who had kicked John. He seized the man's crotch with both hands and hung on like an enraged bull terrier.

The man whose genitals were being pulverized by Herman's grasp expelled a high-pitched screech. "Get him off me," he said.

The other construction worker grabbed Herman's leg and tugged, but this just added yet another element of torture for his companion; not only were his balls being crushed, now they might be pulled off entirely.

Herman would not let go. The louder the man wailed, the tighter his grip became.

A small crowd gathered. One of the men knocked the second construction worker to the ground. Still, Herman clung to his victim, like someone possessed.

"Let him go, Herm," someone said.

"Tickle him." A female voice. Mary Beth Mason, who had known Herman since childhood, said, "Herman's real ticklish." She straddled Herman, then dug her fingertips into his ribs.

"Dang it, Mary Beth, quit it," Herman yelled.

But the tactic worked. Herman relinquished his grip and crawled from beneath Mary Beth.

"See, told you," she said.

The brief fray ended when a police car pulled up. The construction workers went to jail, mainly to protect them from the mob of locals that had gathered around, and John went to the hospital. "Better take him back to Upstate," Herman said. "That bastard kicked him pretty hard."

#

When John woke up his head felt like someone had used it for batting practice. Not everything hurt, though. Stacey sat at his bedside holding his hand. That part felt good, very good.

"Take it easy," she said. "You have a nasty concussion. Your CT scan checked out okay, no acute intracranial bleeding or anything like

100

that."

"Hi." It wasn't much of a response, but it was the only thing he could think of.

She ran her fingertips across the side of his face. "Next time, let's meet somewhere else, okay?"

She sat there, just holding his hand. All the doubt and awkwardness of their earlier meetings simply melted away. The connection he'd hoped for was there, as if it had been all along.

Stacey winced. "John, my hand, you're squeezing too hard."

They kept him in the hospital for two days. Stacey dropped by every day for a visit, then came back to sit with him in the evenings. That was the best time of all, talking, not talking, no matter. Just having her near, he couldn't wish for more.

The hospital discharge planner, a stout lady with a clipboard, came to see him before he left. "You're going to need some help at home," she said. "You can't manage by yourself."

"He's coming home with me," Stacey said. "I'll take care of him."

#

It was all the very best times of his life rolled up into a few days, like that euphoric period that newlyweds share, except no sex. Every time John got amorous Stacey pushed him away. "Not yet," she said. "You shouldn't get excited. Concussion, remember?"

"Just whose orders am I following here?" he asked. He tried to wrap his arms around her, but she wriggled away from him.

"Mine. I'm your doctor and your nurse, and you have to do exactly as I say. Now, come help me in the kitchen."

Her apartment was tiny, an efficiency type that could be traversed end to end in a dozen steps, not the kind of place John could tolerate for long had it not been for Stacey's presence. It was the first occasion they'd had to spend time together, and John knew, if it was humanly possible, that this was the girl for him. Oh, they still had issues, serious issues, between them, but for the time being, none of that mattered.

#

That first evening in her apartment started off nicely enough, great, in fact, even considering that John paced around like a caged bear. Clearly this was a man who did not like being confined in tight spaces, but Stacey could have guessed as much already. She had prepared a pot roast from one of her mother's old recipes, but there must have been a few steps her mom had not written down. The beef was tough and stringy while the vegetables turned to mush. None of which seemed to deter John in the least. A dinner that might easily have fed four adults disappeared in no time at all.

"Delicious," he said. "Didn't know doctors could cook like that."

"Sit still," she said. "I'll clean up."

"No way. I ate most of it, so I can darned well help out."

Stacey had used much of her kitchen space for storage of boxes and odd bits that she had no other place to put, so their workspace was tiny, so much so they had to turn sideways to get past one another. With the proximity and close contact the temperature in the small room was rising too fast. "Can you raise that window above the sink?" she asked. "It's stuck, and I never can get it open."

John pounded the frame a couple of times with the back of his hand, and the window slid open without a whimper.

"You're pretty handy around the kitchen," she said. The cool air rushed in just in time.

"I'm even handier in there." He motioned with his head toward the bedroom.

"Don't even think about it." She thumped his forehead lightly with her knuckle. "Remember your concussion."

He held her gaze just long enough. She felt her resolve melting into the same mushy consistency as those semi-liquid vegetables in her pot roast. Then he winked at her. "Okay, you win…this time."

#

John settled himself on the sofa, and Stacey brought in a bottle of wine and two glasses. She set one in front of John then poured it half full. She took the other glass and the bottle to the worn dark blue armchair, leaving the coffee table between them. There was no pretense of coasters to protect the wooden tops from watermarks. There were already so many circles that a few more could hardly matter.

"Why are you way over there?" John patted the sofa cushion beside him.

She folded her legs beneath her. "Because it's time we had a nice long talk, past time, in fact."

Uh oh. John squirmed in his seat. "I'm, uh, not much for

talking."

"You think I don't know that? You were always the quiet one, used to be, at least. But we have a lot of catching up to do, nine years' worth."

He knew where she meant to start and knew just as well he really didn't want to go back there, not when things were going so well between them. Finally, after all the fits and starts, he was beginning to see daylight. Why go back and dig up old unpleasant things?

"John?"

"Do we have to go back to that?"

"Yes, because that's where you lost Christopher, but it's also where I lost you."

"What do you mean?"

"Cut the crap, John. This is me, Stacey, you're talking to. I remember how it was after Christopher died. How when I'd look into your eyes it was as if there was nobody in there. And nobody could get through to you, not your mom, your dad, not me, not anybody."

John leaned his head back on the sofa, stared at the wall beyond. "I let him down."

"How? You really think you could have stopped him that day?"

"No, by then it was too late."

"I don't follow you."

"I let him down a long time before we ever got into that stupid boat. When we flipped, and he struck out for shore, he must have known he wouldn't make it. I don't think he really wanted to."

Stacey left her chair and sat down beside him. "You're losing me, sweetheart."

"It finally dawned on me that maybe he wasn't really the happiest guy in the world, not like we all made him out to be. You know, everybody's best friend, but nobody's best friend, not really."

She took his face in her hands, wiped tears from his cheeks, then her own.

"You see, that's where I let him down. I should have been there for him a long time before that. Instead, I was just like everybody else, just another hero worshipper."

She dropped her head onto his shoulder. "Oh, sweet Jesus, and this is what you've been carrying around inside you."

"No, just recently. It took me nine years to figure it out. Guess I'm a little slow."

For a while there seemed nothing left to say, so they sat that way, Stacey's head on his shoulder, her arms around his neck.

"I'm so sorry, John. But there's no way for you to know for sure, about your brother, I mean. Maybe you're right, but we'll never know. But I'm not going to stand by and watch you beat yourself up over it any longer. You've suffered long enough, we both have."

"He was my brother, Stacey. He should have been able to talk to me."

She sat up again. "Well, you're going to talk to me now. Got it? You've changed since they fished you out of the lake, and I want to know what's going on."

"Changed, yeah, so I've heard."

"Well?"

He stood, but the walls seemed closer than before. He could cross the entire living area in four or five steps. How could anyone live so closed in, he wondered. But she hadn't asked about his preferences in spacious living, she'd asked specifically about changes in his behavior, something he was not comfortable discussing. There was so much he didn't want her to know, ever.

"John, are you going to talk to me, or am I going to have to beat it out of you?"

"What? You can't do that. I've had a concussion, remember?"

"Yeah, I remember." She walked in front of him, blocking his path. "And you should remember that I have three older brothers, so I know how to fight dirty. I don't have to hit you in the head to hurt you. I know other ways. So start talking or be prepared for some painful consequences."

"You would actually do that to an injured man?" He tried to embrace her, but she pushed his arms aside.

"Try me."

"Okay, okay." He held up his hands in surrender. "What do you want to know?"

"Are you happy now?" Her voice softened, and she held his gaze with her own.

He shook his head. "Sometimes it feels okay being different, but a lot of the time it feels like I'm just running around in circles looking for something. That's why I wondered about Christopher, you know, did he feel the same way?"

"Maybe there's hope for you yet."

She kissed his cheek, but when he tried to embrace her she pushed him away again. "We still have more to discuss."

"Then I'm going to need another glass of wine."

"Half a glass, that's your limit." She took the bottle away.

'I don't remember you being so bossy before," he said.

"John, this I the first time I've had you alone, all to myself. I want so much for us, but there's stuff I need to understand better. You have to help me."

"What else is there?"

"Your ghosts. After you called me about Ms. Arthur, I went back to her room. I found her locket in the desk. She left it there for me. I wasn't there the night she died, so she had to ask you to tell me about the locket."

"So, am I crazy or not?"

"Maybe we both are. Seeing dead people, talking to them, this is not normal. You know that, don't you?"

"Sure, but what else can I do? They turn up whenever they want. I don't call them or anything."

She sat back in the chair, cradled her wine glass in her hands. "Lord, what am I going to do with you?"

"I can think of one thing in particular."

"Stay right where you are. Remember what I said about fighting dirty. I'll do it."

"Are we through talking now? I'm tuckered out."

"Okay, then. Besides, I have an idea."

#

On Thursday afternoon Herman came by to drive John home.

"Make sure he takes it easy," Stacey said. "No hard work, no exertion of any kind."

"Okay. Still feeling rocky, huh?"

"Yeah." John fingered the lump that remained prominent on the side of his head. "What did that guy hit me with?"

"His foot, inside a big old construction boot," Herman said.

"Probably had a steel toe in the danged thing."

"Might have to look him up in a couple of weeks," John said.

"No." Stacey grabbed him by the shoulders. "No more fighting. I'm serious."

"I just want to talk to him, that's all."

She was livid. "If you go fighting, I'll never speak to you again. I swear."

Herman chuckled. "She's got you, Johnny. She's really got you."

He began to miss her as soon as Herman wheeled the truck onto the highway. Yeah, he was glad to be out of that tiny apartment, but leaving her behind, he wondered how his life could ever feel complete again without her.

"Kinda quiet," Herman said. "Pretty little lady doctor getting under your skin?"

"Maybe a little."

"Maybe a lot, seems to me."

#

Stacey waved as they drove off, hoping above hope that they would be back together again soon. There were still gaps in his past, and present as well, that she wanted to fill in, but getting John to open up just a little was as much as she could hope for now. She knew much more about his escapades than he thought, but full disclosure would have to wait for another time. She dared not push him too far yet.

As it was, she tried to strike some balance between her feelings and rational thought, but she was losing the battle. It was as if she were back in high school with him, overwhelmed, gushing, willing to throw away everything for a glance, a word. The nine years in between might as well never have happened.

"Get a grip, girl," she said out loud, but the words were hollow and meant nothing.

It wasn't until the early evening as she was preparing her dinner—she'd thrown out the remains of the pot roast she'd prepared for John—that she got back to the idea she'd had before, Paul Pierce. All the craziness led back to Pierce. Ever since he'd gotten his hooks into John things had gone haywire.

She felt more convinced than ever that Pierce's dismissal of John's behavior as a sequelae of a Near Death Experience was just a smoke screen, something to hide what he was really up to. The key lay with the other people Pierce had treated for cold water drowning. There wouldn't be many of them, but she didn't need a great number. If the findings proved consistent—ghostly visitations, skin biopsies, Dormistan—she had made her case. Whether or not all of this might be tied into his Longevity Center was something she would have to consider later on.

Of course, dropping everything on Dr. Pierce's doorstep was only part of the problem. The real question was whether she could ever get John Merritt back to being John Merritt, the original version. First things first, she told herself. Now she needed information.

The idea seemed solid enough, but getting the data she needed would be something else entirely. She had already learned how protective Dr. Pierce was about his patients. If he got wind of what she planned to do she would be toast. She needed someone who could gain access to Pierce's files without him finding out about it, and that meant Benny.

As distasteful as the thought was, she could come up with no other solution; when it came to hacking into computers it would have to be Benny, the senior medical resident. Heavy, sweaty Benny. Benny whose eyes through his thick horn-rimmed glasses looked like marbles floating in a fish bowl. Benny who pressed up against her at any opportunity. But Benny who was a certifiable genius when it came to computers.

The following day Stacey found him in the cafeteria along with two medical students to whom he was doubtless passing on words of wisdom. Loathsome as he was, Benny never seemed to forget anything. He was a veritable gold mine of medical trivia and always seemed to attract an entourage of students hoping to catch some tidbit that they could use to gain a step on their classmates. The only question was whether the price—being close to him—was worth it.

"Hi, Benny." Stacey maintained her distance and, for good measure, kept a chair between them. "Can we talk?"

The asparagus, the entire stem that he was chewing on, protruded from the side of his mouth like a green tongue. "Huh? Sure. Scram, guys."

The students grabbed their notes and headed for the door.

Benny ignored his napkin and wiped his mouth with the back of his hand, leaving a few green strands trailing up the side of his face. "Stacey, darlin', whatever can I do to you…I mean for you?"

"Settle down, Benny. I need a favor."

"Hey, favors make the world go round. I do something for you, you do something for me. Know what I mean?"

His smile reminded Stacey of a large lab toad that had just swallowed a bug. To complete the picture, all he had to do was belch…and there it was. "Urrrp." He patted his abdomen. "Ahhh, asparagus always gives me gas. What was it you wanted, my dear?"

What she really wanted was to get as far away from him as possible, but she had no alternative. John Merritt would owe her big time for this. "Okay, Benny, what I need is some information."

"You've come to the right man," he said. "Did I say you're looking especially fine today?"

"No, but thanks. What I need is some patient information."

"Why don't you get it yourself? What's the big deal?"

"I tried but I couldn't get the information. If I could get into the computer myself I wouldn't have to bother you."

"It's no bother, Stacey, always ready to help a beautiful woman in distress." He leaned forward, grinning. Some residual from his dinner remained stuck to his front teeth giving him a gap-toothed jack-o-lantern appearance.

"I need to tell you, this might be a little risky. The patients I want to know about are some of Dr. Pierce's, and he's pretty touchy about them."

"No problem. He'll never know." Benny shook his head and smirked.

"You mean he won't be able to trace anything back to you?"

"Catch me? Are you kidding? You are talking to the premier hacker. The system hasn't been made that I can't get into, and I leave without a trace."

"Great, because if Pierce finds out, things could get nasty."

"Not to worry. Just what is his lord and master up to that's so mysterious?"

"He's treated some patients for cold water drowning."

"Oh, yeah. He's the big expert."

"I need to know something about how he's treating them, what medications he's using. I talked to one of them in the hospital, and he was having some bizarre hallucinations. He's called me since he was discharged, and he's still having them."

"Any beautiful women in the hallucinations?"

Stacey shook her head. "He thinks he's seeing dead people."

"Maybe he's just crazy. If I had hallucinations I'd want them full of beautiful women, beautiful naked women."

"I'm sure you would, but I don't think he's crazy. Aside from the apparitions he seems pretty normal. Anyway, I'd like to find out if any of Pierce's other patients have that sort of problem."

"So, you want me to get a list of the patients he's treated."

"Yes. If you could do that it would really be great."

"I can handle that, no problem."

"Thanks, Benny. Thanks a million."

"Once I get the list, you can thank me proper. I'll let you know how. You know, tit for tat." He laughed so loudly that he drew stares from people at other tables.

"I've got to go, Benny."

"Okay, just remember, tit for tat." His barking laughter followed her out of the cafeteria.

#

Damn, what a bitch. Benny had worked for almost three days trying to break into Pierce's computer system. Of all his many hack attempts this was the toughest he'd faced. But he'd finally gotten in, finally gotten the list Stacey was so worked up about. A line of secretions emerged from the corner of his mouth, and he caught it just before it dribbled onto his computer keyboard.

Drooling was not an unusual occurrence with Benny. In fact, whenever he thought about Stacey Patterson, saliva trickled from the corner of his mouth, especially when he had time to visualize her in those special situations, situations where she was totally compliant because she had no alternatives, a situation like he was about to present to her very soon. He picked up the phone.

"Hey, this is Benny. Did I wake you?"

"No. I was already up. Did you have any luck with the records?" Stacey asked.

"Maybe. What are you wearing?"

"That's none of your business."

"Well, maybe I can't remember whether I got what you want or not."

"Benny, I'm wearing a very sweaty running outfit right now. I'm about as attractive as a load of dirty laundry."

"You're all wet and sticky, huh?"

"You can add smelly to that if you want."

"God. Unnnh."

"Benny, are you all right?"

"So good I can't stand it."

"Just stop it, will you? Tell me about the computer stuff."

"Better if I show you."

"Okay. When I get to the hospital I'll page you, and you can show me then."

"No, no, no."

"What? Why not?"

"This is probably very valuable information. It took me days to get into Pierce's files. I don't know who set up his firewall, but whoever did is damn good."

"But you got it?"

"Yeah. And you owe me big."

"What do you want, Benny?"

"Just treat me nice, like you would a boyfriend, tit for tat, remember?" Benny laughed so hard he dropped the half-cooked hotdog he'd been chewing on.

"Benny, please. I need that computer information. I have to have it."

"You know where it is. Come and get it."

"Your apartment?"

"That's the place." Benny leaned back and wiped the moisture from his face with the back of his hand. It wouldn't be long now. He'd busted his ass to get that data for Stacey, and she'd pay for it. If she was half as desperate as she sounded he could make her do things he'd only dreamed about. And best of all he'd get it all on film. He checked the two cameras he'd concealed in his bedroom. Ahh, Stacey. He'd waited a long time for this. He grabbed his crotch. Rock hard. Benny gazed at the bathroom door. Should he? No, he'd save it all for her.

# Chapter 11

Once Herman had driven off around the bend in the road and out of sight, John danced a little jig on his front porch. His dog tried to join in, but only succeeded in tripping John, dropping him squarely on his backside. But the upset did nothing to dampen John's spirits. It seemed as if the murk in his brain was finally beginning to clear a bit, and he could almost envision a future, with Stacey Patterson.

Yeah, there were still a few problems, issues, she called them. Like, how much did she know about the number of women he'd bedded in the last few months? He hadn't been exactly discreet about chasing skirts, and Stacey knew enough people in town to check up on him if she wanted.

But that behavior was all past history now. As firmly as he could, he resolved to keep it in his pants, where it belonged. If that meant taking a half dozen cold showers every day, so be it.

Maybe there was some medication for urges like his, something to slow him down. He would check on that tomorrow, and for sure he would burn the collection of ladies' underwear that he kept in his office at work. It had increased substantially since that day he had stretched Janie Sells out across his desk. God forbid Stacey should ever find out about that.

And he was beginning to have some insight into the changes Stacey was so concerned about, or so he thought. Understanding Christopher's behavior helped him understand his own a little better. And even if he was wrong and Christopher was marching to a different tune altogether, at least he understood that his own sexual antics would bring him no more than momentary satisfaction, nothing on which to build a future.

When it came to ghosts, he'd held back there too. He'd had to tell Stacey about Ms. Arthur. He'd promised, after all. But there had been many others.

In particular he hadn't told her about Elizabeth and her mom, Margaret Simmons. Because he'd made a deal with Margaret.

Margaret Simmons had asked him to lunch on a Sunday just after the first of the month. Once again he'd had to search for a clean shirt, struggle with a tie, shine his shoes. Damned shame, after all that, he had to drive up in his ratty old truck. He thought for a moment about taking the Harley, but that might send the wrong message. He reminded himself that he was meeting a grieving mother, and that he was the one who had given her the most devastating news any mother could ever hear.

No, he would show her all the respect and compassion he could muster. She deserved that much.

He knew the restaurant, had driven past it any number of times. Just never thought he would see it from the inside, way too high class for his tastes. Coburn's Diner was more his speed. He felt like a bumkin.

Margaret Simmons proved as gracious and charming as anyone could possibly be. She embraced him warmly, then insisted he sit beside her, not across the table. She held his hand as they talked, got reacquainted.

"How have you been, John?"

"Me? Fine. And you?"

"Good days and bad days. I've thought about you a lot. I want you to know how grateful I am. You helped me more than you'll ever know."

"But all I did was bring you bad news."

Now the sorrow came out, and no amount of poise or social grace could cover it up.

"Yes, but as bad as it was hearing it, not knowing was even worse. And it meant so much knowing that she was okay. It made me think she had found peace, and maybe, in time, I can too."

He searched so hard for a comforting word, but none came. So he squeezed her hand, and that was enough.

While they ate she asked him so many questions about himself, past, present and future, as he saw it.

He talked on and on. He wasn't forthcoming at first, he never was, but Margaret was quite skillful at drawing him out.

Finally the subject changed to ghosts. "You've seen others?" she asked.

He nodded.

"And they talk to you?"

"Sometimes."

"I have a request. It's a bit unusual, and I don't want you to feel under any obligation. In fact, I don't want an answer now. I'd like you to take some time to think about it.

"After Elizabeth was taken, weeks would go by, and I knew nothing. That was the worst time of my life. Even worse than the day you came to my office. I began meeting with a counselor who referred me to a support group, other parents who had lost children. None of them held any real hope for ever seeing their children again, but they all wanted one thing, one last chance to say 'I love you.' That's all"

She paused for a moment, pushed her dessert around on her plate with a spoon.

"What I want you to think about is whether you would be willing to meet with our group, on the chance that the children might appear, to you at least, so you could give them that message one last time. I know it's asking a lot."

"Yes," he said. He didn't have to consider it at all. "I don't know if they'll come or not, but if they do I'll do whatever you ask."

"I'll be happy to compensate you, of course."

He shook his head. "No, if I can help, I'll do it."

She took a deep breath, exhaled slowly. "I never dreamed I'd be having a conversation like this."

"Me too," he said.

She gave him a time and place. "I'll send a car for you."

"Not necessary. I can find the place."

It seemed such a small thing, one last chance to express love, to ask or grant forgiveness, but he knew better. There was nothing small about it, not being able to say those things you wanted to say, needed to say. He knew because he'd carried that same burden around with him for years now. He had ghosts of his own to deal with. They had not appeared yet, but sooner or later they would. When they did he wanted that last chance at reconciliation. So how could he refuse someone else that same opportunity?

#

Twilight had given way to total darkness by the time he pulled his truck onto the long drive that led to Margaret's estate on East Avenue. Even in the dim light he could see the immensity of the house. The well-lit front porch was lined with columns like an antebellum mansion. He felt that perhaps he should look for the service entrance.

He killed the engine, then sat in the truck for a moment as the metal frame creaked and groaned while it cooled in the evening air. Quick movement at the periphery of his vision. Then it stopped, sat munching grass. Just a rabbit. They weren't all ghosts, he reminded himself.

Thirty yards from the house he could already feel the longing, the hurt, the deep bottomless cavity that was loss. Among those things, fear was not present, not anymore. For certain he'd pay a price for what he was about to do. Human beings weren't equipped—physically, spiritually or otherwise—to act as transmitters of messages from the void. It was like forcing electrical current through a circuit in the wrong direction. Too much for too long and the circuit burned out. How much could he handle?

Bright lights of a car behind him, then, again, darkness. A door slammed. Porch lights reflected off the windows of the car in front of him illuminating the face of the woman who trudged past. The face looked young, but the gait, the posture, were old. Clearly he wasn't the only one who dreaded going inside.

Showtime, he said softly. Damn, but he wished now he'd brought Rebel along. Running his hand through the dog's shaggy coat, feeling the muscles underneath, had the same effect on him as a cool shower on a hot August afternoon. He could sure use that kind of calm and reassurance now.

Margaret met him at the door. She wore the same blue suit she'd worn the first time he'd been to her office. "I was beginning to wonder about you." She took his hand in both of hers and pulled him to one side. "Are you still sure you're up for this? I don't want to put you through anything you don't want."

"I'm ready." He forced a smile, figured she understood.

The entryway into which she led him was bisected by a broad, carpeted staircase that curved upward to a second-level balcony that ran the entire width of the room. To the left lay a sitting room with the largest indoor fireplace John had ever seen. Individual portraits, one obviously Margaret herself, and the other a distinguished looking man with kind eyes, hung above it.

"My husband," Margaret said. "He died about a year and a half before Elizabeth disappeared."

"Oh, God," John said. "I'm sorry. I didn't know."

She turned away, bent slightly at the waist. He didn't know what to do. Should he hold her, try to comfort her? No, he decided. She would deal with this in her own way. The best he could do was be there for her, with her.

After a long moment she straightened up, took a few deep breaths. "The others are waiting. We should join them."

Her guests sat in a small circle, eight of them. Their faces turned toward him like parts of a single organism, etched with impossible mixtures of hope, despair and grief. Just beyond the circle hovered other forms, cloud-like. No surprise there. Still it seemed impossible that only he could see them.

She introduced him to those seated in the circle, but those weren't the names he remembered. Beside or above each seated figure floated another—two beside one woman, sisters?—and these were the names that imprinted themselves in his brain. Not all at once, some were less forthcoming, almost shy. No surprise there, either. They'd been hurt before. Could they trust him?

"I am well-acquainted with Mr. Merritt's unique abilities, as most of you know," Margaret said. She led him to a leather chair at the far end of the circle. Obviously they'd saved it for him.

How did they ever get leather so soft, he wondered. His old saddle, even after years of wear, was still like cardboard in comparison. "Call me John," he said.

"I want to make it clear that John has no financial incentive for being here," Margaret said. "He wouldn't even let me pay for his gas."

The woman who'd walked past him in the driveway—must have been her—caught his gaze, then looked away. Beside her floated the form of a young child. When it ran its hand along her shoulder she turned toward it. Did she know? Could she feel it?

"John has been a great help to me." Margaret took a seat alongside him. "If any of you have questions for him, please, ask."

"Our daughter would be fifteen now." A woman to his left spoke so softly he leaned toward her to hear.

"Eight years she's been gone." The man next to her held her hand. Her husband, besides John, the only man in the room. Eight years he'd said, but both their faces bore the agony as if their child had disappeared only days before.

"Brenda?" John asked.

"Jesus," the husband said.

"Who told you her name?" The woman's voice rose to a sad wail.

John felt every eye in the room bearing in on him, including some that weren't really eyes at all, just points of light, like stars.

"It's okay." Margaret kept her lawyerly voice low and steady, as if she were driving home a point to a jury, a point about which she wanted no doubt, no question. "I told John nothing about your particular losses, no names or anything else. If he's learned anything about your lost children, I'm sure, absolutely certain, he received the message from your daughter or her spirit, at least." She turned toward John. "Am I correct?"

John nodded.

There followed a collective gasp, then silence for a moment.

"Jesus," the husband said again.

"Can you talk to her? No, wait. What was her middle name?"

The spirit form floating alongside the woman made no movement, but her name was in John's head before the question was finished. "Brenda Joyce. You called her B.J. She sends her love."

The woman seemed to dissolve. So did her husband. For a moment, John did too. Oh, how much better it would have been to have someone, something to touch, to hold, but that would not happen. For now, a mere presence, an expression of feeling that remained after the body itself was no more, that would be all, and it would be enough.

"Will you tell her we love her, and we miss her every day?" the woman asked.

"Of course." And that was all, all the questions they could have asked but didn't. Simply sending and receiving one last "I love you," was all that mattered.

And so it went, until the end when roughly the same scenario with the same message had passed between each set—specter and bereaved family member. The faces were different now. The sadness more muted. Even a few quiet smiles.

John propped his elbows on the arms of his chair, wondering if he'd be able to stand when it came time to leave. The process had drained him, as if a plug deep inside him was pulled and much of what made up John Merritt had drained out.

The little group filed out slowly. As they passed John's chair several reached out to touch him—arm, shoulder, one stroked his cheek. The man, B.J.'s father, clapped him firmly on the shoulder. He started to say something but clenched his jaw and moved along.

Margaret sat on the sofa across from him. If looks were any indication she felt just as washed out as he did. She looked around her. "Are they gone?"

He nodded, mindful that they were talking about ghosts.

"She didn't come, did she?"

"Who?"

"Elizabeth."

"No."

"Do you know why?"

"I never do," he said. "They seem to come and go whenever they want."

"Will you come upstairs with me, just for a moment?" She struggled to her feet.

John followed her. He knew where she was going, and he didn't want to be there, but how could he refuse?

Margaret turned right at the top of the stairs, down a short hallway. The walls were covered with photos of Elizabeth—riding a pony, splashing in a pool, a birthday party, then one large portrait of a very young girl sitting on Margaret's lap—mother and daughter. Margaret's feet dragged over the carpet. She looked as if she'd aged ten, no, twenty years in just a few steps.

Even before they reached the room a torrent of emotions—rage, fear, helplessness—struck John like a punch in the gut. The closer they got to the room the stronger the force enveloped him, surged through

117

him. Margaret stepped aside to let him pass, but when he reached the door he could go no farther. Now he knew why Elizabeth hadn't appeared downstairs. She'd been here all along, in this room. Something horrible had happened inside. This wasn't the kindly apparition who had beckoned to him earlier in his kitchen at the ranch. Something powerful raged inside this room, powerful enough to crush him if it chose to. He sagged against the doorframe, clutched it with both hands.

Margaret's voice seemed to come from far away. "John? John? What's happening?"

He had no recollection of going back downstairs, or how he got to the sofa where he now lay, Margaret sitting beside him pressing a damp cloth to his forehead. He felt dampness below too. Oh, God, he'd wet himself.

"I'm so very, very sorry," Margaret said. "I should never have put you through that. I had no idea."

"Me neither," John said.

"You'll stay here tonight," she said. "I have some of my husband's old things upstairs. They won't be a great fit, but at least they're dry."

"No, I'll be okay." He got off the sofa, worried that his urine-soaked trousers might mar the cushions.

"So sorry," she said again. "I'll never ask you to do that again."

"You don't understand. It had to be done, she was waiting for us. And, whenever you're ready, we'll do it again. Maybe next time I'll bring an extra pair of pants."

#

At just past midnight Margaret Simmons stood on her front porch watching John walk back to his truck. He stumbled twice along the flagstone walkway, and she called out to him, but he waved and continued on his way. He'd repeatedly refused her requests that he stay for the night. He hardly seemed in condition to make the drive back to Canandaigua, but, she found, he was just as strong willed as she was herself. He reminded her a bit of her husband in that respect, soft spoken but determined. She was finally able to get a couple of cups of coffee into him, and that seemed to revive him just a bit. At least he'd lost that *deer-in-the-headlights* stare, which had frightened her so much. He'd also accepted a pair of pants from her husband's closet; they were too short in the legs and too big in the waist, but at least they were dry.

She went back inside and turned off the lights downstairs. For all she knew the spectral visitors from before might still be lurking about, unseen and unheard. More likely they'd followed along after the living beings as they left for home. The possibility that they were all surrounded all the time by spirits was both chilling and comforting all at the same time. For sure she would welcome some such spirits, while others she never wished to see at all, ever.

Back upstairs she walked slowly down the hallway where John had apparently encountered a maelstrom just a few hours before. The experience had left her a bit shaky as well, but nothing like the vortex that had buffeted John so severely. As was her habit, she kissed each of the photos of Elizabeth. When she reached the large portrait of her daughter sitting on her lap as a very young child, three years and six months of age, she pressed her hands against the glass that covered the painting. By now the glass was marked everywhere by imprints of her fingertips, her lips, but not for anything would she wipe them clean. Each kiss, each touch counted, had a meaning of its own.

This time when she kissed her daughter's image, something radiated back to her. She felt a warmth she hadn't felt before. "Elizabeth? Can you hear me? I love you." No reply, of course, but it was definitely there, the warmth.

Back in her daughter's room she continued on with her nightly ritual. She wandered around the room, touching things—the assortment of teddy bears that lined the shelves and the small desktop. Elizabeth had a real thing for teddy bears. The upper part of her closet was jammed with the little creatures. Margaret had considered thinning out the lot, donating some of them, perhaps just trashing the older, shabbier bears, but decided against it, thinking that the older and shabbier the teddy, the more time it had spent in Elizabeth's arms. No, she would keep them all, as she would anything else touched and loved by her daughter.

Margaret ended up where she usually did, in the rocking chair in the corner of the room. Elizabeth, while becoming the very embodiment of love and joy and wonder in her brief childhood, had been a fretful baby. So many nights Margaret, Elizabeth cradled in her lap, had rocked far into the night until Elizabeth, and sometimes Margaret as well, were both fast asleep.

Just as when she'd kissed the photo in the hallway, she now felt a special warmth, a presence. "Elizabeth? Darling?" As before, nothing she could see or hear, and she wasn't even sure how she became aware of it. If she'd mentally ticked off the list of the five senses with which we supposedly experience the world, none of them would seem to have been involved. Still, it was there, she knew it.

Any doubts she still had about John Merritt and his *special abilities*, as she called them, had now been resolved. Not even the most gifted con artist, and she'd seen a good many of them in her years of practice, could do what he'd done tonight. The young man was the real deal. Now she was sure.

And Margaret's trust was not bought easily. Even after that first meeting with John in her office when she'd accepted his message from Elizabeth's ghost as gospel, a glimmer of doubt reared its ugly head. That first time she'd been depressed, anxious, and most of all, vulnerable. More than anything in the world she wanted some sign from her daughter. John had brought her what she sought after every minute of every day. Even though the message was dreadful, it was something, better than that void into which she stared each day, wondering.

She was vulnerable too because of her personal belief in an afterlife. The non-analytic side of her brain believed that only the thinnest veil separated the living from the dearly departeds. In her mind the spirits of the dead hung around, just waiting for the opportunity to complete unfinished business. There were things left unsaid, and they wanted to say them. Never before had she been able to peer into that deep darkness, and, except for Elizabeth, she wasn't even sure she wanted to. So when John appeared with his message, Margaret bought into it readily.

Perhaps too readily, she thought later. After the meeting in her office, she had phoned a private investigator and pointed him directly at John Merritt. The weekly reports she received from her investigator painted a psychological picture not unlike her own, that of someone who alternated between two extremes. In John's case, his outward behavior, that of the town playboy, was in total contrast with the image described by people who had known him for years. In his report it was altogether as if the investigator was describing two different people, or, at the very least, someone who had undergone a dramatic change in personality.

120

"I'd cut off my right arm for that boy." This was a direct quote from John's friend, Herman Poulos, who probably thought he was having a casual conversation with a friendly guy in a bar, not someone hired specifically to compile a personal history of John Merritt. John's newly-minted reputation as a philanderer contrasted as well with Margaret's first impression of him, and she was big on first impressions. In her office that day at their first meeting she saw pain, confusion and kindness all wrapped up so tightly that holding it all in check must have taken a great effort. How long could he keep the lid on something like that, she wondered?

The investigator's work turned up little that either confirmed or negated Margaret's impression of John. Even with her doubts he still held the key to her daughter. The loss of Elizabeth changed Margaret in a most fundamental way, as such loss often does. The gaping wound that consumed so much of her energy was the lack of closure in her daughter's death. At times it seemed like a vortex sucking everything out of her, away into some void. She pictured some hellish abode, a black hole where all joy was captured and extinguished, hers included. She found some small salvation in work, but more hours in the office was no answer. Her friends and colleagues noticed, even if she didn't.

Months after Elizabeth's disappearance the state police in western Pennsylvania apprehended the man who was, by his own admission, responsible for her abduction and death. Margaret watched him on TV walking handcuffed between two troopers. This sad looking pudgy individual with a face so bland you could see it a hundred times and still not be able to pick him out of a crowd, had taken the lives of Elizabeth and three other girls as well. But the police could only locate one body, and it was not Elizabeth's. Margaret cleared her schedule, threw a few things into a suitcase, and headed for Pennsylvania. But she was too late. The other dead girls had parents too, one of whom was a former army sniper. He took a room in the YMCA two blocks away from the courthouse where the serial killer would be taken. The distance, just over one hundred yards, was a done deal for the sniper. At that range he could put bullet holes in pennies.

As he was being led in, shackled, encased in a bullet-proof vest, the bland face stopped, turned, and looked back toward the very window where the sniper steadied his rifle barrel on the back of a chair. The entry wound in his left eye was rather small, but the explosion that took off the back of his skull splattered the escorting officers in bloody gore. The bullet ended any chance of learning more about Elizabeth's fate. Margaret never got to hear the man speak. So far as she knew at that moment what he had done to her daughter, and where he had done it, would never be known.

#

The lucrative law practice that now flourished under Margaret's firm hand had been started up many years before by her husband. He was the prototype of the kindly country lawyer, careful and very effective in the courtroom, but never vicious. After his death in a car accident eight years earlier she had run the practice by herself. Quickly enough she imprinted the firm in a different way. She didn't simply defeat opponents, she destroyed them. She became known among her colleagues as "a ruthless bitch."

Along the way she had become something of a community power broker, ending up with becoming president of the board of directors at Upstate Medical Center. Her tenure began with the obligatory tour of the hospital, a center that survived more on its past reputation than its current status. The hospital tour she received under the watchful eye of Dean Donald Westbrook, included a trip through the sparkling new Intensive Care Unit, as well as a face-to-face meeting with Dr. Paul Pierce. Her comment that the new facility must have cost a lot of money was met with raised eyebrows but no further explanation. She filed that observation away for the future, something she would check out in due time.

"Dr. Pierce will be conducting new studies on aging," Dean Westbrook said. "This is one of the most rapidly developing areas in the medical field."

Margaret was already quite aware that care of the elderly, was a hot area. She also knew of the bandwagon effect, not just in medicine but other fields as well, where effort chased money, instead of the other way around. She had no doubt that those who worked in the area were sincere people, many with a true desire to help, but there were dollars to be made, and, from what she'd seen of the rather shabby Upstate facility, those dollars were sorely needed. She'd wanted to ask the dean why a cardiovascular surgeon, Dr. Pierce, was heading up the study program,

122

but before she could raise the issue she was hustled off for a tour of the lab.

The lab tour was conducted by a young Asian man whose halting accent made him very difficult to follow. Worse still, the tour began in the rat lab. While he babbled on about his research Margaret fought off waves of nausea; she hated rats. She held her hand over her mouth and stared at the ceiling as he talked. At least the next area had no live animals. She caught something about tissue culture, but the rest of the speech was lost on her.

It mattered little, though, the dog-and-pony show she'd just been given. She promptly forgot about the research lab. Her expertise lay in different areas. The power brokers at Upstate wanted her for her influence in the community, particularly in the area of fund raising, an area in which Upstate apparently needed all the help it could get.

Back in Dean Westbrook's office, as Margaret struggled to clear the lingering stench of the rat lab from her nostrils, Westbrook led her to a table that filled one entire corner of is work space. In the center of the table sat a two-story model building, surrounded by plastic greenery. "Our new Longevity Center in Canandaigua," Westbrook said, waving his hand across the table. "Over here will be the pool house. This building on the left will be a gymnasium—low impact aerobics, yoga, that sort of thing."

"What's this one?" She pointed to a smaller structure attached to the main building by an enclosed corridor.

"Dr. Pierce will be doing some of his special studies there," Westbrook said.

"Why so far away from the medical center?"

Westbrook rubbed his chin for a moment. He had the look of a man trying to sell an idea that he wasn't completely sold on himself. "That was Dr. Pierce's call. He wanted the separation. I mean, we automatically associate medical centers with illness. He wanted the Longevity Center to have a different image, you know, health, wellness."

Not much of Westbrook's presentation was news to Margaret. The newspaper coverage had described the Canandaigua construction as a spa, and that's exactly how it appeared to her. It made little sense, though, to sink what must have been a huge amount of money into a glorified resort when the medical center itself was in such obvious need of a facelift. "The hospital board passed on this?" she asked.

Westbrook began rubbing his chin again. "We had a large donation up front from a private donor. We'll need additional funding to complete the work, but after it's in operation the center should be self-sustaining. In fact, our projections indicate that it could be a money maker."

#

Margaret dozed in the rocking chair in Elizabeth's bedroom. She could almost feel the warmth of her daughter's small body lying in her lap, but, had she opened her eyes, she would have seen nothing. For the moment, the warmth was enough. She was sure now she'd found a means to some real communication with Elizabeth's spirit. She had taken John to Elizabeth's room hoping to find some evidence of her being there, that she might be there in some form that would allow a reunion between the two of them, even though one of them was dead. Instead she'd seen John pummeled by an angry, violent spirit, action so completely unlike Elizabeth. Next time she would be more careful, because she needed John's help, needed him desperately. He was the conduit. He would help her reestablish the link with her daughter.

# Chapter 12

Had she not been so desperate to get the list of Pierce's patients, a list she was unable to obtain on her own, Stacey would never have even considered Benny's demand that she come to his apartment to retrieve it. She knew exactly what he wanted in return.

"Tit for tat," he'd said, just before she hung up the phone. His laugh sounded like someone who enjoyed incinerating ants with sunbeams directed through a magnifying glass.

But Benny, if she could believe him, had successfully hacked into Pierce's computer system and fished out the information she wanted so badly. Now all she had to do was go get it. If Benny weren't such a smart son of a bitch Stacey wouldn't have worried at all. With any other guy she would go in at her bright bubbly best, blue eyes twinkling, get the list and be gone before he knew what was happening. But Benny was cagey, and the last thing in the world she wanted was a wrestling match with a big greasy guy who looked like one of his parents might have been a walrus. The very thought of being groped by him made her skin crawl

She made herself as unattractive as possible, worn jeans with a hole in the right knee and a faded, baggy sweatshirt that she pulled straight from the laundry hamper. She thought about chewing on a clove of garlic before leaving but decided against it. Garlic breath might ward off vampires, but for all she knew, Benny might actually like it. She shoved her hair beneath a baseball cap and began the slow, unwilling drive to his apartment.

Benny met her at the door. "Stacey, darlin' come right in." He wore green hospital scrubs with what she hoped were old mustard stains on the front.

"I just need the list, Benny. I'm in kind of a hurry."

"Not so fast, darlin'." He managed to get the door shut behind her.

She never thought at all about Benny, about how he might live, but if she had, the scene before her would be about what she expected. He had a lime green sofa in the center of the room with stains on all of the cushions; two looked dried, one looked fresh. "Do you have a cat?" she asked.

"Huh? No."

Two pizza boxes lay on the floor beside the sofa. Against the far wall on a long table sat three computers, far too much power to be under the control of someone with Benny's potential for malevolence. No telling what kind of damage he might do if he set his mind to it. She definitely did not want him as an enemy, but just as definitely was not about to give up what he wanted from her. She scanned the rest of the room looking for the list, hoping for an opportunity to grab it and run.

But Benny must have read her thoughts. "Looking for this?" He waved the list of patients, just out of her reach. "Tit for tat, remember?"

"Please, Benny." She took a step toward him, forced a smile. But when she reached for the list he grabbed her wrist with his free hand. Damn, he was quicker than he looked, and a lot stronger too.

He twisted her arm behind her back. A sharp pain ripped through her elbow as he shoved her toward the sofa.

"Stop, you're hurting me." Her foot caught on one of the pizza boxes, and she slipped, falling face down on the sofa. Benny landed on top of her, still holding onto her wrist.

He grabbed her hair and pushed her face into the fetid cushion. "How do you want it, darlin', rough or easy? I enjoy both ways myself."

Benny released her wrist and wriggled his hand underneath her. As he fumbled with the snaps on her jeans his mouth was right next to her ear. "I been dreaming about this for a long time."

"Wait," she said. "Not so rough. I'll do what you want." Don't panic, she kept telling herself, but she was close, very close.

He eased his bulk up onto his elbows. "That's better. You're gonna do a few special things for me now, right?"

"Whatever you want. Just please get off me. I can't breathe."

As he raised up to his knees she managed to roll beneath him.

There wasn't much space between them, just enough. She drove her knee up into his crotch. His eyes rolled back, he grabbed his groin and sank to the floor where he lay making a noise like a puppy having a bad dream.

"I'm really sorry to have to do that, Benny, but you had it coming." She grabbed the list from the floor where he'd dropped it, then ran for the door. She could wait for a while to review the patient information. Right now she need a long, hot bath.

#

She soaked until the skin on her fingers began to wrinkle, but even that wasn't enough to rinse away the image of Benny hovering over her, his fetid breath on her face. But she had work to do. Wrapped in a cozy fleece bathrobe and fortified by a hot cup of spiced tea, she spread out the patient data sheets on her desk. She could only hope that Benny was as good as his word and had covered his tracks well. If Dr. Pierce ever discovered that she had this information she was history.

The information she found was scant: five patients with dates of treatment along with some demographic data, addresses, phone numbers and such. The top two entries had additional information: dates of death. So, she thought, Dr. Pierce was not always successful with his resuscitations. But as she looked more closely she saw that both patients had died several months after the catastrophic event that had brought them to the hospital. The cause of death was not listed in either case.

Is this all, she wondered. There was no mention of personality changes, nothing about hallucinations. She needed more data, and there was only one way to get it. She would have to visit the patients on the list, interview them herself.

Naomi Wells was the last name on the list, right after John Merritt. That's where she'd start. She grabbed the phone. Naomi sounded suspicious at first, but agreed to a Saturday visit.

Seneca Falls was a pleasant hour's drive southeast from the hospital. Stacey drove along a two-lane road meandering through countryside that was just beginning to awaken from winter dormancy. Irregular swaths of green appeared in an otherwise brown landscape and a few stubborn patches of snow hung on in shady spots, long past their seasonal time.

At the end of a long rutted path, Stacey found Naomi's house, a log cabin invisible from the road. As she drove up, a chorus of barks and yips bounded out to meet her in the form of two golden retrievers.

"Girls, girls, come back here." A young woman wearing jeans and a flannel shirt stood on her porch, yelling at her dogs and waving at Stacey. "They're harmless. I just don't want them jumping on you with their muddy feet. Hi, I'm Naomi Wells."

When the dogs retreated back to the porch, Stacey ventured out, picking her way along the flagstone path that led to the house. "I really appreciate your seeing me today." She extended her hand to Naomi and got a crushing grip in response.

"Come on in. I'll put the dogs on the back porch."

Stacey took the moment to browse around the living room. The logs that formed the walls must have been a foot across, and a huge rack of moose antlers hung over the fireplace. The mix of dark woods and leather furniture suggested masculine decorating preferences.

"Most of the stuff in here belonged to my dad," Naomi said from behind her. "When he died I just didn't have the heart to change anything, although I am having second thoughts about those antlers."

"I see," Stacey said. "You must have been very close to him."

Naomi looked down. "He was my only family. I guess he was my world."

"It's none of my business, I know, but you're a bit isolated back here. Wouldn't it be better to get closer to people?"

"Maybe I'll move someday, but, for now, I'm happy here. I actually enjoy the peace and quiet. And it's easier to work…not many distractions."

"What do you do? I didn't see any shops or anything on the way in."

"A couple of days a week I drive into Seneca Falls. I have a part time job there with an insurance agency processing claims, but mostly I work at home, right here. I scratch out a meager living writing articles for wildlife magazines. My dad got me started. He had quite a following before he died."

"Fascinating, carrying on a family tradition."

"I guess so. I made coffee just before you drove up. Care for a cup?" Naomi brought steaming cups to a small round table that apparently served for both eating and working. "The coffee might be a bit stronger than you're used to," she said.

"Another of your dad's legacies?"

"Yeah. He always said he liked his coffee chewy."

"Delicious," Stacey said, taking a sip. "I certainly can't get anything like this in the hospital."

"What did you want to ask me? I mean, you made a long trip out here, so it must be something you couldn't find out by phone."

"Just a few questions." Stacey retrieved a notepad from her briefcase. "I wanted to verify your dates in hospital, stuff like that."

"Isn't that all in the records?"

"Yeah. Most of it is. There are a few other things I want to ask about, too." Stacey knew better than to approach her target directly in an initial interview. To pose a question like, "Are you seeing ghosts?" to someone you'd just met might close that door permanently. So instead, she let Naomi guide the initial stages of the interview. If she took time to gain the young woman's confidence there would be plenty of time to ask her the more difficult questions.

"While we're at it, maybe you can answer a few for me," Naomi said. "Tell me why Dr. Pierce is keeping me on this medication so long. It's been two months now."

"Medication?"

"Yeah, Dormistan, he called it. I wrote it down, but I still don't know what it's for. I mean, I appreciate all he did for me. He saved my life, after all. But why do I have to keep on taking this stuff?"

If she could have done so without being noticed, Stacey would have kicked herself. The medication, of course. She should have anticipated questions about Dormistan, but she been so eager to find out about spectral visitations and such that she'd completely forgotten about it. "What has Dr. Pierce told you about it?" Her answer was a dodge, just trying to buy time.

"Not much, just that I have to take it every day."

"I'll see what I can find out for you," Stacey said. She cursed silently. It was the same lame answer she'd given John. She already knew a good deal about the history of Dormistan, but still had no real idea about what Paul Pierce was doing with it. She knew better than to dribble out information to patients in small bits, such as the fact that Dormistan was a derivative of LSD and might cause world-class hallucinations. She didn't even know for sure that the Dormistan pill that Pierce was passing out hadn't been altered in some way. The question that kept popping into her mind was about Pierce himself: was he smart enough to reconfigure the Dormistan formula? Stacey didn't believe he was. But if not Pierce, who?

The door behind Stacey creaked and a muscular young man clad only in a towel wrapped around his waist stopped in the doorway. "Sorry," he said. "Didn't know you had company." He turned, after a long appreciative look at Stacey, and went back into the room. He didn't bother closing the door while he dressed.

Naomi blushed furiously. "Please, don't get the wrong idea. I'm not like this. It's just that since I got out of the hospital, I've had…urges, like never before. I mean, all the time. Do you think that's from the medication?"

"Could be," Stacey said. "Sometimes people who have been through experiences like yours experience an increased libido. Nothing wrong with that. so don't apologize." Stacey wrote "libido" on her notepad and drew a circle around it. "Have you had any other unusual effects since you've been taking the medication?"

Naomi's hands began trembling, and she dropped the spoon she was holding. "I guess you mean them."

"Them? Who?"

"The shadow people, I call them."

#

Bobby Pippin, the next patient on the list, lived an hour south of the city. At twelve years of age, he was the youngest person on the list. His family lived in a modest cottage surrounded by maple trees. Stacey could only see the front yard, as the back side of the house was concealed on either side by a line of dense shrubbery.

His mother, who introduced herself as Brenda Pippin, appeared suspicious, and kept looking back and forth from Stacey to Bobby. It required all of Stacey's skills to put the woman at ease. Apparently something in her experience at Upstate Medical Center had set Brenda on edge, and anyone who wanted access to her son would have to go through her first. Only after about fifteen minutes of chit chat, Stacey at her nonthreatening best, did Brenda Pippin appear to relax and permit Stacey to direct her questions at Bobby.

"How did you ever manage to fall through the ice, Bobby?"

Stacey asked him. Indeed, the slightly built boy hardly seemed heavy enough to break through.

"Tubby—that's my dog—chased a rabbit across the pond, and I tried to follow him. I almost got to the other side before I fell through."

Brenda Pippin brought tea for herself and Stacey, and a glass of milk for her son. "That dog, I don't know whether to hug him or shoot him. He ran up to the back door barking like crazy. He led me back down to the pond, and I saw the hole in the ice, but I couldn't see Bobby."

"Were you able to get him out yourself?" Stacey asked Brenda.

"Oh, no, not me. I started screaming and our neighbor heard me. He called 911 from his cell phone. He actually tied a rope around his waist and jumped into the water, but he couldn't find Bobby."

"So the EMT people got him out?"

"No. The firemen fished him out with a big hook. He was so cold and blue. I was sure he was dead." She ran her hand gently through her son's hair, as if reassuring herself of his presence, his life.

Bobby sat, drinking his milk, his face expressionless. "You didn't bring any cookies."

"It'll soon be time for your dinner, dear. Cookies after, not before."

"But obviously they got him to the hospital in time," Stacey said.

"Yes. They all did a wonderful job. I'll never be able to thank those people for what they did."

"How long did Bobby stay in the hospital?"

"Over a week. I guess they wanted to be sure he was all right. Do you know why it took so long? Is that unusual? I mean, he looked just fine after the first couple of days, and it really was torture for him, staying cooped up for so long. And this medication Dr. Pierce has him on, he says Bobby has to keep on with it until he says stop. I don't understand that either."

"Have you asked Dr. Pierce about it?" Stacey's fingers tightened around her pen. Dormistan again, and she still had no proper answers for the woman sitting in front of her. Besides that, she was certain that Pierce did not have clearance for use of his drug in children. The medical literature was full of reports of clinical trials gone bad when investigators tried to treat children as small adults.

"He didn't give me much of an answer. It's hard to get information out of that man."

"When I see him, I'll ask him about it," Stacey said. "Have you noticed any unusual effects while he's been on the medication?"

Bobby looked up at his mother.

"Go ahead, tell her," she said.

Bobby shook his head and looked down at the floor.

"It seems he's acquired some new playmates lately. Several times I've heard him talking to someone in his room, but when I go in there's no one there but Bobby."

"They're real," Bobby said. "They talk to me."

"Who are they, Bobby?" Stacey asked.

"They're my friends. They were scary at first, because I couldn't make them out real clear, but they don't scare me so much anymore. They just appear, then they disappear. I can't touch them, and I guess they can't touch me, either."

"It almost sounds like you're talking about ghosts," Stacey said.

"Maybe I am. Nobody sees 'em but me." Bobby looked up at his mother.

"I asked Dr. Pierce about it. He said they were just hallucinations and they would all go away."

"But it's been a number of months now, right, Bobby?" Stacey asked.

Bobby nodded.

"And look at this." Bobby's mother tugged up the right sleeve of his sweatshirt and pointed out three small, healed indentations in his upper arm. "Skin biopsies, they said, to check the effects of the medication. It's all about the medication. I want it stopped." She gathered her son in her arms. This interview was over.

There were other patients on the list, but Stacey didn't bother. She had what she needed. This was much more than the residual of a near-death experience. John's ghostly visions, just like Naomi's and Bobby's, were due to Dormistan. She was sure of it. What she didn't know was why Pierce insisted they all keep taking the medication. What was his angle?

#

After she got home Stacey changed into sweats and sneakers,

poured herself a glass from the jug of chardonnay that took up most of the middle shelf of her refrigerator, and plopped on the sofa. She balanced her notepad on her knee.

It was all there, the skin biopsies, ghosts, and Naomi Wells appeared to have the same turbocharged libido that John was rumored to have. And the common denominator had to be Dormistan.

But why? What could possibly be so great about this drug?

She knew enough about the regulations covering human investigation to know that Paul Pierce was playing a very risky game here. There was no way any review committee would ever give him permission to carry out clinical trials on a drug with the side effects of Dormistan. And informed consent, the cornerstone of all therapeutic trials, forget about it. John, Naomi, Bobby's mom, none of them had a clue about Dormistan, and Stacey didn't know much more herself.

Clearly she had more work to do. At least if she had to butt heads with Paul Pierce again she would have some ammunition of her own. If he wanted to make threats about her medical career, she could, with the information she had now, just as easily pull the rug from beneath his own.

# Chapter 13

"John, I hate to keep nagging you about this, but if we don't pay the utility bill they're gonna shut us down." Herman slumped in the chair beside John's desk.

"I'm still waiting to hear from that damned builder, Bynum, out at that new Longevity Center," John said. "Until he pays up I'm broke." Indeed, Merritt Constrution Supply, which for years had operated on the thinnest of profitability margins had now hit a financial brick wall.

"I called them again this morning," Herman said. "They won't even talk to me."

"Me either. I could take him to court but that would take weeks, maybe months."

"Meantime we'll be working in the dark." Herman chuckled.

"What's funny?"

"I know what your daddy would do."

"I do too, but that would probably get me thrown in jail," John said.

"Well, bein' nice sure ain't getting us anywhere fast."

"You're right. Maybe I'll take a drive over to that building site. Talk to him personal." John piled a stack of overdue bills on top of another stack of bills, also overdue. It only took a single break in the supply chain, of which Merritt Supply was a link, to completely gum up the system, and, since Bynum was not a local contractor, he could probably care less about who got paid and when. Payment was more a personal matter to John. When he didn't clear up his bills on time it was his friends and neighbors who got shorted. His father would never have tolerated such a situation, and he'd had just about enough of it himself.

"I wanta come too." Herman jumped up. "In case you need any help."

"No need," John said. "Nothing's gonna happen. I'm only gonna talk to him."

"Right. And I wanta' watch."

"Okay, but if you start anything I'll make you wait in the truck." Herman's short fuse could make a bad situation worse, quickly. For that matter, John's own patience was wearing thin. Times past, he avoided confrontation whenever possible, but this afternoon he was almost hoping for some action. His now improving relationship with Stacey had led to sleepless nights and tense days, none of which improved his general disposition. A failed business could hardly improve his prospects with her.

Herman drove John across town, then followed state road No. 12 out to what used to be a century-old dairy farm, now transformed into the spanking new Upstate Longevity Center. There had been a lot of local resistance to destruction of the old dairy farm, considered a local landmark because of the ice cream it served up to tourists during the summer months, but the new owners promised to incorporate elements of the old structure into the new building. The promise of a number of new lucrative construction jobs carried the day, but in the end all of these guarantees proved fictional. The barn and farmhouse were dismantled and carted away, and the construction jobs all went to an outfit imported from Pennsylvania. Bynum Construction neither needed nor wanted local assistance. They purchased supplies from local outfits like Merritt Supply, but payment for goods was slow to appear, and the bills that had begun to accumulate on John's desk were also stacking up on other desks around town.

#

Nobody seemed to know exactly who owned the new structure. Everyone assumed that it was allied in some way to the Upstate Medical Center. Indeed, a delegation from the Medical Center had arrived with much fanfare to inspect progress on the building. Coverage in the local newspapers was enthusiastic but carefully controlled. Reporters complained—privately—about being led around, practically on a leash, to selected areas, while being denied access to others. Oh, to be sure, what they saw was impressive enough, a beautiful indoor pool, a gymnasium filled with the most modern equipment, and a dining area that outclassed anything in Canandaigua. The Longevity Center looked more like a four-star vacation destination than a medical facility.

"We identify wellness and longevity with normalcy. The goal for this new construction will be to promote healing, not through medical intervention, but through active changes in life style." That's what Dean Donald Westbrook had said during one of his trips down from the Upstate Medical Center. It sounded good, everyone agreed, but nobody was sure exactly what he meant.

One local merchant was heard to say, "I'd sure feel healthier if I could spend a few weeks in a place like that."

Westbrook had introduced the man designated as the Medical Director of the new center, Dr. Paul Pierce. Pierce, at least, was a familiar name in the area because of his dramatic saves in a few cases of cold water drowning, John Merritt being one of them. The second man that Westbrook introduced that day, Dr. Hans Riegler, was not known at all. When Westbrook asked Riegler if he'd like to say a few words to the crowd the man simply shook his head and took a step back. Riegler would remain a man of mystery to one and all.

#

Since the upstate winter had effectively halted outdoor construction efforts, the crew from Bynum Construction now raced about in a great hurry to put finishing touches on the main buildings. The ground, softened by melted snow cover, was a muddy quagmire, deeply rutted out by tracks of heavy equipment.

"Dang fools ought to know enough to wait until things dry out a little," Herman said. He pointed to a truck mired in mud up to its rear axle. He followed a gravel path that wound around to the rear of the main buildings, to a square brick structure that bore no signage or identifying marks whatever. A level pathway, also lined with gravel, connected it to the main buildings, but otherwise it seemed as if it didn't belong at all. Its oddity was all the more prominent by being the only structure around that was enclosed by six-foot chain length fencing.

"I ain't been here since they dug the foundation for that place," Herman said. "What do you suppose it is, some kind of warehouse? It's got no windows."

"Can't be just a warehouse. Remember they dug down over ten

feet. There's something underground."

"Wonder what they got down there," Herman said. "From the looks of that fence they don't want people snooping around.

"Whatever it is they bought a lot of pipe from that outfit across town. Wonder if they paid him yet."

Herman stopped the truck, killed the engine.

"What's that thing they put out back? Looks like a water tank," John said.

"That's exactly what it is."

"But the swimming pool is over in the main building."

"That one ain't connected to the swimming pool. The lines run right into that funny looking building. And they put in some kind of monster water pump, shipped over from Japan. Damned thing has a big refrigeration unit. They must have some plans for using a lot of cold water."

"How did you find out about that?"

"I talk to people," Herman said. "I got friends. Maybe if you stopped running around like a crazy man folks would tell you stuff too."

They both jumped when the beefy security guard rapped on John's window with his nightstick. Then he motioned back toward the street with his thumb.

"Ain't real neighborly is he?" Herman said. "Guess he wants us to leave."

"Not yet." John got out.

"Take off." The guard stepped toward John.

"Where's Mr. Bynum, the builder?"

"I said get lost." The guard swung his nightstick at his side. "You understand English?"

"I understand it fine. I'm beginning to wonder about you, though. Where's Bynum? Is he in there?" John pointed at the windowless building.

"Nobody goes in there."

Herman had crept around the rear of the truck and stood just behind John. "Wouldn't get him mad if I was you," he said to the guard.

"So, you're some kind of tough guy," the guard said.

"Shut up, Herman." John turned back to the guard. "I asked you a question. Where's Bynum?"

The beefy man swung his nightstick at John's head, missed and grazed Herman's shoulder. John buried his fist in the man's gut, and his heavy body landed butt-first on the gravel driveway where he sat bent over and wheezing.

"You okay, Herm?" John asked.

"Oh sure, barely nicked me." He walked over to the guard and prodded him with his toe. "See, I told you not to get him riled up."

"That's enough, Herman." John knelt down beside the guard. "Now, I'm gonna ask you one more time, where's Bynum?"

The guard pointed to a small trailer parked in the back corner of the lot. John took off with Herman close behind. "You should wait in the truck," he said to Herman.

"No way in hell. I wouldn't miss this for anything."

"Just don't go stirring things up. All I want to do is talk to him."

John entered without knocking. The florid man behind the desk didn't look glad to see them. "What the hell are you doing in here?"

"Name's John Merritt. Maybe you don't remember me, but you should remember Merritt Supply."

"So?"

"You owe me money. I can't pay my own bills until you pay me, and I've waited long enough."

"So you're here to collect?"

"All I want is what you owe me."

"You'll get paid when I'm good and ready. Now get the hell out of here. You small town yokels think you can just march in and take over."

"I'm not gonna ask you again."

"I've got security here. The guard will bust your head if I tell him to."

"Your guard is sitting on his big fat ass out in the driveway," Herman said. "If you don't watch out you'll wind up the same way."

John pulled the billing statement out of his pocket and put it on the desk in front of Bynum. "There it is. I want my money today."

"I'll show you what you'll get." Bynum reached into the desk drawer and had the revolver halfway out before John kicked the drawer shut.

"Dammit. You broke my finger." Bynum bent over the desk

139

holding his hand.

"He'll break more than that if you don't pay up," Herman said.

"Herman, will you please be quiet?" John said. "Now, Mr. Bynum, I see a safe over there in the corner, and I'll bet you have enough money in there to pay my bills and then some."

"This is robbery, that's what it is. You're a goddam thief."

"Wrong. Robbery is what happens when you don't pay your bills. If you'll just fork over this amount I'll mark it paid in full, and we'll leave."

Bynum extracted a stack of cash from the safe and counted it out. "There, damn you. And you can expect a visit from the cops."

"You have a bag I can carry it in? Wouldn't want people to get the wrong idea." John marked the bill PAID and initialed it. "Check outside, Herman. Make sure there are no unscrupulous types lurking about."

"All clear, John."

"Sorry about your hand, Mr. Bynum. I'd get that checked out if I was you. Doc Simpson can fix you right up, but he's going to want cash."

Back in the truck John kept the canvas bag of cash tucked close against his side.

Herman took a long look at the building. "Wonder what in the world they do in there? Why would they put up a building with no windows and only one door. I've seen prisons prettier than that."

"Whatever it is they don't want anybody looking inside. Doubt we'll ever find out."

"You think?"

"Yeah. If they have any kind of open house party, I don't expect we'll get an invitation."

Herman laughed and pulled out into the street. "Your pappy would have been proud of you today."

That's when John saw his father--his ghost, at least--standing on the corner, waving as they drove past, that familiar lopsided grin spread across his face. Then he vanished, and there was nothing to say he'd ever been there at all.

#

Bynum watched the old truck drive away. Damn, his hand hurt. His little finger stuck out at an odd angle. Broken for sure. He'd call the cops, all right, but first he had to check in with his employer, Reigler. That old gray-eyed bastard wanted to know everything that happened on the job site.

"John Merritt?" Reigler asked.

"Right," Bynum said. "He runs Merritt Supply. It's a dinky local outfit, but their prices were a lot better than I could get anywhere else."

"And you owed him money?"

"Yeah. I got behind in the paperwork. I was gonna pay him all along." Actually Bynum made a habit of skimming from local suppliers. The individual sums never amounted to much, but over the years he'd amassed a substantial retirement fund for himself.

"What was he like?"

"He was pissed off."

"I mean, was he coherent? Was he acting crazy?"

"No."

Bynum clutched his broken hand. What the hell were all the questions about? The man had hardly said three words to him before. "No, he was a mean son of a bitch, but he wasn't crazy. I'm gonna call the cops. I probably won't get the money back, but I can get the bastard picked up for assault, for damned sure."

"No." Riegler's voice was sharp, a command.

"What? Why not? He broke my finger. He punched out my security guard."

"Let it go. I told you before, don't do anything to attract attention. I don't want cops or anybody else snooping around."

"But...."

Click. Reigler had hung up on him. Bynum kicked a chair across the room. He'd had his safe cleared out, his hand busted, and the old man wanted him to sit there and suck it up, like nothing happened.

This damned job couldn't be over soon enough. That gray-eyed spook was driving him crazy, turning up at all hours, sticking his nose into everything, asking a million questions. But when Bynum himself asked a question the old man clammed up.

#

Bynum had a wealth of experience building resorts and spas, but this Canandaigua facility beat them all. Only eight rooms, suites, actually. How the hell could they make money off renting out just eight rooms?

And the rooms were huge. The old man had flown in a special decorator from New York who was driving Bynum crazy. From the way she was spending money you'd think they were building a palace. The kitchen area was filled with top-of-the-line appliances, the sort of stuff Bynum himself had only seen in catalogues. One thing for damned sure, they weren't catering to the local tourist trade. Whoever stayed in this place would pay through the nose, and then some.

But this building out back puzzled Bynum most of all. Riegler wouldn't even tell him what the building was for. Yeah, it was a weird building, all right. Part of it was like a small hotel with rooms, a kitchen and a laundry, but nothing at all to compare to the lavish appointments in the main building. This smaller structure was outfitted more like the cheap roadside motels where you spent the night but didn't linger. And there were no windows; the spaces were all closed up. Who'd want to stay in a hotel with no windows?

Even weirder was that big plexiglass cage in the basement. The walls were thick enough to stop a truck. Every time he came over for one of his unscheduled visits Riegler headed straight for the basement to check it out. He'd walk around that perfect cube—eight feet on every side—rubbing his hands together like something special was going to happen, and he couldn't wait to get started.

He'd had Bynum install a big water pump alongside the cage—one hundred gallons a minute—that would fill the whole thing up in no time. But the water came straight from a refrigeration tank, just above freezing. And the part that raised the hairs on the back of his neck, the part he really didn't want to know more about, was the heavy, reinforced chair bolted to the floor in the middle of the plexiglass cage. With the thick straps on the arms and legs it looked for all the world like an electric chair. Anybody who got strapped into that thing had no chance of escape. Why? Bynum didn't want to know.

He wanted to finish the job, collect his money and go someplace where that gray-eyed sonofabitch could never find him again. But first he had to get a splint for his busted finger.

#

Inside the mysterious building, so unlike anything Bynum had ever built, or even seen before, would unfold the final stages of Hans Riegler's solution to that most important question of all: how to prolong human life span indefinitely.

Hans Riegler was born into a prosperous Austrian family. His father, Peter, a research chemist, had charmed his upper class mother into marrying beneath her social station, and her family money allowed him to pursue his laboratory talents without financial worries. Before World War II burst over Europe, Peter moved his family—wife and young son, Hans—to Switzerland where he had obtained a position with Sandoz Chemicals.

One evening in 1944, Peter brought someone to dinner, a brilliant chemist, like himself, named Albert Hauptmann. For over a year Peter had been collaborating with Hauptmann on a new compound derived from the ergot fungus found on rye kernels. Hauptmann himself had ingested a small amount, 0.25 milligrams, of the synthesized compound—lysergic acid diethylamide, resulting in a frightening hallucinogenic experience. Sometime later he enticed Peter to try it as well, with similar results. Without question they had in their possession a chemical of great power, but with no obvious application other than induction of remarkable altered mental states, sometimes intensely pleasurable, sometimes terrifying.

Young Hans was not given the chance to experience the power of LSD, as his father wanted him first to concentrate on his education. By the time Hans was finished with his studies at the university, his father was actively pursuing work on LSD on two fronts: he continued active collaboration with Hauptmann at Sandoz, but had other secret experiments of his own, funded by his wife's family money. He enlisted Hans into what had become the family business and would eventually become a life mission for Hans. Like any good scientist, Peter always included a control group of subjects in his experiments, but fully informed volunteers, such as those Sandoz might insist upon, didn't always work out. More often than not Peter didn't know himself what to expect when he administered his new drug, so explaining the potential side effects to someone else was next to impossible.

He needed a group of subjects over whom he had absolute control, who would follow his directions exactly because they had no alternative, so he turned to a local orphanage. After a generous gift to the Boys' Home, Peter approached the headmaster with a request; might he not be allowed to test a new medication on a few of the boys?

Young Hans was actively and enthusiastically involved in these early studies, even more so after a chance observation in March, 1956. Eight of the boys were skating on a nearby pond when the ice broke. By chance, there was an even split: four were part of the LSD group, four were taking a placebo. The rescue effort was clumsy and largely ineffectual. Some of the would-be rescuers broke through the ice themselves. The result was that most of the boys spent a long time beneath the ice. When their bodies were finally retrieved they showed no signs of life. They were, all eight of them, laid out in a makeshift morgue.

About an hour after lying in an unheated room, three of the boys shocked everyone. They began twitching, coughing and opened their eyes. All three of them survived. The fact that all of the survivors were ingesting the LSD preparation was not lost on Hans or his father. The accident appeared to have provided both father and son with a new goal for their studies. But they needed a new experimental model. They couldn't very well dump people into an icy pond, besides, spring was approaching.

Other things were afoot as well. As a young man about to take his place in society, it was time for Hans to embark on his grand tour of Europe. There were relatives to visit, museums to tour, artwork to view and music to be heard. Hans wanted to continue working with his father, but Peter insisted on what he considered a vital part of his son's education. His son would become a man of the world, sophisticated in the grand old style of the European elite. The work was important, yes, but there was a world to be seen, and Hans would see it, whether he wanted to or not.

The son's cultural exposure was supposed to last for a year, but went on for considerably longer. At a concert in Paris, he fell madly in love with a young countess and pursued her for several months. His suit failed for two reasons: he lacked his father's charm, and he lacked a title. He lost out to a young man who had both. A very dejected Hans returned to his father's lab more determined than ever to make his mark in the scientific world.

When Hans returned home he was most impressed with the progress his father had made, but first he had to catch up on things that had gone before. "The boys," Hans said soon after his return. "The boys who fell through the ice. What has become of them?"

Peter laid a hand on his son's shoulder. "I am keeping a close eye on them. Come with me." Peter led his son back to his small office where he pulled a notebook from a shelf behind his desk. "Look here. I've recorded height and weight every month and compared it with ten other boys of the same age. The other ten boys have grown as expected, but our three boys are about the same now as when they fell into the pond. Of course, I need a much longer period of observation, but so far they do not show signs of normal aging."

"Remarkable," said Hans. "Truly remarkable."

"Now you see what I meant earlier when I said I've found your life's work. If you can develop this medication and establish a satisfactory data base, the world will be at your feet begging you to give them a way to live forever, begging you for immortality." He emphasized the last word by banging his fist on the desk.

Their discussion ran late into the night. What should they do next? What would constitute definitive proof of their hypothesis? Eventually the topic swung back to the event that had initially signaled the potential of what they had—cold water drowning. Peter had already administered Dormistan to rats, but the drug alone was not sufficient to prolong life span. It was only effective after the rats had first been submerged in icy water for a prolonged period. So, what was there about cold water immersion that allowed Dormistan to work its magic on life span?

While Hans was away on his cultural tour of Europe, Peter had conducted an extensive investigation into the peculiarities of cold water drowning. He knew, for instance, that cold water conducted heat away from the body thirty times faster than heat loss by cold air. He learned also about the mammalian diving reflex, a series of reactions that occurred almost immediately after immersion in icy cold water. Those young boys who had crashed through the ice at the orphanage would have, after a brief period of thrashing about, developed a slowed heart rate, slowed respirations, then cardiac arrest. The survivors would likely have developed tight laryngospasm that prevented aspiration of water, protecting the lungs from injury.

But how could the brain survive oxygen depletion for such prolonged periods? Peter knew that at normal temperatures, an oxygen-depleted brain began to die at around three to five minutes, but the boys from the orphanage exhibited normal brain function after immersion in the lake for up to thirty minutes. He befriended an obscure university professor who gave him the answer: at colder temperatures the brain died more slowly and might survive oxygen depletion for up to forty-five minutes. Peter had guessed as much from his own observations, but it was reassuring to hear it from an academic authority.

So, this bizarre and mysterious event—the mammalian diving reflex—was somehow integral to the age resistance effects of Dormistan. Peter had come this far. The rest would be up to Hans.

Fifty years later Hans would be puzzling over the same issue, but not for want of effort or money. His determination to fulfill his father's legacy drove him like no other force could. And he had money, lots of it, to sustain his efforts. When his mother died she left her entire fortune to Hans. Soon after, her brother, a prosperous merchant, died without an heir, and his holdings were left to Hans as well. With such immense financial resources at his disposal Hans could easily have hired a small army of scientists to help unravel his problem, but he did not.

For the most part he worked alone, because he trusted so few people. It would be too easy for someone to scoop up his father's idea and develop it, leaving the Riegler clan holding the bag. In this race there would be no prize for second place. The first one to market Dormistan would have power beyond measure; the second would only become a footnote in scientific journals.

So when Hans, toiling away in his laboratory with cell culture techniques he had learned years before, discovered the mechanism of the prolonged survival first observed by his father, he did not shout from the scientific rooftops, he did not submit reports to first tier scientific journals. He kept his observations on apoptosis to himself. Even though his discovery that programmed cell death could be slowed, even halted altogether by Dormistan, would have set the scientific community to buzzing like never before, that treasure remained closed away in his own lab manuals, which he kept in a locked safe. Sharing was not a part of his grand plan. Only a select few would reap the rewards of his labor, and he would select them personally.

He had managed to modify the Dormistan molecule so as to remove the immediate hallucinogenic effects, but other problems remained. In addition to the very unpleasant submersion process that remained a necessity, other side effects awaited those who participated, willingly or not, in his studies.

For most of them the thin veil between the current life and the afterlife was torn asunder, and the Dormistan participant found himself able to see and hear ghosts. Some people handled this situation more deftly than others. Some were able to resolve old conflicts, others were tormented by the ongoing presence of those they had wronged, or who had wronged them. But was it too high a price to pay for an indefinite life span? It depends, doesn't it, or so thought Hans. Sure, he saw ghosts, too, but he planned to live for a long, long time, ghosts notwithstanding.

Of course, not all the side effects of Dormistan were unpleasant. The patients Hans treated typically experienced a greatly enhanced libido. His father had made note of this among the boys in the orphanage; when the lights went out at night, it was a sexual free-for-all. Hans considered this a great plus. "Not only can you live forever, you can fuck yourself silly while you're at it," he told his father, who apparently agreed.

On his seventy-eighth birthday—although he appeared, at most, half that age—Hans packed up his belongings and moved to America. The craze for eternal youth was such a big part of the American psyche that he felt sure people would even submit to drowning to achieve it. But first, he needed a collaborator, someone licensed to practice medicine, someone who could be bought. He spent months scouring medical journals, searching for someone with expertise in reviving victims of cold water drowning. His own success in resuscitation procedures left something to be desired. He was able to salvage only about sixty-percent of his subjects, and disposing of his failures proved quite a nuisance.

Success rates published in the American medical literature were much higher, approaching eighty percent, even after submersions of forty-five minutes. This achievement seemed due in large part to the use of cardiopulmonary bypass technology in the drowning victims, so Hans narrowed his search to cardiovascular surgeons who had experience with the technique. One name appeared in the literature with some frequency—Dr. Paul Pierce. Once he had performed his usual extensive background check, Riegler discovered that the good Dr. Pierce had made a few bad decisions—professional as well as personal—along the way. He was one of those whose grasp always exceeded his reach, whose ambition lay just beyond the borders of his own talent. In other words,

Pierce was vulnerable, made to order for Riegler's own plans. Pierce could be swayed by opportunities that promised rapid success, and rapid money. Dazed by the prospect of a rapid rise in the medical hierarchy, he probably wouldn't ask too many questions, and, by the time he did, it would be too late.

# Chapter 14

Stacey made a quick stop at the Ladies' Room just before her three o'clock appointment in Paul Pierce's research lab. Pierce, like a number of other physicians, took Thursday afternoons off, most of them for golf outings. How Pierce might spend his afternoon was of no interest to her, so long as he was nowhere near the lab.

She had called Lawrence Konrad, who directed Pierce's lab, earlier in the week. Just a medical resident who wanted a look into the world of medical research, that's all, so she said.

She fussed with her hair for a moment, then did a quick touch-up with lip gloss. She undid the top button of her blouse, toyed with the second button for a moment but decided against it.

Konrad was a breast man, she knew. She had met him at a chamber music concert a couple of months before. She was no great fan of chamber music, but had gone at the insistence of a friend who didn't want to go alone. Konrad had performed a cello solo that, surprisingly, she enjoyed. When her friend introduced them after the performance, Konrad's gaze seemed riveted to the top of the rather low cut dress that Stacey wore.

"God," her friend said later. "He looked like he was ready to lick your chest."

Oh, what the hell, she thought as she tapped on the door of the lab. She undid the second button.

Konrad was all smiles as he held the door open for her. From the direction of his gaze she decided that the second button had been a good idea after all.

"So, all ready for your tour?" He stood about her own height, and had a neatly trimmed beard tapered to a point at the tip of his chin.

"Yes, thanks so much for taking the time to show me around. Do you find plenty of time to practice your cello?" she asked.

"Every day." He smiled. "We have formed a quartet, two violins and a bass player. We've just begun playing together, but when we're more proficient we'll arrange some performances. If you wish I'll let you know about them."

"Thanks, I'd like that very much."

He took her arm and led her down a short hallway into a small windowless room where two technicians sat hunched over a bench. They did not look up when he walked by.

"Just routine stuff in here," Konrad said. He walked on toward a set of double doors.

Stacey had done her homework before the visit. She had plied her friend with questions about Konrad, no point in going in unprepared.

"I didn't think he was your type," her friend said.

"Maybe I've just developed an interest in the cello."

"Yeah, like hell."

Konrad, she learned, came with a very impressive resume. He had completed a doctorate at a university in Austria, then migrated to the U.S., where he'd worked in skin pathology at Columbia University for several years. His list of publications was quite extensive, too much for someone of his youthful appearance. By her own estimate he would be in his early thirties. How could someone so young have been so productive?

One thing for sure, people like Konrad didn't come cheap. Pierce, or someone, would have had to lay out big bucks to get this young man.

"I'm surprised you're interested in what we're doing here. Most of the medical trainees don't seem to care at all."

He still held her arm, and she was beginning to wonder if he was ever going to let go.

"I wasn't sure what kind of project you were interested in, so I thought we'd start in here." He held a door open for her that led into a longer corridor. At last he released her arm, and Stacey resolved to keep a safe distance away from him.

"Hope you don't mind rats."

"Just so long as they're in cages."

"Now for the good stuff. Welcome to the wonderful world of basic science." Konrad made a sweeping movement with his arms, as if he were a conductor on a podium. "Not many people really know what's going on here, but we're doing some neat stuff." He seemed almost desperate to talk to someone, anyone. Understandable, she figured, considering his company most of the time consisted of rats.

"Thanks," Stacey said. "But go slow. I'm not up to speed on what you might be doing down here." She walked past a door marked Ladies' Changing Room. The heavy door that opened onto the corridor closed silently behind her. There was no turning back now.

"You go in here," Konrad said

"I…I don't have to," she said.

"Oh, it's not a bathroom," he said. "It's where you'll change."

"I have to change?"

"Right. We're going into a sterile environment. Nobody comes in wearing street clothes."

Stacey opened the door and went inside. She hadn't counted on anything like this. The far wall was lined with numbered gray lockers, but no locks. Then she spotted a faint red dot in the corner of the ceiling. A camera. The bastards. So they wanted to film her undressing. Could be for security purposes, or just someone's sick hobby. Either way, it was illegal, another piece of information she would file away should she ever have another confrontation with Pierce. She pulled a chair over so that she could just reach the camera, took off her lab coat, and draped it over the prying lens. She scanned the room, but never detected the second camera located just above the door where she entered.

Each locker contained a sterile bunny suit, so named because of the baby blue color. Stacey was quite familiar with the curious get ups because the same apparel was used in the surgical operating rooms. After she'd changed into the sterile outfit, including slipcovers for her shoes, she rejoined Konrad who now wore a blue suit as well, and followed him into the lab.

They passed maybe a dozen people working at various lab stations. Nobody even looked up. This section apparently wasn't Konrad's domain.

"Running a lab this size must take a lot of money," Stacey said.

"Lots," he said. But on that topic he would say no more.

Stacey had an Oh My God moment. She had underestimated Pierce. The man controlled an incredible amount of real estate and resources where both were at a premium. Just the week before, Dean Westbrook had sent around a memorandum announcing a new round of cost cutting steps, and while everyone else was tightening their belts, Paul Pierce was living like a king.

"Does Dr. Pierce have much time to spend in here? I expect he has such a busy schedule you'd hardly ever see him."

"Yeah, mostly Dr. Riegler is here," Konrad said. From the scowl that formed when he said it, he apparently did not enjoy Dr. Riegler's visits.

"Who is Dr. Riegler?" Stacey asked. "I don't recall hearing that name."

"He works with Dr. Pierce. He pretty much runs things in the lab. Dr. Pierce comes in from time to time, but he doesn't seem that interested in the basic stuff."

So, Pierce had a silent partner after all. Stacey made a mental note of the name. That would explain a lot. From what Konrad had just told her it seemed the lab belonged to Paul Pierce in name only. But who the hell was Dr. Riegler?

They walked down a short hallway, Stacey's shoe covers slapping loosely on the floor. "Been a while since I've been in the basic science world, as you call it. What on earth is that?" She pointed at a large unit embedded into the wall, containing row after row of tiny cylindrical spaces. Each held a sleeping rat. The glass looked thick and it was colored a deep green, so the rats were not clearly visible.

"Shhh," Konrad said. "Don't wake them up." He laughed at Stacey's puzzled expression. "Actually you couldn't wake them up if you tried. They're medicated. Some of them have been asleep for months."

"But, what about nutrition, hydration?"

"Look up close. See the little tube? That goes into their rectums. They get everything they need through that."

"Good heavens. What's the longest you've kept them asleep?"

"I'm not supposed to divulge that kind of information, but I'll tell you--one year. We probably could go longer, but that's it so far."

"But lab rats only live for a couple of years," she said. "I remember that much, at least." Actually, an even shorter life span would be fine by her; she hated rats, in cages or out.

"About three years, actually."

"What are they like when they wake up?"

"That's the next stop. Follow me."

They walked farther down the corridor and made a left turn into an even larger room. Cages filled with rats were stacked at the far end of the room, and the counter tops were covered with tiny mazes, wheels, ladders, and other devices that Stacey had never seen before.

"This looks like an amusement park for rats," she said.

"Right on. Actually it's an obstacle course. We measure the time it takes them to complete various sections. See, the technician is starting a group out now."

The lab tech started off a group of six rats one by one, timing their entry into and exit from the maze. Next they ran through a long tube placed on an incline, also timed.

"They're fast," Stacey said.

"They've all done this before, and they learn quickly. Plus they get a nice reward at the end." Konrad pointed to a cage at the end of the table where the rats that had just completed the course were busily chewing up a large chunk of cheese. "That's imported cheese," he said. "Nothing but the best for our rats. Now, look at the next batch."

The technician released a second batch of six rats into the maze.

"What's different?" Konrad asked.

"That's a sad looking group of rats," she said. "They're skinny. Some of them have lost parts of their fur. And they're slow. Look, two of them didn't even make it out of the maze."

"What's your impression of the second group?"

"I think they're either sick or a lot older than the first group. They look like they're pretty near the end."

"What if I told you they were the same age as the first group?"

"No way. That's impossible," Stacey said. "If anything they look twice as old as the first group."

"Remember the sleeping rats that you saw on the way in?"

She nodded. The hair on the back of her neck began to prickle. Something quite remarkable was going on here. Be patient, she had to remind herself.

"We started off with a matched group of twelve rats. When they were all one year old, we split them into two groups. One group of six was put under for a year. The other group was kept normally, like we keep all the rest."

"So the group that was kept under didn't age as rapidly?" Stacey shook her head in disbelief. The difference in the rats was amazing. What was Pierce—or Riegler, whoever he was--onto here?

"That's the idea. While the other group was aging normally, the rats we kept in the incubator didn't seem to age at all. That's why they look so young in comparison."

"Unreal," she said. "You can actually stop the aging process." She struggled to keep her voice even, calm.

"I don't know that we completely stop it, but we can sure slow it down a lot."

"How on earth do you do that?"

"If I told you that I'd have to kill you," Konrad said with a nervous laugh. "Just joking, of course. It's a medication we give them. I can't say any more." He walked a bit further. "And it gets even better. Look at this bunch."

A large cage set off to one side contained about a dozen rats, copulating as if their lives depended on it.

"But…" Stacey shook her head. Rats could be disgusting, sure, but this was above and beyond anything she could imagine.

"Yeah. They're doing it like crazy." Konrad laughed out loud.

"Is this from the medication too?" Stacey asked.

"Sure is. You know, like marijuana makes you want to eat, our medication makes them want to copulate. Think about it. We can increase life span and libido all at once. Can't get any better than that, right?"

"Amazing. Simply amazing. Let me ask you one other question. Are you doing any similar studies with humans? I mean, everybody's going to want this."

"No, no, no. This is basic stuff here. The rats seem to tolerate it well enough, but we don't have any idea how human subjects would react. It would be neat to find out, though. Just think, if we could slow down the aging process in humans. …"

As he spoke about the possibility of human studies, Konrad's demeanor changed. He stopped making eye contact and his voice dropped to a whisper, as if he were speaking to himself, not to her. Was he being truthful? Did he have information about Pierce's other patients? He seemed very close to divulging information that should be kept secret. All she had to do was give him time, time to slip up and say more than he should.

"So, you just give them this medication, and the rats stop aging." Trying to remain calm and objective was becoming more and more difficult. She took several deep breaths before she spoke. The question that had arisen was fantastic in its implications: had Pierce or Riegler or whomever really discovered the key to immortality?

"No, no," Konrad said. "I wish it was that simple, but we have to do something else first." He led her to a smaller room that contained two large plastic vats, each filled halfway with water. "This one on the left, the water is kept at room temperature, always sixty-eight degrees. The one on the right is refrigerated, thirty-five degrees. If I had any rats to spare just now I'd show you what happens, but our next shipment won't arrive until tomorrow, so you'll just have to take my word for it. If I drop one rat into each vat, they'll both thrash around for a few minutes, then the one in the cold water just sinks to the bottom. The one in warm water keeps swimming around until it can't swim anymore."

"So, they both drown, one a little sooner than the other."

"Actually, no. You've heard of the mammalian diving reflex, you know, where people survive immersion in cold water, sometimes half an hour or longer?"

"I've heard of that, yes." For sure she'd heard of it. She had personal accounts in her own apartment…John Merritt, Naomi Welles, Bobby Pippin, to name a few.

"Dr. Pierce is the real expert in this. He's revived a lot of people who have fallen through the ice in the winter. What saves them is this mammalian diving reflex, everything shuts down. Then if they can get them here soon enough, Dr. Pierce hooks them up to his bypass machine, and a week or so later they walk out of the hospital, good as new. But it takes really cold water before the diving reflex kicks in."

"So, these rats you put in cold water, you're able to revive them?"

"Most of them, yeah."

"But I don't understand the connection between the diving reflex and the fact that you can keep rats alive for so many years."

Konrad screwed up his face as if he'd just bitten into something sour. "We don't either, not exactly. Somehow the diving reflex shuts off a number of physiologic systems, and the medication keeps them shut off. Come with me. I have something else to show you that might convince you."

Before he opened the door to the room Konrad handed her a surgical face mask, then donned one himself. Just inside the door he took two pairs of sterile latex gloves and gave one to Stacey. The room had no windows. On the far wall a large laminar flow hood emitted a low humming sound, the only noise in the room. Konrad led her past a series of incubators, each filled with stacks of petri dishes.

"What are you growing in here?" she asked.

"Skin biopsy tissue."

"From rats?"

"Human."

She realized that Konrad was now showing and telling her things he probably should not be showing or telling anyone. But, like most enthusiastic researchers who were working on a hot project, he couldn't seem to help himself. Her suspicions were confirmed when she saw the labels on the petri dishes he took from one of the incubators: Merritt, J., Welles, N. He'd apparently forgotten his earlier assertion about having no experimental data on human subjects, but she was not going to remind him just now.

The microscope under which he passed the petri dishes projected an image onto a computer screen. "This first sample is normal human skin tissue. We can usually keep it alive for about two weeks. See, lots of the cells here are forming vacuoles in the cytoplasm. Some of them are already dead.

"Now, look at this." He slid another covered dish under the microscope. The label on the corner of the plate said Merritt, J.

For the moment Stacey was thankful for the surgical mask that hid her face. The answers to John Merritt's questions about the small biopsies cut from his upper arm lay right in front of her.

"Just check this out." Konrad's voice went up an octave or two. "These cells are over three months old, and we've replated them five times. They look just as healthy as the day we took the biopsy."

"My God," she whispered. "How?"

"Here's another one." He was on a roll and wouldn't even slow down to explain. He pushed another plate under the microscope head. "These have only gone through about four platings, but they look as good as new, right?"

"What's the longest you've been able to keep the cells alive?"

"Usually around four to six months we get some bacterial contamination, and that ends it. Otherwise, who knows? For all we know the cell lines might be immortal." Konrad replaced the petri dishes in the incubators. "Dr. Riegler thinks the longevity is because normal apoptosis, you know, programmed cell death, is shut off by what we're doing, so long as we keep them well fed and warm, the cells go right on living, way past normal."

"Odd, I've just never heard of Dr. Riegler"

"He's in and out at odd times. I never know when to expect him. He doesn't do any teaching or anything like that, but he's worked on the apoptosis angle for years and years. It's like, been his whole career."

"Just one more thing," Stcey said, "you can interrupt apoptosis with the mammalian diving reflex, but how do you keep it turned off?"

"Excellent question. That's the medication effect, keeps the cells from dying. And the effect seems to last as long as the medication is taken. Right now we have to give it to the rats every day, but Dr. Riegler has somebody in the Pharmacology Department working on a long-acting dose that we'll only have to give once a month, maybe even less frequently. Amazing, huh?"

"Definitely." She had more questions, dozens of them, but she didn't want to arouse Konrad's suspicions. So she thanked Konrad profusely, promised to attend his next concert, then headed back to the changing room.

Her fingers trembled as she buttoned her blouse. Now she knew the whole sequence: shut down apoptosis with the mammalian diving reflex, then keep it shut down with Dormistan. If the effects she'd seen in the skin biopsy specimens could be extended to an entire organism, Pierce and his mysterious partner Riegler had discovered a way to prevent aging. It apparently worked well enough with rats, but how about humans? That, obviously enough, was just what was being done with John and Naomi and Bobby Pippin, and who knew how many others? They were all unwitting subjects in a bizarre longevity experiment, and, if

157

she could believe what Konrad had just shown her, the scheme worked.

How much would this information be worth? Priceless.

Be careful what you wish for. The old phrase had never seemed more true to Stacey than it did now. She had the information she sought, but what was she going to do with it? The work that Pierce and his mystery man, Riegler, were doing was probably illegal, but how could she hope to stop it? With all the money and resources Pierce appeared to have at hand it would be like trying to stop an onrushing train. He would crush her like a bug.

But first things first. She knew enough to explain John's behavior and that was her primary goal. If she could set him straight, get him off Dormistan, maybe they could get on with their lives…together.

She weighed the various issues he brought to the table—her table: still trying to atone for his brother's death, Dormistan, the drug that allowed him to communicate with the dead, that pushed his libido into overdrive, and, most damning of all, might well render him immortal, all the while she would grow older.

"John Merritt," she said aloud. "You are one complicated man, and you damned well better be worth the trouble."

# Chapter 15

"You have a visitor." Pierce's secretary warned him as he trudged toward his office, head down, eyes focused on the floor in front of him.

"What? Who? You know I don't see anybody first thing." On those mornings when he had no surgery scheduled he liked to ease into the day, coffee, the newspaper, a little navel-gazing. In contrast to some of his more industrious surgical colleagues who could hardly wait for the opening bell so they could begin cutting into human flesh, Pierce favored a more calculated approach to the day, hoarding his precious energy reserves in anticipation of any crisis that might arise. Of course, not everyone interpreted his actions as he intended. Some of those who did not or could not understand called him just plain lazy.

"I couldn't stop him." His secretary held up her hands in surrender. "He said he'd wait inside, and in he went."

Pierce glared at her with a look that said, "You can be replaced," and went into his office. His sanctuary had been invaded, and he was not happy.

Hans Riegler, compact, immaculate with his cane and crew cut looked up, but didn't speak.

"Oh, I didn't expect you." Pierce fussed about, making a big show of hanging up his jacket and donning his white coat as if to say business as usual, in spite of his trembling hands. "Can I offer you coffee or anything?" He would likely remain in this state of apprehension until he determined Riegler's mood for that day. The man could be totally charming and gracious, or vicious; there seemed to be no in-between state with him.

Riegler shook his head, his face an expressionless mask.

Pierce crouched behind his desk, feeling a bit more secure behind the wall of mahogany. He needed the physical barrier between them. Riegler didn't look pleased. "What can I do for you?"

"Things are going slowly, too slowly." The man's voice was flat, metallic.

"This kind of work takes time. And with the weather warming up I doubt we'll have many more people falling into icy ponds until next winter season. I am pleased with the results we have so far," Pierce said.

"Pleasing you is not my concern."

"But, what else can I do?" Pierce shuffled papers, moved things around on his desk, anything to avoid the glare directed at him from Riegler's unreadable face. "All my patients are accident victims. If there are no accidents, I have no patients."

"And that seems to be a problem."

"It's one I can do nothing about. I can't very well start drowning people." Pierce laughed nervously.

Riegler smiled, but the effect was not reassuring. "I believe I can help you with that aspect of our problem, as you call it."

Pierce took off his glasses, annoyed at the chattering noise they made against his desktop as his hands continued to shake. "What are you proposing?" He asked the question, but he really didn't want an answer.

Much of his dealing with Riegler had been conducted on this basis; Pierce took the money and didn't ask questions. Because there was so much money, limitless, so it seemed. How quickly Pierce had become accustomed to luxury, as if he'd been born into it, which he most certainly was not. He now drove a new Mercedes 300SL and parked it with the dean's accommodation, in a reserved space all his own. The three suits he'd had made by Riegler's Parisian tailor made him the best dressed physician on staff.

And now the hook was set in too deep for him to wriggle off. Riegler owned him.

"How many patients can you handle at a time?" Riegler asked.

"I have two intensive care beds set aside for my own use. That was our agreement with the Dean."

"Are those beds in use now?"

"Uh, no."

"And you say you expect patient accrual to fall off sharply now, until next winter, so all our time and money will be wasted while you sit around and wait for the weather to change."

"Yes, but it's unavoidable."

"No, Dr. Pierce. In fact, it's quite avoidable. It's time to move on to the second phase of our program. The Canandaigua facility is nearing completion, so we shall no longer be dependent on the weather, and you can release those ICU beds back to the hospital. You will make arrangements for the increased level of activity at our new location. You must move that little cardiopulmonary bypass machine of yours to our new Longevity Center."

"But the bypass equipment belongs to the hospital," Pierce said. Sophisticated equipment came under the heading of capital expenses, a listing that was reviewed by a half dozen committees before it was ever brought on line. Reversing the process, actually removing such instrumentation from the medical center, would be like trying to force a river to run uphill. Pierce knew that much, at least.

"I've spoken with our friend, Dean Westbrook. The necessary arrangements have been made."

Pierce was aware that his jaw dropped, but he could do nothing to stop it. This man, Reigler, cut through red tape like it was tissue paper.

"But, what about staffing, nurses, technicians?"

"I have taken care of that. I have selected all of them myself."

"Can you trust them?"

Riegler laughed. "Trust has nothing to do with it. They will do exactly as I say, no questions asked."

"I'll need Chang to operate the bypass machine."

"He will be coming to the Center, of course."

"But, patients," Pierce said. "We have no patients in warm weather."

"I have a mechanism for supplying you with subjects, patients, if you prefer. When you have everything in place they will be delivered to the Canandaigua facility. If there are complications, deal with them there. No transfers back to this hospital. Much too risky."

"What are you planning to do…drown people?" His nervous twitter was hollow, forced.

Riegler looked directly at Pierce and tapped his cane on the floor. "Just concern yourself with what happens at the Longevity Center. Leave everything else to me."

"You can't do that, what you're talking about." Pierce's voice broke. He'd known all along that this moment would come. Riegler was not a man to be slowed down by a simple change in the weather.

Riegler leaned forward, pointing his cane at Pierce's head. "Don't ever again presume to tell me what I can or cannot do. Do you understand?"

"Yes, sir."

"You're about to become rather busy, Doctor. I suggest you prepare yourself."

The panic that had begun to gnaw at his gut moments before now transformed to nausea, and he wondered if his breakfast might reappear in the middle of his desk. He was about to become an accomplice to a most unlawful act. And even worse, he had, at some level known about this all along.

He and Reigler had never had specific discussions about this second phase, but Pierce knew well enough that the man would never be content to plod along collecting data on the few patients foolish enough to fall into freezing winter lake water. No, they were in the final stretch run now. Riegler wanted more data, and he wanted it quickly.

The scientific implication of their work with apoptosis, dazzling though it might be, wasn't the point, not to Riegler. He wanted a product, and he wanted results. Let others toil away in the laboratory uncovering the mysteries of apoptosis. The finish line was in sight now, and very soon the biggest trophy of all—unlimited prolongation of the human life span--would be his to control, his to sell to the highest, the very highest bidders.

But first, there were unpleasant things to be done. Pierce slumped down in his chair. He was boxed in, and he had put himself there by his own ambition, his own greed. The so-called cardioprotective effects of Dormistan that allowed him to get the drug past the hospital committee that reviewed projects on human experimentation; that was all crap. Neither he nor Reigler cared about protecting hearts, even though cardiac difficulties were a prominent feature as patients were re-warmed after cold water drowning. They were interested in something else entirely. Their experiments were modeled after work done by Riegler many years before.

"Those children you showed me, years ago…." Pierce said.

"I suggest you never saw those children, Dr. Pierce. Forget about them. They were orphaned after the war. Their chances of survival were slim. I gave them life, a very long life."

Riegler ended the conversation as he ended most conversations, he simply got up and walked away, leaving Pierce to mull over alone some of the things he had seen and done. At the door he turned and looked back at Pierce, as if he were considering something unpleasant.

Pierce glanced down at his trembling hands. How had he ever gotten into such a mess? No matter. He was in too deep now. He couldn't get out even if he wanted to. "When can I expect the first patients?"

"I'll call you when the first delivery is to take place," Riegler said. "They'll be arriving rather late so as not to attract too much attention. I expect you to personally supervise their admissions and care. Good luck."

"These new people I'll be getting, how long will we keep them submerged?" There seemed no point in creeping around the subject any more. The specifics were all that mattered now. Riegler was calling the shots, and Pierce was just following orders.

"Thirty minutes."

"Dear God, we'll really be drowning them."

"That's the idea, you idiot. Haven't you heard anything I've said?"

Pierce's head hung down until his chin rested on his tie. "It's inhuman. That's what it is, inhuman. If anyone ever found out…."

"Hardly something for you to quibble about at this stage, Dr. Pierce. Real medical breakthroughs only come to those with vision, those who take action. People won't give a whit about how we developed Dormistan. They'll be too busy lining up to get their own prescriptions filled. Open your eyes, man. Dormistan is the fountain of youth. We'll be selling immortality. We have the power to slow down the aging process, and perhaps prevent some of those nasty diseases that come from just getting old. Everyone will want it, but only a few will get it, and those lucky few will pay dearly."

"And afterward, the patients you send, after they leave the Center? What happens then?"

"Not your concern, Dr. Pierce. Not your concern." Riegler's cane tapped sharply against the hardwood floor as he headed out the door.

The temperature in the room seemed to drop as Pierce remembered that trip to Zurich, the children from years ago who, in spite of a youthful appearance, lurched about, their movements lacking the true fluidity of youth.

# Chapter 16

The girl was full of surprises; John had to give her that much. One minute it seemed Stacey wanted nothing to do with him, the next she calls up and invites herself out to see him. "I'm off this weekend," she had said. "You wanta' get together?" Just like that.

"Oh, yeah, I'd love to, but...," John said, looking out at the half-finished repair of Nacho's stall he'd started earlier in the morning. The rambunctious gelding had kicked loose several of the boards at the back of his stall, and John was carefully checking to make sure there were no nails sticking out that the horse might rub up against.

"But what? You're going to stand me up? Don't tell me you have other plans."

"No, nothing like that. I just got so far behind here. I haven't done any work around the place for weeks."

"I could come and lend a hand. I'm not helpless, you know."

"That would be great. But this is kind of dirty work. I got horse poop on my boots."

"Is that worse than human poop?"

John laughed. This was definitely his kind of woman. "Poop is poop, I guess. When can you come out?"

"I'll be right out in the morning. Oh, do you have any food?"

"Glad you reminded me. I'll make a run to the market this evening. Anything special you like?"

"Surprise me. I'll bring lunch."

"Bring your work clothes, woman. I'm talking real manual labor here."

"You're scaring me something awful. I expect to be suitably

165

compensated, you know."

Her laugh made his skin tingle. Something had changed. It was as if she had decided he wasn't so bad after all. You got a second chance here, he said to himself. Don't blow it.

#

Spring came as such a special event after the typical long, often brutal, upstate winter, like a reward for having stuck it out instead of fleeing south as so many residents regularly did. But those snowbirds, as they were called, usually missed the magic of seasonal change. To watch a formerly barren landscape dust itself off and show new signs of life was like watching a desert area burst forth in green after the fall rains.

Seasonal events had a stabilizing effect on people, John in particular. The front page of the newspaper, the evening news on TV, all suggested that the world was sinking into chaos. But even a brief trip outside, seeing nature's changes taking place right on schedule, was an affirmation. For weeks now he'd watched those undulating ribbons of Canada geese wending their way north. One cloudless night, standing on his front porch, he'd stared upward as a flight passed in front of a full moon. Their honking set Rebel into a barking fit, as if the dog was answering their wild calls. John could feel it himself. Those geese, they had to know something, right? If the world was going to hell in a handbag, why bother to make such a long trip? And now, to make things even better, Stacey was coming for a visit.

Saturday morning clouds gave way to a bold blue sky, and John smiled his approval. Rebel raced around the yard barking.

"You're in a good mood, I see. You must know we've got company coming. Maybe I should give you a bath."

The dog yelped and ran behind the house.

"Just as well," John said. "I got plenty to do without chasing you around."

He walked down to the barn and hoisted up the beam that held the double doors closed. He ran his fingers along the wood, now polished over years of handling by generations of Merritts. His connection could not have been more real if he'd grown roots into the spot where he stood.

Nacho and the little bay mare in the next stall were already stamping their hooves as John entered the barn. The fresh air of the outside gave way to the musty mix of confined animals, stored hay and harness leather.

John poured their morning rations into their feeding troughs along with those for the two geldings across the way. "Eat fast, guys. Then you're all going out to the pasture." He dragged the stack of pine boards from the back of the barn up beside Nacho's stall. He'd just strapped on his tool belt when he heard Rebel barking.

"Is this dog rabid?" Stacey yelled from her car.

"I think he's just glad to see you. I am too."

Stacey skipped from car to barn and wrapped her arms around his neck. "Show me."

"What?"

"Show me you're glad to see me."

Somewhere between the softness of her lips, the fresh scent of her hair and the warmth of her body pressed against his, John lost all sense of time and place.

"There," she said, pulling away from him. "Now I feel welcome."

He pulled her back but she wriggled out of his arms. "I thought you said there was work to do."

"Did I say that?"

"You most certainly did. Now, come on and help me." She walked to the rear of her once-red Toyota and popped open the trunk. She thrust a picnic basket into John's arms.

"Wow," he said, testing the weight of the basket. "Feels like you packed enough to feed a whole crew."

"Just want to make sure you've got plenty of energy for what you want to do, and what I'll want you to do later." She kissed his cheek and jumped away before he could grab her with his free arm.

"Do we have to wait?"

"Work first. Reward later," she said. "Now, come on, show me what you want me to do."

He led her inside, handed her a shovel and a pair of work gloves. "You sure you're up for this?"

"I've seen stalls before," she said. "And unless you've figured out a way to potty-train your horses, I know exactly what the shovel is for."

She looked around for a moment. "You know, I haven't been in this barn since that winter when you took me for a sleigh ride. Do you

167

remember that?"

"Sure, I do."

"Where is it?"

"The sleigh? I put it back in the shed."

"Well, just make sure you get it all cleaned up again before winter. I want another ride, several of them. And bells, don't forget the bells. And next time you better not flip us over."

"That was the best part."

They worked steadily until just past noon. To John's surprise Stacey appeared no stranger to a pick and shovel as she mucked out the two stalls with a vengeance. During the late morning she stripped off her work shirt leaving her in a tank top that stopped short several inches above her navel. At least three times after that John hit his thumb with the hammer.

"Lunch time," he said after the last whack on his thumb, already swollen and throbbing.

"Thank God." Stacey wiped her brow. "I'm not used to this kind of work. But I must say, it's a nice break from that dreary old hospital."

He slipped his arms around her bare waist and drew her close. "I thought you were having a good time shoveling horse poop."

"I'm having a great time. Now feed me before I pass out."

They spread the contents of Stacey's picnic basket on a table midway between the barn and the house. The limbs of four white oaks intertwined making a bower of spring buds above the picnic spot.

"How long has this been here?" Stacey ran her fingers along the two-inch thick oak planks that made up the table. "It looks ancient."

"Been here as long as I can remember," John said. "I'm not sure who built it. I think maybe my granddad. There's one just like it, a little smaller, in the kitchen."

"You have a picnic table in your kitchen?"

"Sure, why not?"

"No reason not to, if it's as sturdy as this one." She swept off the top of the table with a small towel and spread a cloth over the bare boards. "So, I guess you have a lot of great memories, family picnics out here."

"Yeah. Lots of great memories. I'm working on one right now, in fact." He embraced her, pressing her back on the table.

"I think I'm lying in the potato salad."

"I'll lick you clean."

#

"This has to be the most unorthodox picnic ever." Stacey pulled on her workshirt . She folded her jeans and laid them on the bench beside her.

"Why, just because we had dessert first?"

"I guess you could say that."

She laughed, and the sound reminded John of wind chimes in a summer breeze.

"Can't say I wasn't warned." She spread mayo on a slice of French bread. "They always say, watch out for the quiet ones. Of course, you haven't been exactly quiet of late."

John watched her smile, the way she moved. She slid a thick sandwich across the table toward him.

"You don't mind me sitting around half-dressed?" she asked.

"The only thing better would be if you took everything off."

She laughed again, and again the sound turned him to jelly. "This is the best day ever," he said.

"That's what I wanted to hear." She twined her fingers through his. "Now tell me you're not going to chase after all those other girls anymore."

"What other girls?"

"Come on, you know what I mean."

"It's not like that," he said, mostly to convince himself. But it didn't work. He was different now, and not just because of the urge to peek up every skirt that passed by.    "Do you like yourself better this way?"

He sipped the iced tea she'd poured for him. "In some ways, I guess, others, not so much."

"You know what I want? I want my old John back, the quiet one who used to blush whenever I smiled at him. The one without ghosts following him around all the time." She pulled his head down to hers and kissed him.

"Like I said, the best day ever." He lifted her onto his lap, her bare legs wrapped around his waist, and they sat, wound together. Wisps of cloud ran past the afternoon sun tracing patterns on the ground, but they didn't notice. For John it was as if he held the entire world in his arms. He wanted nothing more, needed nothing more. Then he felt Stacey stiffen in his arms. "What's wrong?" he asked.

"Oh, my gosh. Please, tell me, when we were making love on the table, there weren't any of your little ghost friends watching."

"No, absolutely not." He lied, of course. They were always around now. Often they were no more than wisps of cloud themselves. Even Rebel seemed more accepting now of the spectral visitations.

Stacey jumped off his lap and pulled on her jeans. "I can't get used to this, John, having an audience around, one I can't even see. This is just too weird. What on earth do they want from you?"

He walked to her and wrapped his arms around her, surprised to find that she was shivering. "It's mostly simple stuff, like a message. You know, like good-bye to somebody, or something they didn't get a chance to say while they were here."

"And you're the messenger."

"Sometimes. It seems to help them somehow. Remember your patient, how she wanted me to tell you about the locket she'd left for you? You'd do the same if you could. I know you would."

"I don't think so. The very thought of ghosts floating around, talking to them. No way. I could never do that."

She pulled out of his arms. "I have a confession. I did something. You might not like it, but I had to do it."

He put his hands on her shoulders and drew her back to him. "I told you not to get yourself in trouble because of me. I can handle this myself."

"I got a list of some of the other patients Dr. Pierce is treating with Dormistan, the medication you're taking."

"You want to see if they're crazy too?"

"You know better than that. I went to see two of them. They had fallen through the ice, same as you. And Dr. Pierce brought them back. And the medication you're taking, they're taking it too."

"Are they crazy?"

"No, they aren't, and neither are you." She jabbed her forefinger into his chest. "It's all the medication, the ghosts, the personality changes, everything. All you have to do is stop taking the pills, and everything should get back to normal."

"You learned all that just from visiting a couple of his patients?"

"Not exactly, I snuck into his lab at the Medical Center. He's doing some amazing things, but that doesn't justify using you and the others as guinea pigs. Anyway, I am definitely not comfortable with your seeing ghosts, let alone talking to them. What if you just stop taking that medication for a while, just see what happens?"

"That doesn't change anything. Not seeing them doesn't mean they're not still there, and sometimes they need somebody like me to speak for them, since they can't. Besides, it's not that simple. Come on, let's take a little walk."

He led her down a path that ran behind the barn and up a small hill with a stand of pines at its crest. Three dogwood trees in early bloom stood at the south edge of the pines. The hill lay in a north-south direction, so it caught a direct view of sunrise and sunset as well. The center of the little pine grove had been cleared out, and the grass was neatly trimmed. Three tombstones sat in the middle. "The Merritt family graveyard," John said. It was a place he visited frequently, looking for closure but never finding it.

Stacey stopped short. "Why are you bringing me up here?"

"Some things you need to know about my family history."

"I already know about your brother, John. Everybody knows about the accident."

"There's more," he said. He took her hand and tugged her along with him. "My family." He pointed to the tombstones. "My granddad there on the left, died in his sleep, 1980. No fuss, just went peaceful. He was my favorite."

"Do you ever see his ghost?"

"A couple of times. Never says much. Always nice to see him though. Dad is next to him. He died a year or so after mom left. Broken heart, old Dr. Simpson said. He's where I got my love for horses, I guess. He liked them more than he did people. Now we get to the hard one. Christopher, 1990, he was twenty. You know that story."

"It was an accident, John. I know it, you know it, everybody knows it. What you're doing now, obsessing over it like this, it won't help your brother, it won't help you, and it won't help us."

He shook his head and walked away a short distance, finally stopping to lean against one of the pine trees that ringed the gravesites.

"I've got to get this straightened out," he said. "With Christopher, at least."

"So this is what all the craziness is about, right here. And what if Christopher never shows up? Are you just going to keep on taking those damned pills, hoping someday he will?"

Stacey took a few steps away from John, away from the graves. She stood facing back down the hill, arms clasped tightly across her chest. "What about me? What about us? Do you know how hard it is to get used to this, you seeing things I can't see, talking to them? I mean, I know why you do it, but that doesn't make it any easier. Sometimes you just have to accept things you can't fix, let them go."

"I've tried. I've tried for so long." The words came harder now, as if his throat was closing up. "You know the last thing my mother said to me? It was right after we buried Christopher. We were walking back to the car. She was a few steps in front of me. She stopped and looked me straight in the eye. 'You killed my son.' All my fault."

Stacey ran back to him, took his face in her hands. "Oh, God, John, that's the worst thing I've ever heard. Damn her to hell. And you know it's not true."

He shook his head. "But that's what she said, and I'll never forget it." It all came rushing back at him, the sudden squall, the wave that caught them broadside flipping them both into the foaming lake. Christopher swimming away, then disappearing. "I begged him to stay with the boat, but he swam off anyway."

"It wasn't your fault. There was no way you could have saved him. You're lucky you were able to save yourself."

"But why did he even try? He must have known he'd never make it. Maybe he thought he could get help. Maybe he thought he could save me if he made it to shore."

She pulled his face down close to hers. "You can't change what happened, John. You can't fix it. Why can't you see that?"

"I have to know, did he die trying to save me? Is that what my mother meant?"

She rested her forehead against his chest. "What I see is, you're stuck in an impossible situation. For that matter, so are we."

"What do you mean?"

"I mean you can't let it go, and I can't stand by and watch you go on like this. I just can't. We go through this over and over again. It's like this big wall between us. We never seem to get past it."

"I guess I'm a hard man to love."

"You big jerk, I've loved you since tenth grade. No, I won't stop loving you, but I have to stop seeing you. I can't take this anymore."

She turned and walked back down the hill alone. She stumbled several times, like someone walking with their eyes closed.

He wanted to run after her, but could not. His feet felt nailed to the ground. Maybe he'd been right in the first place; he was crazy as a bat.

# Chapter 17

Saturday morning, overcast with clouds hurried along by a northeast wind, one week to the day since he'd watched Stacey walk away, leaving him standing by his family graveyard, John wheeled his Harley into the barn, a new speeding ticket folded in the pocket of his jeans.

After putting his horses out to pasture he had decided on an early morning cruise down the Interstate. About ten miles out, his jaunt was interrupted by flashing red and blue lights that seemed to have appeared out of nowhere.

The state trooper who pulled him over stood tall, rail thin in a crisp uniform that looked as if it had just come from the cleaners. He took long slow strides, stopping at John's left shoulder. He took off his sunglasses and held them dangling between his thumb and forefinger. "John Merritt, is that you?"

John recognized him immediately. Terry Baker had been a classmate of Christopher's and a pallbearer at his funeral.

"Hey, Terry, it's been a long time."

"Man, what in the world were you doing just now? I clocked you at ninety-five, and the road isn't even dried out yet. That's crazy, man. I mean, I could see Christopher doing something like that, but you always acted like you had some sense, at least."

"Yeah, sorry. Had a lot on my mind."

A light drizzle set in, cutting short their conversation. "Look, I'm going to have to write you a ticket. I called in a high speed pursuit, so I have to do it. I'll knock down the speed to seventy. Judge Weaver is doing traffic court now, so he'll probably let you off with a warning."

"Thanks, Terry. I really appreciate it." Judge Weaver had been a friend of his father's, and, with a little luck, that family good will might get him out of a jam.

Terry wrote out the ticket and handed it to John. He put his hand on John's shoulder. "You be careful now, you hear me? I don't want to go to any more Merritt funerals."

They shook hands, and John promised to buy Terry a beer at their first opportunity. He took secondary roads back to his house, narrow lanes flanked by rows of wildflowers, and by the time he pulled into his drive the cloud cover had broken up, yielding to a bright blue sky.

He parked the bike, then trudged back to the house. Usually an early morning ride, particularly one at high speed, cleared his head, but not today. He was still mired in the same muddle that had hung over him all week. That sinking feeling of loss that had set in as he watched Stacey walk away still dogged him. He thought about going into town, but in his current state of mind he'd get into trouble for sure. All he needed was a disorderly conduct citation to go with his speeding ticket to cap off a lousy week.

The safe thing, he decided, was to stick to his routine. Saturday morning he usually put in an hour or two cleaning up the house, not very exciting but a damned sight safer than tearing around the countryside.

He wandered from room to room, picking up the few stray items he'd left lying around the house. Since his single existence as a single man was practically monastic, there was little in the way of clutter to bother with. He went through the entire house with the vacuum cleaner, more out of routine than need. Rebel was now banished to the kitchen area; fleas followed the dog wherever he went, and confinement seemed the only solution.

The Merritt farmhouse was old—old, hell, it was ancient—but sturdy. Now sturdy didn't seem quite sufficient. What had satisfied him before didn't cut it now. More and more he felt himself tugged between his old ways and wanting something new. The new item in the equation was Stacey, but she had walked away, and he'd done nothing to hold her back.

As the only resident, John confined himself to the bedroom he and Christopher used to share, the single bathroom and the kitchen. He could make the entire short trip in the dark. He had no use for the entry room off the front door his mother had called the parlor, and seldom spent time there. Wasted space, in his opinion. The only item of interest in the entire room was an old photo of his grandparents sitting side by side, holding hands. He saw hope in their faces, plans for a future together. What might they think if they could revisit their old homestead now? One single Merritt prowling around like a lost soul, with occasional visits from ghosts.

The bedroom his parents had shared he considered off limits, a space as private now as when they'd both slept there. When he gave it any thought at all, John still found it hard to imagine his parents sharing the same bed. Did they cuddle on cold winter nights, he wondered? A more likely scenario had them each far over on opposite sides of the bed. Still, at some point his parents must have met in the middle. How else to account for the births of himself and Christopher?

Had he and his brother been a little less similar in appearance there might have been some doubt about lineage, but each of them bore the strong jaw and deep, penetrating blue eyes that distinguished their father. Only in behavior did John and his brother differ, and, in recent months, even that difference had diminished. Fortunately for John, he had, over the years, built up enough good will in the community that most people were willing to overlook the wild side he seemed to have developed.

And then there was Stacey. She was the best thing in his life now, no doubt about that, even considering the peaks and valleys that seemed to characterize their relationship. Problem was, when she wasn't around, which was most of the time, he couldn't seem to keep his dick in his pants. Any woman, any time, and his penis went on full alert. Most mornings when he woke up the damned thing was standing there on full alert forming a little teepee in his sheets. To make matters worse, world had apparently filtered out into the community. Girls he scarcely knew approached him, phone numbers scribbled on scraps of paper were shoved into his pockets. Half the time he couldn't even remember who had put them there.

With all the windows in his house open, he heard the car stop out front before he saw it. A bright red Camaro convertible—Janie Sells. John had only seen her a few times since that day he'd stretched her across the desk in his office. What the hell was she doing here now? He stood by his front door as Janie extended one long, very bare and very tanned leg from her front seat. There followed another leg, equally long, equally tanned, then a pair of cutoff jeans that barely covered her crotch. "Nice tan," John said. "Been away?"

"Tampa," Janie said. "I got a job down there. Moving out next week, so I thought I'd drop in, say good bye."

What followed was inevitable, as soon as she stood and made a token effort to tug down her shorts. She wore a sports bra top that she peeled off right there on the porch. "See, no tan lines." Soon after he got a look at the entire package, and, just as she'd promised, no tan lines above or below.

He stumbled backward into the house, Janie undulating in front of him. They got as far as the sofa in the parlor. So far as John knew that old piece of furniture had never before been put to the use they gave it. One leg of the sofa cracked beneath them, and Janie, bouncing away on top of him, laughed, but did not stop.

Afterward he lay there dazed, watching as she reassembled her meager wardrobe. She tossed her panties at him. "Something to remember me by." Then she was gone.

Scarcely had her car pulled away when he heard another arrival. He recognized the creaking door of Herman's truck. No doubt he would have seen a half-naked Janie leaving; she would have made sure of it. Christ, where were his pants?

A very chastened John, shirtless, shoeless, shuffled out onto the front porch. "What's up, Herm?"

What had just happened between John and Janie could not have been more apparent if Herman had been there watching them do it. The only clear sign of Herman's mood were his ears; when he got mad his ears turned bright red, and they were practically glowing now. Herman glared at him across the porch. It didn't take long for him to make up his mind. "We're gonna have it out, John, right now. Just you and me." Herman, a head shorter than John and outweighed by more than fifty pounds advanced with his fists clenched, boxer-style.

"What the hell, Herm?"

Herman took a swing at John and connected with a light blow to his jaw. "Let me know when you've had enough." He took another roundhouse cut that John parried with his forearm.

"Cut it out." John took a couple of steps back. "What's got into you?"

Herman was a little winded from the action, but he kept coming. "You been acting like a jerk, and it's gonna stop. You hear me?" Herman wound up for another punch, but John stepped in and pinned his arms to his sides. Unable to swing his fists, Herman began stomping John's bare toes.

"Ouch, dammit. Quit that." John lifted him off the ground, but Herman began kicking him in the shins. Rebel had been watching from the porch and now joined in the fray. But he didn't go for Herman; instead, he nipped John in the leg.

John yelled and hopped up and down, still holding onto Herman. "You've turned my own dog against me. He bit me."

"I'd bite you too if I wasn't afraid I'd lose my dentures. Now put me down."

"No more punches?"

"That depends."

They sat side by side on the front steps. Rebel approached John warily, his head down and his tail between his legs, then lay down at his feet. John wagged his finger at the dog, then rubbed his leg where Rebel had nipped him. "I'm gonna remember this."

"You leave that dog alone. Next to me he's the best friend you got."

"Some friends. One bites me, the other tries to kick my ass."

"You had it coming, and you know it."

John started to reply, but Herman held up his hand. "You're gonna listen to me now. Ever since you got out of that hospital you've been acting like an idiot, and it's got to stop. If that pretty little lady doctor ever finds out what you've been doing out here she'll do a lot worse than bite you. Hell, John, you got me madder than I been in years, even got your dog mad at you. Don't that tell you something?

"If I hadn't known you before, hadn't known what a good kid you used to be, why, I wouldn't give you the time of day now. You're just like all the other nobodies around here, running around with their heads up their asses, talking about all the girls they've screwed, and they don't know the first thing about being a man."

"But, when Christopher ran around, everybody liked him. Why is it any different for me?"

Herman smacked his palms down on his bony knees. "Your brother. Dammit, I knew that was it all along. And you still don't get it, do you?" He grabbed the porch railing and pulled himself up. "See, you made him out to be God Almighty, like everybody else did."

"You better not say anything bad about Christopher. He was a great guy."

"I'll say whatever I want about anybody, and that includes you. Christopher was a good enough fella, I guess. A little confused sometimes."

"You're crazy. Christopher had it all together. Everybody said so."

"And everybody didn't know shit." Herman jammed his hands in his pockets, suddenly looking very old. "I'm only gonna say this once, John. I'm too tired and wore out to repeat myself. The only one who ever needed to prove himself was your brother, not you. That's why he ran all over the county acting like a fool. Even your ma could see that."

John felt a chill, like he was standing in a cold rain. "I thought she just liked him better than me."

"She liked him, sure, but she was worried sick about him most of the time. She was scared he'd never amount to nothing. That's why she spent so much time with him."

"I don't know if I understand this or not."

Herman laid a gnarled hand on John's shoulder. "See, you got nothing to prove, never did. Only, you're the only person in the county too dumb to see it. People liked you just the way you were, so quit trying to be your brother. Let it go."

"That's what she said."

"Who?"

"Stacey." He didn't want to tell Herman about their little spat, and certainly couldn't tell him about the ghosts that had become part of his daily life.

"I guess I messed up some," he said.

"You messed up a lot. But it's nothing you can't fix. The John Merritt I used to know was as good a man as you'll ever find, better than most. That's all you need to do, bring him back."

"Thanks, Herm."

"Sorry I hit you."

"Somebody had to do it. I'm glad it was you."

They sat for a while, as only old friends can do, no need for talking.

"You okay now?" Herman asked. Afternoon shadows had begun to creep across the lawn.

"Better, thanks."

They embraced, the awkward hug of men not used to being hugged by other men.

"And you treat that little lady doctor right, you hear me?"

After Herman had driven away, John went back inside for his shirt and shoes, then began a lonely trek up to the little graveyard at the top of the hill. The sun sat directly overhead now, and he cast no shadow, as if he weren't really present. He gazed at the grave markers. Somehow the answer had to be here, but he was no longer sure about the question. He had received the same advice from both Stacey and Herman: "Let it go." But he could not. He'd been gnawing on that same bone now for nine years, and just letting go without some answers was not an option.

Herman's revelation about their mother's concern for Christopher added a new level of complexity. What had she understood that John had not? All those years that he had idolized his brother, had he ever really known him? Like everyone else, he had, as Herman reminded him, kept Christopher high on a pedestal. But what if he had wanted something else? What if, instead of the girls and the glamour, he had craved something with more depth, more meaning? It was a thought John had entertained before, but never found out because he never asked.

He plopped down beside the grave and buried his face in his hands. Warm tears oozed between his fingers. For a man who never cried, he seemed to be doing a lot of it lately.

"I'm sorry, man. If I had you all wrong, I'm sorry. Maybe if we'd just had more time." Now he understood the heartbreak of those bereaved family members who sought contact with their dead children. Like them, all he wanted now was one last chance to talk, to say those things he'd never said while his brother was alive.

Well, if that meant taking more of those crazy pills, visits from ghosts, so be it. No matter what it cost him, he would press on, not so much to ease someone else's pain, but to ease his own. Let it go? Not likely.

# Chapter 18

John slept well that night, but Rosita Gonzalez, two months shy of her nineteenth birthday, hardly slept at all. Pressed in together with all the others in the airless back of the truck, she had no room to sit, let alone down. She caught her breath in short gasps, pinching her nose shut with her fingers to close out the stench of unwashed, sweaty bodies. When she finally succumbed to exhaustion she slumped against her neighbor, an equally exhausted man, and together they swayed and lurched as the truck bounced along unpaved roads.

Her journey had begun on foot just before daybreak with six others from her village. They were led across the border into Arizona where they joined a larger group. Most were young adults, like Rosita, along with a few elderly men and women, and even a few children. The two men who led them seemed in a great hurry, and they stopped for nothing. They marched on in silence until the sun crested the mountains. Along the way several simply gave up and fell by the wayside. She never saw any of them again.

Rosita carried only a small bottle of water and two pieces of chicken in a tattered knapsack, along with a few items of clothing, also tattered. The shoddy footwear in which she started the hike fell apart after the first mile, so she kicked them aside and continued walking in her bare feet. Sometime during the night someone had snatched her knapsack away. When she cried out, the man in charge smacked her in the face.

"Quiet." His voice sounded like the hissing of a snake.

They walked single file through a series of switchbacks. The banks were too high for Rosita to see above them, but she could tell from the position of the sun that they were still headed north. How long since she'd eaten? At least a day, she guessed. And no water for at least that long.

She stumbled along now, weak and hungry, barely able to keep up. Others were less fortunate. When they slumped to the ground they were simply left behind, forgotten.

The sun was well past its zenith when the man in charge stopped the column. Surely they would be given something to eat now, some water, at least. Instead, he motioned them toward a truck, partially concealed by desert scrub.

"Water, please." The moan rose from the group like a chorus.

"Get in," the man said. "Or I'll leave you here. I swear it."

They crawled inside, those behind pushing those who struggled. When it seemed that every available inch of space had been filled, the man slammed the door of the truck, leaving them in darkness. Some would be left behind. Rosita heard their cries, but could do nothing to help them.

She no longer had to walk on her cut, bruised feet, but found her situation even worse than before. The inside of the truck reeked of human waste and vomit, and was even hotter than the desert at high noon. From several of the women, prayers rose in a high-pitched wail.

Thoughts of time and place were lost to Rosita and her companions now, replaced by hunger, thirst, fatigue and the unbearable stench that enclosed them. They were carried along on a journey that seemed without end. A couple of times the truck stopped, but the rear door remained closed. They no longer begged for release; such pleas would do no good.

#

Shortly after nightfall, the driver pulled the truck off the road and waited beneath a rocky overhang until the black van with tinted windows that had followed them for several miles pulled alongside. A compact, swarthy man known only as Mr. Ortiz climbed out of the van, stretched, farted, and walked to the parked truck. He was followed by two others, one of whom carried a shotgun in the crook of his elbow.

Mr. Ortiz walked around to the back of the truck. He could hear children crying inside. Fools--who would bring a child on a trip like this?

Ortiz slipped on work gloves; the metal door handle was still hot to touch, and his hands were soft. A coyote by trade, he'd branched out and now was making more money than ever for doing less work. In short, he'd moved up into management, leaving the grunt work to others. He ran three, sometimes five crews, depending on who was in jail and who was out.

He held one hand over his nose as he opened the back of the truck; twenty to thirty people—he'd lost count---jammed into a small, hot space for more than twelve hours raised quite a stench.

The half-moon shining in a cloudless sky reflected off the upturned faces as he opened the gate. He motioned for them to get out. Many fell to the ground, victims of heat and dehydration. That was the first cut. He didn't want weaklings. He paid no attention to those who faltered. They were on their own now. He lined up the others at the back of the truck.

He motioned to one of his men for a flashlight. He walked over to the portly man on the end of the line and prodded the man's torso with his finger...flabby. Ortiz drew his lips back, exposing his teeth and indicating to the man that he should do the same.

The man still had most of his own teeth. Ortiz waved him over to the side. His weight was a drawback, but he'd do in a pinch. The fat ones were harder to bring back, or so he'd been told. Bring back from what? He didn't know, didn't want to know.

After he'd looked them over—he took extra time with the younger women--Ortiz selected four of them, two men and two women. He would only need two of them at one time, but it was safer to have a couple of spares, just in case.

He pointed to the black van parked alongside the truck. Three of the Mexicans turned and started walking, but one young woman clung to the hand of her young child.

"Leave it. You are going to make a lot of money," Ortiz said to her. "You'll be able to buy anything you want for your child."

Still she clung to the child's hand. One of Ortiz's men crept up behind her and twisted her free arm up behind her back. She let out a little cry and released the child's hand. He dragged her toward the van.

"Where will you take them?" the truck driver asked as Ortiz slipped a small role of bills into his hand.

185

"Not your concern. Better for you if you don't ask questions. I'll let you know when we need more."

"As you say." The truck driver turned to the rest of the now illegal aliens he'd just trucked across the border into southern Arizona. "Get out. Go away," he said, waving his arms at them.

"Water, please. The children are so thirsty." An old woman, kneeling, raised her hands to him.

"It's your own fault. You're a fool for bringing children along. Now, get out of here. Otherwise you'll all be caught and sent back. Then you can pay me again." He got in the truck and drove off.

Ortiz climbed into the van with his four passengers, and the two men who sat in the back. The man carrying the shotgun rested it across his lap.

"Water, please," one of the women said.

Ortiz passed a quart jar of water into the rear. Had the light been better, the silt and slime in the water would have been apparent.

"Let's go," Ortiz said. "We've got a long trip."

#

They traveled through the desert in darkness. Sometimes Rosita Gonzales saw the lights of towns off in the distance, but the van stuck to secondary roads and the lights remained far away. After what seemed like a very long time the driver pulled off the road. The sun had risen now and the countryside was greener, a welcome respite from the monotony of the desert. Rosita was glad to get out and stretch her legs. Her traveling companions did the same. The men in the back of the van didn't say much, but Rosita didn't like the way they looked at her. Men had looked at her like that before, and the outcome was always trouble.

The men urinated beside the van. One of them shook his penis at Rosita. She and the other woman were allowed to go off a few steps by themselves, but not out of sight of the guards who laughed as the women squatted on the ground.

"We got to eat," the head man said, the one they called Mr. Ortiz.

They drove for another hour on the interstate, now in broad daylight, passing road signs that Rosita couldn't read, before Ortiz took an exit ramp off the highway.

Up ahead, Rosita immediately recognized the golden arches that meant burgers and fries. Her mouth began to water, but then she remembered that the coyote who drove them across the border had taken every cent she had.

Mr. Ortiz ordered for all of them, and Rosita felt her stomach knot up as the aroma of the food filled the van.

"Not yet." Ortiz kept the bags in the front seat.

They drove to a little roadside park, and Ortiz pulled the van by a picnic table in the far corner, partially shaded by a large maple that was just beginning to sprout its spring finery.

When Rosita started to get out of her seat, Ortiz yelled at her. "No, you four, you stay inside. You eat in the van."

He got out along with the two guards who squeezed past Rosita and her companions. One of the guards tried to force his hand down Rosita's blouse as they passed.

Slow down, Rosita told herself. If you eat too fast you'll get sick. She looked at the woman who'd sat beside her the entire trip without speaking a word. Her eyes were red and her cheeks were coursed with the tracks of many tears.

"I'm sure your child will be fine," Rosita said. "The others will take care of her, and you'll be together again soon."

The woman leaned her head against the window, her eyes closed.

"You must eat something." Rosita held a burger under the woman's nose.

The woman shook her head and pushed Rosita's hand away.

"Give it to me, then, if she doesn't want it, I do." One of the men tried to snatch the burger from Rosita, but the other man grabbed his wrist.

"No. She has to eat. We all do." The man, in spite of his youthful appearance, had the saddest eyes Rosita had ever seen, but his voice was kind and reassuring. What great tragedy must he have endured?

They spent the next night in a forested area on a ridge above the interstate. Rosita marveled at the number of headlights passing beneath them. The lush greenery was like nothing she'd seen before. The canopy of trees was so dense it blocked out the stars. She turned to the other woman. "Have you ever seen anything like this?"

Then one of the guards grabbed her arm and dragged her off into the bushes. She was too weak to fight him off.

She woke the next morning where he'd left her, curled into a ball, making herself as small as possible. Indeed, she felt small, and ashamed. The others would know. How could she face them?

"Where the hell is she?" Ortiz's voice was high-pitched, angry.

When Rosita walked out from behind the bushes he grabbed her face and turned it toward the sun. "Which one of you bastards hit her?"

Both of the guards shrugged, but said nothing.

Ortiz got right in front of the one who'd beaten and raped Rosita. "Touch either one of these women again I'll cut off your balls. You dumb sonofabitch. They won't pay full price for damaged goods."

They were back on the road, driving into the rising sun. At least Rosita knew the direction they were traveling, but little else. She turned to the man with the sad eyes. "I wonder where they're taking us."

"I think we're headed for New York. The last sign said we're about two hundred miles from there."

"You can read the signs?" Rosita's eyes grew wide.

"You can't?"

Rosita shook her head and looked down in shame. Why had she divulged her ignorance so easily?

"But you speak English so well," the man said.

"My grandmother taught me. But she didn't teach me to read, because she didn't know how herself."

"You'll learn in no time. You seem very smart. I'm sorry they hurt you last night."

Rosita felt her face redden. She asked no more questions. Never in her life had she felt so dirty. If only there were some way she could get back home, but that wasn't possible. Her family was depending on her. She had to find work, send back money. Her four younger brothers had never owned shoes. Her aging grandmother did what she could, but clearly something else had to be done, and Rosita had to do it.

There had been no plan, no discussion. Many of the younger people from her village had tried to cross the border. Most had been caught and sent back. The few that made it sent money home. Not much, but anything was better than nothing, which was what most of them had. On the day Rosita left, her grandmother took a rusted can from beneath a loose board in the kitchen and gave the small roll of dollars it contained to her, and pointed north. Nothing else need be said.

Rosita was caught by the border patrol on her first try. She was detained for a day, fingerprinted and taken back across the border with about thirty others who'd failed.

She cried all the way back to her village. But failure was not an option. Her grandmother stood in the door of their hovel. When Rosita tried to enter the old woman turned her back and blocked the entrance. Rosita must try again.

Her third try was successful, but it left her penniless. She had no idea how much money she had, so she handed it all to the coyote, thinking he would give her back anything above the cost of the trip. He pocketed all of it and motioned for Rosita to get into the truck. He fondled her buttocks as she climbed over the tailgate.

In some ways the current trip in the van was more difficult. Sure, it was much more comfortable than the truck—she had a place to sit-- but before, she'd known where she was going. Now there were so many questions. Why had they picked out Rosita and the three others? Where were they taking them?

They never stopped except for food and gas. Bathroom breaks were taken by the roadside. Rosita cared less and less about the coarse comments the men made as she and the other woman were forced to relieve themselves in full view.

She must have fallen asleep. Her neck was stiff from sitting in a cramped position. They were in a small town. They drove through quickly without stopping. She saw a shop front with a name—Canandaigua—but she didn't know what it meant.  She looked at the man with the sad eyes, but he was asleep.

Her bladder began to scream at her, and she knew she must go soon or she'd wet herself. But there were no bushes to squat behind, only cars parked along the street. Where could she go?

When she felt she could hold it no longer, the van pulled into a parking lot behind a building. The streetlights illuminated a square brick structure with no windows.

"Thank God…finally." She heard Mr. Ortiz say. Except for barking out instructions he'd said little during the entire trip.

Ortiz unlocked the side door and shook the man with the sad eyes. "Wake up and be quiet."

The man stumbled to his feet

"Come on, be quick." Ortiz's voice was harsh.

The bright lights inside burned Rosita's eyes, and she began to tear up.

"Sorry looking bunch, but they'll have to do." The man who spoke was no taller than Rosita. His hair was gray and cropped short. Rosita had never seen anyone so well-dressed except for the few times she'd seen television. His cane made a sharp tapping sound on the floor as he turned and motioned for them to follow.

"Men in there, women in here," he said, pointing to two doors.

Rosita and the other woman were pushed through a door into a small room with two cots and a single chair. She heard the door lock behind her. The bathroom caught Rosita's eye just as her bladder gave her one final warning. She made it just in time.

The bathroom was small, barely enough room for her to turn around, but to Rosita it seemed luxurious. She turned on the water in the shower and held her hands in the stream for a moment. How bad could it be if they were treating them so well?

\#

The room was cold, and Rosita shivered in her thin gown. She looked across at the impassive face of the tall doctor who was asking her questions in a thick accent she'd never heard before. He never looked up, just wrote on the pad in his lap.

But she didn't have so much to complain about. For the two days she and her companions were kept in the strange new place she hadn't been treated badly. No one had hit her or even yelled at her. The food was good and there was lots of it, much more than she was used to having. If this was life in her new country, it was okay by her. Soon she would find work and make money to send back to her family.

She'd had no opportunity to explore her new surroundings. Except for the twice daily exercise sessions when they were taken out in a group and walked along the corridor, they were kept locked in their rooms. Confinement under lock and key troubled her, but perhaps it was some sort of quarantine to make sure she was healthy before they turned her loose.

The doctor motioned toward the table in the center of the room. Rosita lay down as he instructed. Her flimsy gown was secured by a single tie at the neck. He loosened the tie and jerked the garment off her, leaving her naked under the bright light. In contrast to his haste during the interview, he took his time with the examination as he poked and prodded in places Rosita had not been poked and prodded before.

After a long time, he motioned for Rosita to get up. He was breathing heavily now. She retrieved the gown from the floor where he'd thrown it and covered herself as best she could.

The doctor pushed a button on the wall and an attendant entered to escort Rosita back to her room. Her roommate sat waiting in a corner, her face a big question mark. It would be her turn next. Rosita shrugged and gave her a little smile.

The attendant took her roommate by the arm. The woman resisted and he yanked her to her feet. He muttered something Rosita didn't hear. Her roommate, as always, seemed close to tears. She returned after a short time, hugging her flimsy gown close around her body, just as Rosita had done. A nurse carrying a metal tray of instruments followed her into the room. Starting with Rosita, the nurse swabbed off an area of her arm with alcohol, then jabbed a small silver tube into her skin and twisted it several times. Rosita tried to pull away, but the nurse held her firmly. The nurse tapped the small piece of Rosita's skin into a tube filled with a clear liquid. Then she repeated the procedure on Rosita's roommate.

The following day the nurse returned and repeated the punctures on both of them. She ignored Rosita's queries about the procedure. The roommate asked no questions at all.

#

Meals were served in their rooms. Rosita could hardly wait. She had no way of knowing the time, and her stomach growled in anticipation. But today there was only one tray. The attendant placed it in front of her roommate, nothing for Rosita. Then he took Rosita's arm and led her out of the room.

The elevator was spacious, large enough for many people. They seemed to descend several floors. The area where they got off was very cold, and, once again, Rosita shivered.

Two attendants she hadn't seen before, large powerful-looking men, each grabbed one of her arms and led her to a smaller door. They entered single file, pulling her along between them.

What was this place? In the middle of the room sat a large glass box. Pipes ran back and forth across the floor. In the center of the glass box there was a large wooden chair with straps hanging from its arms and legs. The chair reminded Rosita of a photo of an electric chair from an American prison. God, were they going to kill her?

She was shivering uncontrollably now. "I am cold," she said to the guards who paid no attention. The floor was wet, and her flimsy sandals were soaked immediately.

They pulled her to the glass box and forced her to sit in the chair. Her gown fell open in the back and she gasped when her skin touched the cold frame. She was freezing, partly from the room temperature but more so from fear. While one man held her in the chair, the other fastened straps around her wrists and ankles, then another around her waist. She couldn't move more than an inch or so in any direction.

The men left and closed the door behind them. She yelled after them, but if they heard, they gave no sign. One of them pulled handles at the top and bottom of the door, shutting it tightly. Rosita heard the roar of a large machine, then a gushing sound. Cold water, icy water rose along her feet and ankles. She screamed and struggled against the restraints as the water rose up her legs. It was so cold she could hardly breathe. In a matter of moments the water was up to her neck and soon around her face.

Rosita could still see the lights from the ceiling as the water rose over her head. Then she saw other lights, beautiful colors swirling about, then nothing, as she drowned.

# Chapter 19

A perplexed Paul Pierce sat across the table from Hans Riegler who was chatting amiably about the relative virtues and shortcomings of the cabernet they were sharing. The restaurant, a new establishment on the western edge of the city, was French, the menu was in French, the wine list was predominantly French vintage, but Riegler, who was himself quite fluent in French, had ordered a California cabernet, an expensive one. What might have seemed an almost blasphemous choice in someone else fit perfectly with Riegler's unpredictable nature. Pierce had long since given up on trying to guess what his dinner companion's next course of action might be; now he simply aimed to be prepared for whatever popped up, tonight's dinner, for instance.

Pierce's bewilderment had begun much earlier in the day when Riegler had called and announced they would meet for dinner at eight. There was no inquiry about whether Pierce was free, whether he might already have plans for the evening. Riegler's invitation was delivered much like a royal edict; there was only one answer: "Yes, of course."

The unexpected dinner arrangement played havoc with Pierce's afternoon as he tried to anticipate Riegler's intentions, even though he knew his ruminations would more likely be wrong than right. He forgot his two o'clock lecture to the third-year medical students, and begged off with a lame excuse about a sore throat. When a prospective faculty member—a young Harvard-trained cancer surgeon, attractive and female as well—showed up for an interview scheduled weeks in advance, Pierce drew a complete blank. Who was this person? The interview began in shambles and went downhill from there. Only after the young woman left did Pierce notice that his secretary had written a reminder in red about the appointment on his desk calendar.

"It's only dinner," Pierce mumbled in the parking lot. He'd dropped his keys in a puddle beside his car. But why today, he wondered? In all the years he'd worked with Riegler they'd never done anything remotely social, just the two of them together. Even now Riegler remained a total enigma. Pierce didn't know where the man lived. Had it become necessary to contact him by phone or by mail, Pierce knew no number to call, no address to write on an envelope. Riegler seemed to congeal from the elements of thin air, sometimes several times a week, sometimes Pierce wouldn't see him for a month.

Riegler had arranged a small private room at the restaurant. He addressed the waiter in rapid French, none of which Pierce understood. "A veal dish. I think you'll like it," he said to Pierce.

When the waiter left, Riegler began speaking softly, so that Pierce had to lean forward to follow him. He spoke automatically, in a monotone, as if he was reading from some mental checklist. "Everything has been arranged," he said. "All of the equipment, all of the technical staff are in place. We are ready to begin work, Dr. Pierce." He raised his glass. "To our success."

The preparation of which Riegler spoke had included construction of a small recovery room complete with all manner of monitoring equipment. Pierce himself had supervised the preparation of the recovery room, secretly hoping that the expense alone would be enough to bring Riegler to his senses, make him see the impossibility of what he was doing. But Riegler never even blinked as he scanned the figures that Pierce gave him.

They would process ten "patients," procured by Riegler himself. This was the aspect Pierce wanted no part of, hoping to shield himself in ignorance. Who were these people? Where did Riegler get them? What would become of them afterward? Pierce didn't want to know any of this.

These mysterious patients would be treated and housed in a special building for five weeks. "They will receive our new Dormistan preparation," Riegler said. "Only one pill per week. Dr. Konrad's skin culture studies should verify its effectiveness."

Riegler swirled his wine glass, took a sip, then smiled approvingly. Pierce was already finishing his second glass. "All this preliminary work will be finished by September," Riegler said. "Then we shall be officially open for business."

"The spa."

"The Longevity Center, Dr. Pierce."

"I still don't understand how you will get people to come here for this type of treatment. I mean, you can't very well advertise what we'll be doing here."

Riegler chuckled. Pierce had seen him like this a few times before, the way he leaned back in his chair, how his eyes seemed to focus on some distant spot that Pierce could not see, could not even envision. In the few conversations they'd had about the people who would come to the Longevity Center seeking treatment, Riegler always referred to them as clients, a group altogether different from those unfortunates on whom they refined their technique, from whom they collected their preliminary data. This latter group about whose origins Pierce knew little, and wanted to know even less, Riegler referred to as patients.

This same group Pierce referred to as victims, which seemed more appropriate, only, how could they have become victims of cold water drowning so late in the spring, after lake water temperatures had begun to rise? If this question bothered Riegler at all, he gave no sign. The patient group seemed to hold only slightly more importance for the man than laboratory rats, a group to be experimented upon, then disposed of. The clients, now that was a different matter altogether.

"Our clients will come from all over the world. They will have two features in common: an insatiable desire for eternal youth and the ability to pay for it. Many groups have tried, and continue to try to accomplish what we've accomplished here, but none have had our success. Our clients will not appear in response to some article they've read in one of your medical journals. They will come because I invite them. Invitation only, that's what will bring them here.

"They will, of course, be people of quality, people of social worth, none of your imbecilic Hollywood types whose only redeeming assets are large breasts and a willingness to display them. In fact, I intend to supervise the selection process personally. Those who receive the blessing of an indefinite lifespan will be people who deserve it. They will be people used to the very best things life has to offer. They will arrive in New York in their private jets where they will be met by our limousine driver who will bring them here. Even now I am recruiting a staff who will possess the skills and training required for catering to the whims of the elite."

"So, they won't be from around here."

"I can promise you that," Riegler said. "In fact, most will be European, people with class, with titles, people who understand discretion, and, most of all, people with great personal fortunes."

The question tumbled out of Pierce's mouth before he even thought about it. "How much, approximately."

Riegler scowled. Clearly the question made him angry. "A base price of one million dollars, but actual costs will be considerably more. And then there will be the ongoing costs of the medication. Perhaps it sounds too expensive, but ask yourself, what would the prospect of eternal youth be worth to you?"

Pierce knew the answer to that one. He couldn't afford it, not yet anyway. Riegler's intent sounded like the creation of some sort of master race, and Pierce, himself, would never make the cut.

"We shall sever our ties with your medical school. After our preliminary work is complete we shall have no more need to process skin biopsy specimens, so our lab—your lab—will revert back to the school."

"And Dean Westbrook? What about him?"

"I will handle him. Not your concern."

Their waiter returned pushing a cart on which sat a single covered dish. He removed the cover and placed the dish in front of Pierce. Nothing for Riegler.

"That looks quite tasty, Dr. Pierce. I hope you enjoy it. The bill is already taken care of." Then Riegler left, leaving Pierce to eat his dinner alone.

#

A few weeks later, Rosita Gonzales, one of their patients, a source of preliminary data whose only mistake was trying to cross the U.S. southern border illegally, was waking up in the small recovery room adjacent to the drowning chamber. The resuscitation procedure had turned into a debacle with Pierce screaming at the staff as they tried to carry out a very complicated procedure in very cramped quarters. The bulk of the cardiopulmonary bypass machine, when placed alongside the patient's gurney, effectively blocked passage across the room, so anyone who had to get past had to practically hurdle the instrumentation.

Indeed, Rosita was lucky to be breathing at all. The first subject had not been so lucky. During the resuscitation attempt he'd developed a complicated and refractory cardiac arrhythmia that killed him. Pierce, knowing that under better circumstances, the man's death might have been prevented, was distraught. But Riegler was undeterred. "Luckily we have a spare," he said, and directed Pierce to carry on.

They didn't complete the third case, the spare subject Riegler had thought to provide, until shortly past six AM. Pierce was exhausted in body and spirit, and the spiritual depletion was the worst of all. Riegler had dangled a golden apple in front of him, and he'd grabbed it instinctively, not fully considering the cost. Now the full weight of his actions fell upon him with crushing force. In the past twelve hours he'd violated every professional principle he could think of. The face he saw the next time he looked in the mirror would never look quite the same again.

But Riegler seemed as fresh and enthusiastic as ever. He clapped Pierce on the back. "A good night's work, eh?"

"What about the first one?" Pierce asked. They had a body to dispose of, after all.

"All taken care of," Riegler said. "Yes, a very good night's work."

#

The bizarre sights in the room began to take shape as Rosita emerged once again from her drug-induced coma. This time she didn't struggle even though the breathing tube in her throat terrified her. As much as she wanted to pull it out, she couldn't reach it. Her hands were trussed up in restraints and a large strap stretched across her abdomen, holding her flat on the bed.

"How are we feeling today, Ms. Jones?" The nurse didn't look directly at Rosita, but instead adjusted dials on the bewildering array of instruments that sat beside the bed.

Who was she talking to? Who was Ms. Jones?

"I'm glad you decided not to thrash about so much." The nurse walked to the sink and washed her hands. "It won't help, you know."

Rosita could not respond. The tube in her throat made it impossible for her to speak.

"We'll probably take the breathing tube out later today, Ms.

197

Jones." The nurse left, not once having looked at Rosita's face. "Then you'll be able to talk."

Jones. That was it. The whole thing had to be a huge mistake. They thought she was someone else. As soon as she could talk she'd tell them. Boy, would she tell them.

#

For the moment Rosita had to keep a tight grip on her sanity. There was that terrible dream where she was strapped in a chair as water rose around her...cold, icy water. It all seemed so real, but it was impossible. It had to be a dream. No one could be cruel enough to do that to her.

Besides, she had other things to worry about. Last night her father had appeared at the foot of her bed smiling at her. But that had to be a dream too. He'd been dead for over ten years. Then she drifted off. Sometime later when she awoke, other shadowy forms stood at her bedside, people she'd never seen before. They didn't look well, not at all.

Worst of all was her total loss of any sense of time. Was it day or night? Just like the little room where they'd held her before, her ICU room was so shut off from the outside world that she had no way of knowing. She slept when they gave her medication, not when she wanted to. Since childhood her entire life had been run according to the celestial clock—she got up with the sunrise and went to bed when darkness prevailed. Now she had no clue of those events. Someone had even taped over the face of the wall clock in her room.

"I am Rosita," she said over and over again to herself. "And I will get through this. When they find out who I am, they will let me go."

Sometime later—a few minutes, hours, days, she couldn't tell—the nurse came back and injected more medicine into her IV. Rosita's last memory of that was her father smiling at her from the foot of her bed.

When she awoke, her throat hurt terribly. She tried to speak and managed only a feeble croak, but that was more than she could do before.

The tall, stern-looking man in the long white coat who stood by her bed made her skin crawl. He must be the doctor. If she could explain to him about the mistake—she wasn't Ms. Jones after all--he'd surely let her go.

"Don't try to talk now," he said, holding up his hand. Like the

198

nurse, he never seemed to look directly at Rosita.

"Please, Doctor, I must talk to you," Rosita said as she tried to raise herself up on her elbows.

"Settle down, Ms. Jones," the nurse said, "or I'll have to give you more medicine."

Rosita's head fell back. She had to make them understand. Her name wasn't Jones. This was all a mistake.

Tears flowed down her face, tears she couldn't reach because of the restraints that bound her wrists. There was her father again. As best she could tell, he'd simply emerged from the wall. This time he had a worried look.

"What can I do?" she asked. "Please, help me."

"Who are you talking to?" The nurse came back into the room holding a syringe.

"You don't see him?"

"See who?"

"My father is right there."

"You're hallucinating, Ms. Jones. I think you need to rest." She locked the syringe in place and pushed its contents into the IV.

"No, please. I need to talk to someone. Won't you untie me?" Rosita jerked at the wrist restraints. Too late. She felt herself overcome by the powerful sedative. Back to sleep, back to that terrible dream. Once again icy waters engulfed her body, and no one heard her screams.

Rosita awoke in a different place, a room much like the room where they'd kept her when she arrived. Her new surroundings seemed much quieter, not at all like the hospital room. There were no windows, of course, and none of those large machines that had filled her hospital room. Even so, her wrists and ankles were still bound, and she had no recollection of being brought to the new place. How much was dream and how much was real? She hardly knew the difference anymore.

Somehow her father had come along with her, but he still had that worried expression.

Why wouldn't they look at her? The two women in white uniforms worked around her bedside, giving her no more consideration than if she were a pillow.

"Please, untie me. I have to pee."

"You have a catheter." The nurse reached beneath Rosita's gown and pulled up a clear tube filled with yellow liquid. "See, your urine flows right into the bag."

Without a word, the woman at the head of Rosita's bed took a syringe from the tray beside her and flushed it into the IV.

"They said this one would be trouble," Rosita heard her say.

As she slipped once again into oblivion, Rosita watched her father's kindly face twist into an angry scowl.

#

The third day the nurses untied Rosita's restraints and helped her off the gurney. "Careful," the nurse said. "You're going to be a bit dizzy." As soon as Rosita's feet hit the floor her knees gave way and she collapsed. The nurses helped her into bed.

As Rosita lay back the nurse placed a small tray with a few instruments alongside her. She swabbed off a section of Rosita's arm with alcohol, then pierced the skin with the tip of a small silver tube. The puncture burned like fire, but Rosita didn't resist. By now she'd undergone the skin biopsy procedure several times, and she knew that any resistance was futile.

"If you'll behave yourself, we won't have to use the restraints any longer," the nurse said as she applied a bandage to the wound in Rosita's arm.

"How long will I be here?" Rosita asked.

"About two weeks."

"Then I can go?"

"That's up to Dr. Pierce."

# Chapter 20

For two weeks Rosita was confined to her little room. The lights were turned on and off by someone outside. Rosita had no control over them. Beyond the walls of her room she heard the roar of large vehicles and equipment, noises that went on late into the evening, but she had no way of knowing what was going on. During the long two weeks of her confinement she had only two visitors: the nurse who returned twice to repeat the skin biopsies, but who would not answer any of Rosita's questions, and Gaudio, the small man who brought her meal trays.

Gaudio, at least, talked to her, although their conversations were very brief. He was always looking back over his shoulder toward the door as if fearing they might be overheard. To her surprise and delight Rosita learned that Gaudio had, himself, along with his wife and two children, crossed the southern U.S. border from Mexico some four years before her own attempts. He had done seasonal labor picking fruit for a couple of years before he got a job at the Longevity Center where Rosita was now confined. He talked freely about his family. His major fear he told her was deportation. His employers at the Center knew he was in the country illegally and had stressed that, should he break any of their rules—such as he was doing now by fraternizing with Rosita—he and all his family would be shipped straight back to Mexico.

While Rosita took some comfort in seeing a friendly face regularly, particularly one with whom she shared so many background experiences, Gaudio would answer none of her many questions about the reason she was being kept in a locked room. When would they release her? When she tried to describe to him her terrible dream of being drowned in icy water, he looked away as if he didn't want to hear that story. After a few attempts she no longer pressed him for information. If anything, his fears seemed equal to her own.

#

It was not ignorance that kept Gaudio from providing Rosita with information. He knew quite a lot about what went on in the small building behind the Center, too much, in fact. He knew that Rosita's drowning experience was a real event, not a dream, because he was inside the room when she was strapped into the chair. The image of her struggles as the icy water rose up around her would never leave him. He knew too what happened to those who did not survive the drowning chamber. He had helped dig holes into which their lifeless bodies, wrapped in wet bed sheets, were buried. In time the construction crew would pour a foundation layer of concrete over the gravesites, sealing them away forever.

And what about his friend, Rosita? What would become of her? Gaudio had heard rumors that none of those confined there now would ever be allowed to leave—alive. Somehow he had to find a way to help her escape. Somehow he would have to stop the man responsible for this horror, the man they called Riegler.

Of course, he had no idea of how he might accomplish this, only that he must do it. Besides, he had other things to consider. Keeping himself and his small family safe in the U.S. required that he remain anonymous, and employed. The small jobs he'd picked up during those early years barely kept them clothed and fed. His wages now far surpassed anything he'd earned previously. Confronting Riegler would be to risk it all. But the image of Rosita and the others as they fought in the chair while the frigid waters engulfed them burned in his mind. If he didn't do something he could never face himself, or his family, again. Being a party to murder and doing nothing to stop it made him just as guilty as Riegler and the others.

#

While Gaudio deliberated and agonized, Rosita's two weeks at the Center were fast drawing to a close. One of the other attendants, a large man almost twice Gaudio's size had been making crude comments about what he planned for her before she was taken away. He urged Gaudio to come join in the fun. "Plenty there for both of us," he said. "And she won't be around to tell anybody."

Gaudio's preparations for Rosita's escape were meager. He'd brought in one of his wife's dresses and a pair of her shoes. He thought about underwear, but when he compared his wife's small chest to Rosita's ample bosom there seemed to be no point. In fact, he was sure the dress itself would not fit, but his choices were limited. A shopping trip was out of the question, and he dared not ask his wife for assistance. The less she knew about the situation, the better. He concealed the items of clothing in his locker, along with a two-foot section of lead pipe he'd found lying on the ground outside. Not much to work with, but it would have to do.

When the fateful day arrived, the gigantic attendant clapped Gaudio on the shoulder. "Come on, I've been waiting to get at this one." He walked off toward Rosita's door.

"I gotta take a leak first," Gaudio said. He ran back to his locker to retrieve the items of clothing which he wrapped around the lead pipe. By the time he reached Rosita's room the attendant had her pressed down on the bed and had stripped off her gown. "Shut the damned door," he yelled.

When the attendant, kneeling between her outstretched legs rose up to undo his pants, Gaudio hammered him across the back of the head with the pipe. The big man collapsed on top of Rosita, blood oozing from his wound. Gaudio pulled him off Rosita, and he landed on the floor with a loud thud. Surely someone must have heard, but no one came to investigate.

Gaudio thrust the small bundle of clothing at Rosita. "You must run," he said. "Get away from here."

Rosita didn't hesitate. She was barely able to get into the dress, and the shoes didn't fit at all. She threw them aside. "What about you? What will you do?"

What indeed, he wondered? Most likely he'd just killed a man, a very large man, and now he must dispose of the body. But first, Rosita. "Go. Run as far as you can." He pulled a small roll of cash from his pocket. "It's all I can spare."

"No, I won't take your money. I'll stay and help you."

He grabbed her by the shoulders and shook her, hard. "If you stay here they will kill you. Do you understand that?"

Her face contorted, as if something she feared had suddenly

taken form. "It wasn't a dream, then."

"No, it wasn't. If you want to live you'll leave now."

She stared into Gaudio's face for a moment, then hugged him so hard several buttons popped off the front of her dress. "Where should I go?"

"Not toward town. Head east. You can hide in the forest. I'll try to find you there."

After Rosita ran from the room, Gaudio plopped onto the bed and said a prayer for her, and one for himself. If her chances of escape were small, his own were not much better. He grabbed towels from the bathroom and wrapped them around the man's head, trying to soak up the gore that still oozed from the wound. Then he wrapped the body, still warm, in bed sheets. Now what, he wondered? He couldn't possibly lift the man, but he couldn't leave him lying on the floor. Discovery of the dead attendant would mean a fate worse than deportation; Gaudio could spend the rest of his life in jail, or he might wind up in one of the holes he'd helped dig, dumped there with Riegler's other "failures."

He started dragging the body toward the door when he heard the sharp click of an unmistakable tread in the hallway—Riegler. No time for anything fancy now. Gaudio grabbed his lead pipe and hid behind the door. When Riegler entered Gaudio struck him as hard as he could. Rumor had it that Riegler could not be killed, that he had and would live forever. Gaudio had heard these rumors, so he hit him several times more. More towels and more bed sheets that he gathered from the adjoining rooms.

Late into the night Gaudio sweated as he dug a deep hole in a section of level ground that he knew would be the base section of a new building. Shortly before dawn he threw in the last shovelful of sod, covering two bodies, Riegler's on the bottom. The next morning the trucks loaded with concrete would come and pour a six-inch layer over the tomb, burying the evil forever.

#

Rosita inhaled deep gulps of fresh spring air, the first time she'd been outside—and free—in weeks. But she had scant time to enjoy her freedom. If they caught her here she'd likely never see the light of day again. "Head east," Gaudio had told her. She took one long look toward the late afternoon sun, then turned her back on it and began to run.

Rosita was young and strong, but her weeks of incarceration had weakened her. She'd barely made a hundred yards down the main road, a two-lane blacktop already rutted by the weight of the heavy trucks going to and from the Longevity Center construction site, before she had to stop to catch her breath.

She walked into a small stand of pines beside the road, and was sitting beneath one of the trees when she saw the police car drive past, headed back from where she'd just come. Oh, God, were they out looking for her already? From that point on, Rosita continued her journey at a safe distance from the road, ready to hide from any oncoming traffic, in particular, vehicles marked Canandaigua Police. Her progress was slow, and she hesitated before crossing any open spaces.

By the time darkness set in she guessed she'd only traveled a few miles from the Center, certainly not a safe distance. But her progress in the dark was even slower. She kept tripping and falling over objects she could not see. In short order her knees and elbows were bruised and bleeding. Even her feet, toughened by years of going without shoes, could not hold up in the rough terrain that she now crossed.

Finally, late in the night, her body failed her. Exhausted, hungry, thirsty and fearful she lay down at the base of a tree. For a moment, before she let sleep take her, she wished for the comfortable bed back at the Center. But that was a false hope. Without Gaudio's help who knows what those people would have done to her by now. Her last thought on that day was a prayer for his safety, and her own.

#

John Merritt was only half awake as he drove toward town shortly past eight in the morning. During the night something outside the house had set Rebel off, and the dog's incessant barking roused John from a pleasant dream, about Stacey. He let the dog out through the kitchen door, and it raced off toward the edge of the woods out back. When Rebel didn't return after a moment, John took a flashlight and his dad's old twelve-guage from the closet, and headed off toward the sound of the barking, now interspersed with yelps of pain. He found his garbage can overturned beside the back door, litter strewn all around.

By the time he reached Rebel, the dog had a bloodied snout and a black bear up a tree. John considered shooting the animal, but decided against it. The situation was his own fault, after all. Leaving garbage outside was an open invitation to the local wildlife. He waved the barrel of the shotgun at the bear. "You come around here again and I'll shoot your ass off."

By the time he got Rebel's wounds cleaned it was almost six o'clock. He'd missed a night's rest, but worse still, his Stacey-dream had been shot to hell. He fed the dog, made coffee, and got dressed for work.

His first thought when he saw the dirty, disheveled girl running toward his truck was that he'd fallen asleep at the wheel and was dreaming. Then he remembered, most of his unexpected visitors of late were ghosts. This was one he hadn't seen before.

His first clue that this encounter was something other than spectral occurred at the door of the truck. Ghosts, in his experience, never bothered with doors. They passed right through them, open or closed, didn't matter. But this one latched onto the door handle with both hands. When she finally got it open she jumped onto the seat alongside John.

"Please, help me. Please."

No ghost, not this time, something even stranger. This was a live one for sure, even though he'd seen ghosts that looked better than the bedraggled specimen of a girl who sat across from him.

"I can pay you." She pulled a wad of cash from the pocket of her dress.

"I don't want your money. I'll take you into town. There's a doctor there, and you look like you need help."

She dug her fingers into his arm. "No, not that way." She pointed back the way he'd come. "Go there, please."

"There's nothing out there, just my ranch."

"Take me there. I have to hide or they'll get me again."

First ghosts and now this obviously crazy woman. Why couldn't he just have a normal morning like everybody else? Why did all the weird ones come his way? There seemed no point in asking who was after her, or why. She was obviously in a state of panic. He turned the truck around and headed back toward his ranch.

She said nothing else until they pulled up to his house, just kept looking around like she expected something straight from hell might be gaining on her. Every time they passed another vehicle she dove down to the floor until he motioned for her to get up.

Rebel waited for them on the front porch.

"Is your dog friendly?" she asked.

"Most of the time."

Rebel walked slowly up to Rosita, lay down in front of her, then began licking her bruised feet.

"Dang," John said. "Never saw him do that before."

"He's hurt." Rosita kneeled and stroked the wounds on Rebel's snout. Her dress, already dirty and tattered, looked as if it might split at the seams.

"He got into a fight last night. You hungry?"

"Yes, please."

He led her into the bathroom. "You can clean up in here. I'll fix some breakfast, and I'll try to find something for you to wear."

Breakfast was the easy part. Clothing for a young woman, much more difficult. He finally came up with a sweatshirt and an old pair of gym shorts he hadn't worn since high school.

A short time later a strikingly pretty girl, even considering the scraped knees and matted hair, joined John in the kitchen. "I am Rosita."

"John," he said. He placed a plate of scrambled eggs and bacon on the table, along with a cup of coffee. "Dig in."

She did. He thought not even Rebel could make food disappear so fast. He poured a cup of coffee for himself, then refilled hers. It was time to talk. She had a lot of explaining to do. She talked like she ate— rapid, no stopping. Frequently he had to ask her to repeat herself, mostly because he couldn't believe what he was hearing.

"Drowned you, you say? On purpose?"

"Yes, yes, and there were others."

Later he would wonder at the bizarre coincidence of that morning. Her story was preposterous, at best. Any normal person reacting to such an encounter would dismiss her as a complete lunatic. But John had had a number of crazy experiences of his own of late, and was not so quick to write her off. After all, for months now he'd had encounters with ghosts, seen them and talked with them. He too had spent time submerged in icy water and knew well enough that such an experience could do very strange things to a person. But his own mishap had been accidental. The thought that someone would subject another person to something like he'd been through on purpose was just too much of a stretch.

'You don't believe me." Rosita hung her head like a child who had been caught in a lie.

"Let me see your arm."

She pulled up the sleeve of the sweatshirt revealing a series of small puncture wounds in various stages of healing.

John slipped his own shirt off his shoulder and showed her the small scars on his own arm.

Rosita threw her arms around his neck and sobbed onto his shoulder. Rebel whimpered and resumed licking her feet.

Some things had been settled between them. A bridge of trust had emerged from their shared experience, but big issues remained. Truly evil things had been done, and, unless he intervened, might very well continue. First off, he needed reinforcements. He called Stacey at the hospital and gave her a very sketchy version of Rosita's story. When he'd mentioned to Rosita that he'd like to drive her to the medical center she became hysterical.

"No doctors. No hospital."

Rebel growled at him. So, Stacey agreed to drive out to the ranch.

"And maybe you could bring some clothes, if you can spare any."

"Are you saying she's naked?" Stacey's voice was shrill.

"No, no. She's wearing some of my stuff, but it doesn't fit so good."

The idea of calling Margaret Simmons popped into his head as if from out of nowhere. He knew he needed some kind of legal input, but when he mentioned the police Rosita became hysterical again.

"They'll send me back," she said over and over.

Of course, Margaret chaired the Board of Directors at Upstate, and the Longevity Center from which Rosita had escaped was associated somehow with the medical school, so from that angle the idea seemed logical enough. But there was an intuitive component to the choice. At some deeper level he knew that Margaret should be there, and that she should meet Rosita.

And when Margaret—not her secretary—answered the phone, she didn't seem at all surprised to hear from him.

# Chapter 21

By eleven o'clock, under cloudy skies, the little parking circle in front of John's house was filled. Herman had parked what he always referred to as the "company truck" next to John's own battered pickup. He'd dropped by "just to see how things were going," but John figured he'd come by to patch up things after the little spat they'd had a few days before.

Stacey parked next to Herman, and the row ended with Margaret's own gleaming Town Car, looking completely out of place compared to the three more modest vehicles. John wondered at her willingness to drop everything and drive down, but then, his life had been filled with unusual occurrences of late, so one more could hardly matter.

Margaret, tall and imposing in a dark suit, still wore her lawyer face when she got out of her car, but that changed into a warm smile as she joined the small group assembled on John's porch.

Introductions completed, John ushered them into the parlor. For once he felt thankful for this seldom used sitting area that he had long considered wasted space. But the star attraction, the one they had come to see, Rosita, was nowhere to be seen.

"Where is she?" Margaret asked.

"Hiding in the bathroom," John said. "She's still scared half to death."

"I brought a scrub suit for her to wear," Stacey said.

"Maybe we shouldn't have all come at once, probably frightened her even more," Margaret said, "but we all need to hear her story."

They all sat waiting in the front parlor, the room that was never used, while John coaxed Rosita out of the bathroom. After about ten minutes she followed him into the room, Rebel close by her side looking ready to shred anyone who raised a hand to her.

Surprisingly Margaret approached the frightened girl first and introduced herself. She held Rosita's hands while she talked. The bond between them seemed automatic, inevitable, like something that was meant to happen all along. She led Rosita to the sofa where they sat side by side, Margaret's arm draped across Rosita's shaking shoulders. Their conversation seemed perfectly casual, Margaret offering up questions about Rosita's home town, her family, things she liked, things she didn't. Even Rebel seemed to relax, apparently satisfied that this lady in the blue suit wasn't so bad after all.

It was as if there were no other people in the room, just Rosita and Margaret. "The people who hurt you, I'm going to make sure they can never do anything like that again."

When Rosita began her story she looked straight at Margaret, like a girl describing a bad date to her mother. From the time she began she needed no further prompting. The whole horrible event came out in a torrent. No one interrupted her, no one asked questions. Shortly past noon she stopped, then she buried her face in Margaret's shoulder.

When Rosita raised concerns about being sent back to Mexico, Margaret drew her closer. "Don't worry about a thing. I'll take care of you. I have a big house with plenty of room for both of us."

"I just can't understand why anyone could do something so horrible," Margaret said.

"I think I know," Stacey said. "I went into Dr. Pierce's lab at the medical school." She told them all about the rats with their life spans extended far beyond normal, about the apparent necessity for prolonged immersion in cold water to bring the normal aging process to a halt before Pierce's medication took over. She also told them about his silent partner, Riegler.

"What about all those skin biopsies they did?" John asked. "Rosita had them too."

"That's how they test the medication effects. Normally skin cells in tissue culture only survive a few weeks, but yours seem to go on indefinitely."

"You're saying I could live forever?" John said.

"I don't know, maybe, as long as you're taking the Dormistan pills."

"How come you didn't tell me this before?"

Stacey looked down at the floor, wrapped her arms around herself. "I sort of made that decision for you, for us. I wanted us to have a normal life, together. I couldn't stand the thought of you staying the same while I grew older. Growing old without you..." She shook her head.

John cradled her face in his hands. "No way you're going to grow old without me. Whatever happens, we're going to do it together."

"That's more like it," Margaret said. "If I ever saw a young couple made for each other, it's the two of you."

"But, without the pills I can't, you know, help you," John said.

"Never you mind about that. We'll get by just like we always have." Margaret looked back at Rosita. "Besides, things seem to have worked out, pills or no."

"Maybe I should make some coffee," John said.

Stacey followed him into the kitchen. "Don't you make a habit of bringing stray girls home with you. The ghosts were bad enough, but live ones, definitely not." She wrapped her arms around his neck. "You're spoken for, remember that."

#

John couldn't remember a more awkward moment than his present situation—three women all at once in the parlor. He couldn't recall this ever happening before, even when his mother was still around.

The only person who seemed even more at a loss than he was Herman. John walked over beside his best friend. "Heck of a mess, huh?"

"I gotta hand it to you, John, when you stir things up, you do it right."

Coffee helped, as it usually does. It gave Stacey something to do. She played hostess while Margaret and Rosita continued their love fest on the sofa. The change in Rosita was remarkable, no longer timid or fearful, her smile lit up the room.

John felt like the proverbial fifth wheel. They really didn't need him, well, except for Stacey. Now Christopher could have pulled it off, charmed them all, had them eating right out of his hand. But John, since he had dumped his Dormistan supply in the garbage, had felt his old

211

shyness returning. No, not shyness exactly. He no longer needed to be the center of attention. He no longer felt the need to be Christopher. The realization buzzed around him for a moment before he caught hold of it. The battle he'd been fighting for all these years was over. He didn't have to win it. Finally he could just walk away from it.

"John." Stacey's voice seemed to come from another room, but she stood right beside him shaking his shoulder. "Are you okay? Seemed like you drifted off."

"I'm fine, never better," he said, and he meant it.

"We were wondering where this place would be, where they confined Rosita," Margaret said. "It would have to be close by."

"I'll bet I know exactly," John said.

"We ought to take a ride out there, John, see what's really going on," Herman said.

"I'm coming too," Stacey said. "Somebody has to keep you two out of trouble."

In short order John, Herman and Stacey were crammed into the front seat of his truck headed for the Upstate Longevity Center. Rosita refused to go along so Margaret stayed behind with her. Before they drove away John trotted off to his tool shed, and returned with a pair of bolt cutters and a nine-pound sledgehammer.

"What do you plan to do with that?" Stacey asked.

"That's in case they don't invite us in."

The mist that had settled in at sunrise now fell as rain. John turned on the wipers, but the dust on the windshield became an impenetrable muddy screen. "Have to wait for a minute," he said.

"Don't you have one of those windshield cleaner things?" Stacey asked.

"They weren't making them back when this truck was built." He felt a flush of shame at the decrepit condition of his old vehicle, parked as it was near to Margaret's Town Car. Still, it had its good points, Stacey in the middle, her hip snug against his own, something not possible with the newer bucket seats. Could be worse, he thought.

They'd only covered a couple of miles when Stacey patted his arm. "Relax."

He realized he had something akin to a death grip on the steering wheel. He'd stood aside, removed, while the women had questioned

Rosita about her ordeal. He was bewildered, overwhelmed by what he'd heard, particularly by some of the gaps Rosita filled in. Now he found himself in a state of rage, both for Rosita and for himself, and others as well. Pierce had played him for a fool, an experimental toy, and he'd done even worse to Rosita. If he got a chance at Pierce he'd smash the man, Riegler too if he was around. It would be a cold day in hell before they played their little games with anybody else.

About twenty minutes into their drive he slowed and pointed to a small stand of pines on the left. "That's where Rosita came from. She'd been hiding in the trees."

"What did you think when you saw her? Must have been quite a shock," Stacey said.

"First thought was another ghost."

"You're still seeing them?" Stacey asked.

"Not so much anymore, not since I chunked those pills in the garbage."

"Good move, and good riddance." Stacey gripped his arm.

About two miles farther on, John turned off the main road onto a broad gravel path that led to the brand new Upstate Longevity Center. As if on cue, the rain shower halted, and a few streaks of sunlight cut their way through the cloud cover.

"Good heavens," Stacey said. "This place is huge. Margaret told me she'd seen a model of it, but I had no idea it would be so big."

Indeed, the campus spread over almost five acres. The main building, which they now faced, had a fountain in front, some twelve to fifteen feet across, complete with a ceramic cherub in the center. Presumably, when in operation, water would spout from some orifice of the cherub, although exactly which orifice was not clear. The entrance itself, framed on either side by fluted columns, was an all-glass affair that led into an atrium, also framed in glass. From where they now sat you could see halfway through the building without even setting foot inside.

"Who could afford to stay here?" Stacey asked.

"Nobody I know, for sure," John said. He followed the path around the building, then stopped just short of the trailer where he'd had his earlier encounter with the builder, Bynum. A couple of Bynum's trucks were parked off to the left, but otherwise there was no sign of activity. The guard that had challenged him before was nowhere to be seen.

"Looks like they've shut down," John said.

"How on earth are we going to find the place, you know, where Rosita…" Stacey's voice trailed off, as if she didn't want to finish the question.

"I think I know," John said.

"You've been here before?"

"Herm and I drove out when they were first starting the construction." He pointed to a two-story building, so plain and box-like that it looked out of place among its more stylish surroundings. "They dug down about ten feet below ground for that one." He didn't tell her about the massive water pump and refrigeration unit he knew had been installed in the basement. The less said, the better, he figured. Stacey was already digging her fingers into his thigh. She didn't need to hear more about the grim specifics. "You don't have to go in there," he said.

"I'm going. I have to see it."

Yet another surprise, the door was unlocked. John thought for certain he'd have to bash it in with his sledgehammer. He led the way down a central corridor with six doors, three to a side, with Stacey and Herman following behind. All six doors stood open. The rooms inside were identical, small bedrooms each with a tiny private bathroom. In two of the rooms the beds were unmade.

At the end of the corridor stood a larger door with a bar handle in the center. It looked sturdy enough that John doubted he'd be able to smash it, even with his hammer. A few feet from the door the little party of three stopped, they hesitated; they knew that beyond this door was where the unspeakable took place. John felt Stacey gripping his arm with both hands.

Maybe, he thought, he'd get lucky. Maybe Pierce was inside, or that other guy, Riegler, the one Rosita was so afraid of. If so, no power on earth could keep him from punching that guy's lights out. He pressed down on the handle. A latch clicked open. He hit the door with his shoulder, and it swung open. They were in.

Sometimes seeing is still not believing. They knew what they would find; Rosita had told them that much. Even so, seeing the heavy chair bolted to the floor, its restraining straps hanging down, all enclosed in the clear plastic cubicle that filled much of the room, seeing the six-inch pipes that ran into the cubicle, knowing that both Pierce and Riegler might have stood where they were standing now, watching as Rosita and probably others as well were engulfed in icy water, it was all too much to take in.

Stacey wheeled in the doorway and ran back down the hall. John stomped around the room looking for something to break, someone to bash.

Herman remained in the doorway. He kept saying "hell no," over and over again.

John and Herman walked back down the hallway to where Stacey stood, shaking by the door. They said nothing, scarcely dared to breathe, not wanting to inhale the evil of that place. When he opened the door John saw a man standing there, his right hand partially encased in a plaster cast, holding a heavy chain and padlock in the left—Bynum himself.

"What the hell?" Bynum took a step back when he saw John. "I almost locked you inside."

"Where's Riegler?" John asked.

"Disappeared. Don't know where he went."

"You know what they did in there, don't you?" John walked slowly toward Bynum, fists clenched. He still wanted to smash someone, and Bynum would have to do for now.

Bynum looped the chain around his left hand. "Look, they tell me what they want, and I build it. That's all I know. I swear."

"Bullshit."

"Stop." Stacey grabbed John's arm. "Let him lock it up, for good."

#

By the time they got back to John's house the clouds had gone, and the sun gleamed in a clear blue sky. Margaret and Rosita were strolling arms linked a short distance away. Rebel followed at their heels. As the two of them walked back toward the truck their smiles burned away the gloom inside, much the same as the afternoon sun had dismissed the cloud cover. "Rosita is coming home with me," Margaret said. "To stay."

#

That most eventful Tuesday still held one last surprise for the group, although it was not a shared discovery. Stacey learned of it as soon as she got back to the hospital; the whole place was buzzing with the news that Dr. Paul Pierce, Chief of Cardiopulmonary Surgery, had committed suicide, an overdose. He'd obviously put some thought and planning into the act. Oral medications are not always reliable. An uncooperative stomach might regurgitate them, leaving the job only partially complete. So Pierce made sure. He put a couple of pillows into his bathtub, then hung a bag of intravenous fluid into which he'd injected enough Versed to kill several adults, from the shower rod. He'd stuck the needle into his own arm, then taped it in place. Altogether a very neatly done piece of work, according to the EMTs who took his body away. Stacey listened to all the inevitable speculation, but did not join in the conversations. She knew far too much already.

John heard the news on his kitchen radio as he prepared his dinner in the microwave oven. His rage reaction had run its course by now, leaving him with that deep fatigue that follows in the wake of such trauma. Perhaps Pierce had possessed a thread of humanity somewhere deep inside himself, and he'd done the only thing he could do to make amends. A bad ending to a bad situation.

Rosita, after a brief tour of Margaret's mini-mansion, was still in a state of wonder over the luxury around her that would now become her new life. She kept inquiring about her duties, her chores, and Margaret kept assuring her that she hadn't brought her there to be a housekeeper. Rosita's role, she would learn in time, would be to fill the hole in Margaret's heart left by her daughter's death.

She and Margaret were sitting together on the sofa watching the evening news when they saw the announcement of Pierce's death. The surgeon's wife, looking surprisingly calm, said he'd been working very hard and had seemed depressed lately. It sounded like an old cliché—the devoted physician so dedicated to his work that he doesn't know when to stop. The truth, Margaret knew, was a different story altogether.

Rosita screamed when a photo of Pierce appeared on the TV screen. "That's him. That's the man."

"Don't worry, dear." Margaret pulled her close. "He can't ever hurt you again."

# Epilogue

Mid-morning, Friday, early May, John stood out front of his little house staring back at it, wondering how it might look in the coming months, the coming years. Stacey would be out tomorrow. She'd been staying over every available weekend with him now. He'd spent the morning fencing in the new vegetable garden she'd wanted.

"You need more fresh veggies in your diet," she'd said. "All that microwave stuff isn't good for you."

"Is that medical advice?"

"Just plain good advice. My mom told me."

"There's a nice market in town," he said.

But no, she wanted to grow their own. So he fired up the old Farmall tractor, amazed that it still ran after sitting idle for over six months, and tilled a spot to the east of the house. The new garden area got good sun for most of the day. He'd balked at the idea of a fence, but Stacey insisted. "Deer, rabbits, raccoons…they'll eat everything."

She had a point, so, up went the fence.

She'd also begun what he recognized as a subtle campaign to transform his dwelling. He was about to learn some of the differences in gender preferences. What had served him well enough for years now wouldn't cut it any longer. New kitchen, new bathrooms(s), she had plans all right.

Her suggestion about setting up a medical practice in Canandaigua took him by surprise.

"What about that cardiology position you always talk about?"

"That's way off in Boston. I think I need to stay around here, keep an eye on you."

Yeah, change was coming. If he wanted the girl he'd have to

adapt, take her as she was, and he definitely wanted the girl.

Part of the process would involve learning to accept himself as well. He'd spent most of his life defining himself and being defined by what he wasn't—he wasn't his brother. Now he was set on a new path, getting to know himself, to accept himself.

The upheaval of the past few months—his own near death, ghosts, the horror at the Longevity Center—had he not got caught up in all of that he might very well have gone on as before, always wishing he was someone else, never quite measuring up.

#

They all came through the awful experience different people—he, Stacey, Rosita and Margaret. They no longer talked of spirit worlds and thresholds. The here and now seemed quite enough, for each of them. Margaret had found fulfillment in her care of Rosita. His and Stacey's life paths were converging now, along lines of normalcy—no ghosts, no craziness. The townspeople of Canandaigua approved. "A lovely young couple," everyone agreed.

Early one Wednesday afternoon, John grabbed a hoe from his tool shed, then trudged off toward the little hillside where lay the Merritt family burial plot. Weeds seldom grew there because of the shade, but he didn't like to go up there and just stand around. Still, he needed to visit the place. It made a connection, a bridge from past to present, even to the future.

As he walked he re-ran a conversation he'd had with Herman earlier in the week, just after lunch.

"You're about the closest thing to family I got," Herman had said. "And I ain't getting any younger."

"You're strong as a horse, Herm."

"Not any more, I'm not. Anyway, I was thinking, when my time comes, if you could find a spot for me up on that little hill with your folks, I'd sure appreciate it."

The request had stopped John in his tracks. "Are you okay? Is there something you're not telling me?"

"Oh, I feel fine. It's just, when you get to be my age you start thinking about things. It would take a load off my mind to know that I had a place."

"Whatever you want, my friend, I promise. And you are family, always have been."

The conversation was doubly troubling because, for a while, John had been taking the antidote—Dormistan—to the very condition Herman feared, aging and dying, and he'd thrown it in the garbage. He could understand why some people might want to stay young forever, but he didn't share that sentiment. It was unnatural. What next, eternal spring? Eternal summer? Pick your favorite season and have it year round. No way. Mother Nature was a damned sight smarter than he was. Seasons, and people, all changed for a reason, and he was just fine with that arrangement.

He hacked away at a few dandelions that had grown up beside his father's grave. Not much to do, really, he was just going through the motions. He looked around for Rebel, and saw that the dog had stopped halfway up the hill. John whistled, but Rebel would come no closer. When he turned back toward the gravesites he understood why; he saw a figure hovering at the edge of the clearing. A ghost? He hadn't seen any since he'd stopped taking that damned medication. As the figure drew nearer he recognized Christopher. John felt a surge of anger. Why now? Why had his brother's ghost taken so long to appear when so many others had passed in and out of his life? It had been Christopher he'd sought all along.

"It wasn't up to me," came the ghostly message. "It was all you."

"What the hell are you trying to say?"

"You were looking for forgiveness, but you were looking in the wrong place." Now the specter was much closer and much larger. A cloud of Christopher seemed to fill the entire clearing.

John couldn't see through the fog that enveloped him. He had to prop himself up with the hoe handle. Even though he'd rehearsed this conversation a thousand times, now there was no need for him to say more. Christopher knew all of it.

"What happened at the lake that day,that was my own fault, not yours. Just lucky I didn't get us both killed. So, you see, it was never up to me to forgive you. You had to forgive yourself. I think you've done that now. Good-bye, little brother."

The hoe fell from his grasp, and John slipped to the ground. He woke sometime later to find Rebel licking his face. The sun had reached the tips of the pine trees in the distance. John pushed himself up into a sitting position. He gave Rebel a pat on the head. "Be dark soon, boy. Guess we better be headed home."

# About the Author

Mike Owens has undergraduate and medical degrees from the University of North Carolina in Chapel Hill. He obtained his MFA degree in creative writing from Old Dominion University in Norfolk, VA. He has worked extensively with hospice programs and is the author of two textbooks on care of the dying: Care of the Terminally Ill Cancer Patient (2002), and Primary Care Issues for End-of-Life Care (2003). His first novel, The End of Free Will, was published in January, 2014.

Mike lives in Norfolk, VA, with his wife, Marilyn, and their dog, Molly, a highly critical eleven-year-old Weimaraner.

# Coming Soon

# All Burned Up. A Love Story

Nothing left to live for, that pretty well sums up eighteen-year-old Daisy's outlook on life after an explosion leaves her blind and horribly disfigured. Her only option, as she sees it, is to make an end of things as quickly as she can.

But Linda, a nurse who befriended Daisy during her six months of hospitalization, begs her to meet with a new therapist, a man she will describe only as Arthur.

He's huge, black, has only one eye, and has two long scars down the side of his face. He also has a booming laugh that rattles windowpanes. Slowly but surely he breaks through Daisy's shell. He draws out her fear and anger, redirects them onto himself. He teaches her new lessons about life and suffering, then forces her to confront that most frightening emotion of all—love.

www.ingramcontent.com/pod-product-compliance
Lightning Source LLC
Chambersburg PA
CBHW060140130626
46556CB00006B/2428